"I want to marry you," Donald said.

"Marry? Marry me? You . . . you want to marry me?" Of a sudden she stopped laughing, she even stopped smiling, and she looked down at her hands which were now joined tightly on her lap. Yesterday Will Headley, the man she loved and had thought one day to marry, had written her a letter, which by its very charm had seared the delicate vulnerable feelings of her first love and forged her whole conception of life into a different pattern.

Yet Donald was a man, and he wanted her—and Will Headley didn't.

THE MALLEN STREAK

THE
MALLEN STREAK
Catherine Cookson

THE MALLEN STREAK
*A Bantam Book / published by arrangement with
E. P. Dutton & Company, Inc.*

PRINTING HISTORY
Dutton edition published January 1973
2nd printing .... April 1973
Bantam edition published May 1974
2nd printing

*Bantam Books are published by Bantam Books, Inc. Its trade-
mark, consisting of the words "Bantam Books" and the por-
trayal of a bantam, is registered in the United States Patent
Office and in other countries. Marca Registrada. Bantam
Books, Inc., 666 Fifth Avenue, New York, New York 10019.*

BOOK I

THOMAS MALLEN

ONE

High Banks Hall showed its sparsely-windowed back to beautiful woodland and the town of Allendale in the far distance, whilst its buttressed and emblazoned and many-windowed face looked out over its formal gardens on to mountainous land, so austere and wild that even its short summer beauty brought no paeans of praise except from those who had been bred within the rigours of its bosom.

Away to the South lay Nine Banks Peel; to the North was the lovely little West Allen village of Whitfield; but staring it straight in the face were the hills, for most part bare and barren and rising to miniature mountains which, on this day, Tuesday, the twenty-fifth of February, 1851, were thickly crusted with snow, not white, but pale pink, being tinged for the time being by the straining rays of a weak sun.

The Hall was fronted by a terrace bordered by an open balustrade, its top festooned with round stone balls, and each pillar at the top of the steps which led to the drive was surmounted by a moss-stained naked cupid.

The doors to the house were double and of black oak studded with large iron nails which gave the impression that it had withstood the attack of a fusillade of bullets. Over the door was a coat of arms composed of three shields, above it a Latin inscription had been cut into the stone which roughly translated read: Man is compassionate because he gave God a mother.

At first the inscription appeared to have religious

connotations, but when dissected it proved to many to be blasphemous.

Thomas Wigmore Mallen who built the Hall in 1767 had himself composed the inscription and had explained to those interested the deep significance of the motto, which was that God, in the first place, had been created of man's need, and the need had been brought about by the frightening mystery of both birth and death, more so the latter. And knowing that no man came into the world except through woman, man felt compelled to be compassionate towards the omnipotent image he had created. Therefore, even in pagan times, even before Christ was heard of, man had given to his particular deity a mother; but with this difference, she was always untouched by man, a virgin who could give birth.

Thomas Wigmore Mallen was an avowed atheist and the devil took his soul. Everyone knew this when he was found stone dead seated against a tree with not a mark on him, his horse cropping gently by his side.

It was said, among the hills, that the Mallen streak began with Thomas Wigmore Mallen, but then no one hereabouts had known his forbears, for he had hailed from away in the Midlands. However, it wasn't long before he had spread his distinctive mark around the vicinity of his new house. No matter what colour the hair of a male Mallen the white tuft started from the crown and thrust its wiry way down to the left temple.

Strangely, the streak never left its mark on the women of the family, and again not on all the males either. But it was noted that the Mallen men who bore the streak did not usually reach old age, nor did they die in their beds.

Yet the present owner of the Hall, Thomas Richard Mallen, nicknamed 'Turk' by his friends, seemed to be an exception, for he was hale and hearty at fifty-five, and on this day his voice could be heard booming through the length of the house, calling on his guests to get ready and to have sport while it lasted, for in two days' time the hare-hunting season would end.

The guests had not come to the Hall merely to join the hare hunt; most of them had been there for the past
4

three days. They had come originally for the wedding of Thomas's daughter, his only daughter by his second marriage.

More than half the county, they said, had been invited to the wedding, for it wasn't every day that a Northumberland miss married an Italian count, even if a poor one; and Thomas Mallen had gone out of his way to show the foreigner how things were done in England, especially in the North-East of England.

The festivities had gone on for two full days . . . and nights; only an hour ago four carriages had rumbled away, their occupants hardly able to stand on their feet. And this went for the women too. When Thomas Mallen entertained, he entertained. Mallen was a man, everybody said so. Could he not drink three men under the table? and had he not fathered more brats in the countryside than his bulls had heifers? Some mothers, it was said, were forever dyeing their youngsters' hair with tea, but some children, one here and one there, seemed to be proud of the white tuft, and the evidence of this had just now been brought to Thomas by his son, Dick.

Dick Mallen was twenty-three years old and in looks a younger replica of his father, but in character there were divergent traits, for there was no kindness in Dick Mallen. Thomas could forgive and forget, life was too short to bear the inconvenience of malice. Not so Dick Mallen; Dick always paid the slightest slur with interest, creating an opportunity to get rid of the debt, which might have been only a disdainful look, or a snub. Yet a snub to young Mallen was worse than a blow; it indicated condemnation not only of himself, but also of the house.

Both Mallens were laws unto themselves; whosoever dared question that law—and there were many in the county who did, a few openly, but the majority slyly— would be brought to book by the sole male heir to High Banks Hall.

Thomas's two sons by his first marriage had died, the second of them only last year, since when Dick Mallen had gambled more, drunk more, and whored

5

more, three very expensive pastimes, and over the last three days he had excelled himself at the trio.

Now prancing down the main staircase with very little sway to his gait, for he, too, could hold his drink, he paused and shouted into the throng below, which looked for all the world like a hunt meeting without the horses.

'D'you hear me, Father! He's arrived; your hill nipper's arrived. I glimpsed him from the gallery.' He thrust his arm backwards.

Most of the faces down below were turned upwards, and the ruddy countenance of Thomas Mallen was split wide in a grin, showing a mouthful of blunt teeth with only two gaps to the side, and he cried back at his son, 'Has he now? He's early; the passes are still snowed up. Well! well!' He now turned to the dozen or so men and women about him. 'Do you hear that? My hill nipper has arrived, earlier than ever this year. November when last he came, wasn't it?' He was looking across the hall now at his son who was threading his way towards him.

'Nearer December.' Dick Mallen pulled a face at a friend and dug him in the ribs with his elbow, and the friend, William Lennox, who could claim relationship with another of that name who was Lord of the Bedchamber to Prince Albert, pushed his young host in the shoulder, then flung his head back and laughed aloud.

In his twenty-eight years William Lennox had stayed in all types of country houses but he would swear that he had never stayed in one quite like this where everything was as good as a play. He turned now to a man at his side who was thrusting down a dog from his thigh, and said, 'What do you think of that, eh? He wasn't lying in his boast, his bastards do risk the mountains just to get a peep at him.'

Carl Breton-Weir merely answered with a tight smile, thinking cynically that this house appeared like a factory for the manufacture of bastards of all kinds. If it wasn't that to-night he meant to recuperate with good interest all the money he had purposely lost to his host and his friends he would leave now. But to-morrow, if all went well, he would go, good and early. And he wouldn't be sorry to see the back of them all; coarse

6

bores, every one of them. They had afforded him amusement at first but one quickly tired of this kind of amusement . . . Where were they going now? And these damn dogs all over the place. 'Get down! Get down!' He flung the dog from him.

'She likes you; she likes you, Carl.' Dick Mallen was laughing at him now. 'You must have a smell about you she recognises.'

At this there were great guffaws from the men and open titters from the four women present. Kate Armstrong, an overweight woman in her late forties, decked, even in her outdoor garb, with jewellery, one piece of which would have kept six of her husband's miners for a year, slapped out at her daughter Fanny, who at twenty-eight was still unmarried and could, they said, tell a joke as good as any man, saying, 'That Dick. That Dick . . . I tell you!'

There was Jane Ferrier, small, fat and as giggly as a girl, which mannerism sat odd on her forty-three years. Her husband owned a number of glass works in New-castle, and to see the extent of their wealth you had to visit their home and be blinded by the chandeliers.

Then there was Maggie Headley. She had a name for being careful with the grocery bills, although her husband, Ralph, owned not only a brewery and a candle factory, but a coal mine also.

Among the men present was Headley's son, John, and his close friend, Pat Ferrier, both two happy men, at the moment, for they had made enough out of their friend and host and his London guests during the last two nights to keep them in pin money for some consid-erable time.

'Where was he, in the same place?' Thomas was again calling to his son, and Dick Mallen, who was making for the hall door, cried back to him, 'Aye, the same place. I wonder his legs don't give out by the time he reaches there.'

'Seven miles over and seven miles back he has to go; done it since he was that high.' Thomas measured a distance of four feet from the ground. An' I can't get near the beggar. And he won't speak, not a word. Skites off; that is after he's had a good look at me.' He gave an exaggerated heave to his chest and preened himself, and his voice now couldn't be heard for the laughter. 'Come on, come on, we'll change our route, we'll go round by the Low Fields.'

The whole party now swarmed out on to the terrace, where, below on the broad drive, three keepers were waiting. Led now by Thomas, they went through the gardens, skirted the lake, crossed in single file the narrow bridge over the stream that led to the River Allen, then bunched together again and, with the exception of the keepers, laughing and shouting to each other, they stumbled over the stretch of valley called the Low Fields, which edged the north boundary of the estate, and so came to a ridge of shale hills.

After rounding the foot of the hills they were brought to an abrupt stop by Thomas, who was standing, his arm outstretched, pointing.

Before them, about twenty yards distant, a zig-zag pathway cutting up the side of a steep hill met up with the lower mountain road which, at this time of the year, was the only passable road between Alston and Whitfield. At the foot of the mountain and to the right of this pathway was a high peak of rock, accessible to the ordinary climber from one side only, and on top of the rock sat a boy.

From this distance the boy looked to be about twelve years old. His thin body was dressed warmly, not in the rough working man's style, nor yet was he dressed like that of the gentry, but his great coat had a collar to it which was turned up about his ears. He wore no cap and his hair, from this distance, looked jet black.

The whole company looked up towards him and he down at them.

'Why don't you rush him?' It was a quiet voice from behind, and Thomas answered as quietly, 'We tried it. He's as fast as the hare itself; he could skid down from that rock quicker than I can say Jack Robinson.'

'Have you never got any nearer to him?'

'Never. But one of these days, one of these days.'

'Where does he come from?'

'Oh, over the mountain, near Carr Shield.'

'Well, you could go and see him when the weather's fine. Haven't you thought of it?'

Thomas Mallen turned round and gazed at the speaker; his blue eyes were bright and laughing as he said, 'Yes, yes, I've thought of it; but then'—he spread one hand wide—'if I were to visit all my streaks I'd have no time for my estate. Now would I?' Both hands were held out in appeal now and as the laughter rang over the mountain and echoed into the next valley the boy suddenly disappeared from view, and they didn't see him make for the pass although they stood for some time scanning the hills before them.

TWO

It had snowed for two days, thawed a little, then froze, and the five guests left in the house had skated on the lake. They were Frank Armstrong, his wife, Kate, and daughter, Fanny, and Dick Mallen's two friends, William Lennox and Carl Breton-Weir.

Thomas Mallen had allowed his two nieces, Barbara and Constance Farrington, to join the company. It had been a great day for the children, for they were seldom, if ever, allowed to mingle with the guests. When Thomas was at home alone, which wasn't very often, he had the children brought down in the afternoon to share his dinner, and he would laugh and joke with them and make funny remarks about their governess, Miss Brigmore. The two girls loved their Uncle Thomas; he was the only man in their lives and they had lived under his care for six years now, having been brought to the Hall when Barbara was four and Constance one year old. They were the children of his step-sister, who had, against repeated warnings by him, married one Michael Farrington, a man with only one asset, charm. Michael Farrington had deserted his wife when she was carrying his second child but Thomas had known nothing of this until he had received a letter from her telling him that she was near death and begging him to take into his care her two small children. It says much for the man that he immediately made the journey to London and spent two days with her before she died. Then he brought the children from what, to him, were appalling lodgings, back to the Hall.

First, he engaged a nurse for them and then a governess. The nurse had long since gone, but the governess, Miss Brigmore, was still with them, and Barbara was now ten and Constance seven years old.

The children's world consisted of six rooms at the top of the east wing of the house, from which they descended by a back staircase once a day, if the weather was clement, to the world below, accompanied on such journeys by Mary Peel, the nursery attendant. If the coast was clear and Mrs. Brydon, the housekeeper, or Mr. Tweedy, the steward, or Mr. Dunn, the butler, weren't about Mary would take them through the kitchen and let them stop and have a cheery word with the cook and kitchen staff, and receive tit-bits in the form of rich sticky ginger fingers, or a hot yeasty cake split and filled with jam and cream, two delicacies which were forbidden by Miss Brigmore, who was a believer in plain fare for children.

The children adored Mary Peel and in a way looked upon her as a mother figure. Of course, they both knew that Mary was very common and of no account; all the staff in the house were of no account, at least those below Brown, who was their Uncle Thomas's valet, and Taylor, who was Uncle Dick's valet. But they were aware that even these two personages did not come any way near Miss Brigmore's station. Their governess, they knew, was someone apart from the rest of the staff. Miss Brigmore had not stated this in words, but her manner left no one in doubt about it.

The girls had never experienced such pleasure as the afternoon spent on the ice. They squealed and laughed and caused great amusement as they fell on their bottoms and clung to the legs of first one escort and then the other. Barbara fell in love with Mr. Weir and Constance with Mr. Lennox, because both these gentlemen went out of their way to initiate them into the art of skating. Their Uncle Thomas, too, did his share in their coaching; only Uncle Dick did not take his turn with them for he skated constantly with Miss Fanny Armstrong.

On the side of the lake they ate hot chops which they held in a napkin, and their Uncle Thomas let them sip from his pewter tankard. The drink was hot and stinging and they coughed and their eyes watered and everybody laughed. It was a wonderful, glorious day.

They were still under the spell and talking about it at half-past six when Miss Brigmore retired to her room to have her supper. This was the only part of the day, with the exception of their exercise time, or when they were in bed, that they were free of Miss Brigmore's presence; but even now they weren't alone, for Mary Peel sat with them. But Mary didn't count. They could say what they liked in front of Mary; being with Mary was as good as being by themselves. Even when she joined in their conversation, as now, it didn't matter.

'No right to talk about Mr. Armstrong in that manner, Miss Barbara,' she said, lifting her eyes from one of their nightdresses, the front of which she was herringboning.

'Well I don't like him, Mary.'

'What's there to dislike about him? He's a fine man; he owns a mine, a big mine, away . . . away over the hills.'

'How far?'

'Oh, a long way, Miss Constance; a place I've never seen, near the city, they say; beyond the Penny Hills, and that's a mighty long distance.'

'Have you to be rich before you can be good, Mary?'

'Ah! Miss Barbara, fancy asking a question like that: have you to be rich afore you can be good?'

'Well, you said he was a good man.'

'Well, so he is, according to his lights.'

'What lights?'

'Oh, Miss Constance, don't keep asking me questions I can't answer. Sufficient it be he's a life-long friend of the master's, an' that should be enough for anybody.'

'Is it true that Miss Fanny is going to marry Uncle Dick?'

Mary now turned her head sharply and looked at the thin, dark girl sitting to one side of the round table, her paint brush poised over a piece of canvas, and she asked sharply, 'How did you come to hear that, Miss Barbara?'

'Little pigs have got big ears.' This came from the

12

fair child sitting opposite, and the two girls leant across the table towards each other and giggled.

'Little pigs have got big ears' was a saying constantly on Mary's lips, and now she reprimanded them sternly, saying, 'Aye; well, little pigs have their ears cut off sometimes when they hear too much.'

'But is she, Mary?'

'You know as much about it as me, Miss Barbara.'

'I don't, Mary. You know everything.'

Mary Peel tightened her lips to suppress a smile, then said in mock harshness, 'I know this much, as soon as Miss Brigmore enters that door I'll tell her to smack your backsides.'

Again they were leaning across the table. They knew that Mary didn't like Miss Brigmore and that whenever she could she opposed her; as for Mary giving them away in anything, they would have sooner believed that Miss Brigmore's God was a figment of the imagination, like the ogres in fairy tales.

'When are the Armstrongs going home?' Barbara now asked.

'The morrow, as far as I know.'

'Oh.' Both the children now sat straight up in their chairs, but it was Barbara who said, 'That means that to-night there'll be carry-on and high jinks and divil's fagarties.'

Mary Peel rose hastily to her feet and, coming to the table, she looked fearfully from one to the other, saying under her breath, 'If Miss Brigmore hears you comin' out with anythin' like that, you know what'll happen, not only to you, but to me. An' I'm warnin' you, for she'll have me kept downstairs and then you could have anybody up here, Nancy Wright, or Kate Steel.'

'Oh no! no!' They both grabbed at her hands, crying softly, 'We were only teasing, Mary.' Barbara looked up into the round, homely face which to her was both old and young because twenty-seven was a very great age for anyone to be, and she said, 'We like your sayings, Mary, we think they're nice, much better than Miss Brigmore's.'

Mary nodded grimly from one to the other. 'Well, I can tell you this much, Miss Brigmore wouldn't agree

13

with you. And how do you know anyway about the ... about the divils, I mean carry-on?'

'Oh'—they looked at each other and grinned impishly—'we sometimes get up and creep down to the gallery. We hid in the armour box last week. It's a good job it was empty.'

'Oh my God!' The words came as a faint whisper through Mary's fingers, which she was holding tightly over her mouth. Then giving her attention wholly to Barbara, she whispered, 'Look you, Miss Barbara, look, now promise you'll not do it again. Promise? ... In the armour box! How in the name of God did you get the lid up, child?'

'Well, it was very heavy but we managed to get in. But we couldn't get out.'

'You couldn't get out?' Mary had dropped her hand from her mouth and she gaped at them for a moment before she asked under her breath, 'Well, how did you then?'

'We knocked on the lid and called, and Waite opened it.'

'Waite?'

'Yes.' They were both nodding at her.

'What did he say?'

'He just said what you said.'

Mary screwed her brows up trying to recollect what she had said, and when she seemed to be finding some difficulty Constance put in with a smile, 'He said, "Oh my God!"'

Mary sat down suddenly on the third chair at the table and, picking up the corner of her long white, apron, she passed it round her face before leaning towards them and again saying, 'Promise me on God's honour you'll not do anything like that again ... Now come on, promise?'

It was Connie who nodded her promise straightaway, but Barbara remained quiet, and Mary said, 'Aw, Miss Barbara.'

'Well, I cannot promise you, Mary, 'cos I know I'll break my promise. You see, I like watching the ladies and gentlemen at their games.'

Again Mary put her hand across her mouth. Then

14

the sound of a door closing brought her to her feet and all she could say to Barbara was, 'Oh Miss! Miss!' before the governess entered the room.

Miss Brigmore was of medium height. She would have been termed very pretty if she hadn't looked so prim. Her hair was brown, her eyes were brown, and her mouth was well shaped. She had a good skin and a well developed figure, in fact her bust was over developed for her height.

Miss Brigmore was thirty years old. She had come from a good middle class family, and up till the age of sixteen had had her own governess. The fact that her governess's wages, together with that of the eight other staff her father kept in his house on the outskirts of York, and the establishment of his mistress in the heart of York, were being supplemented by the clients of his bank, wasn't made public until Anna Brigmore was almost seventeen.

Her mother did not sustain the shock of her husband's imprisonment but Anna did. When she buried her mother she also buried her father. When she applied for her first post of governess she said she was an orphan; and she actually was an orphan when, at twenty-four, she entered the service of Mr. Thomas Mallen of High Banks Hall in the County of Northumberland, there to take charge of his two nieces.

On her first encounter with Thomas Mallen she had not thought, what a gross pompous individual! for her heart had jerked in her breast. She was not aware that most women's hearts jerked in their breasts when Thomas Mallen looked at them. He had a particular way of looking at a woman; through long practice his look would convince them that they were beautiful, and interesting, and above all they were to be desired.

During her six years in the Hall Miss Brigmore had made no friends. She had been brought up to look upon servants as menials, and the fact that she was now earning her own living did not, in her mind, bring her down to their level.

Miss Brigmore now looked at the children's embroidery and her brief comment was, 'You have been idling; go and get ready for bed,' and turning towards

15

Mary Peel she added, 'See to them.' Then she went through the day nursery and so into the school room. Taking from the shelves three books, she sat down at the oblong table and began to prepare the lessons for the following day, but after a moment or two she pushed the books aside and rose to her feet, then went to the window where she stood looking out into the darkness. Yet through the darkness she pictured the lake as she had seen it earlier in the day. She could see them all in pairs, with hands crossed, weaving in and out; she could see the children tumbling about; she could hear the laughter, in which she did not join.

She, like the children, preserved a vivid memory of the skating party—because the master had looked at her from the ice. He had not only looked at her, he had laughed at her. But he had never asked her to skate. No one had thought to ask her to skate. And she could skate; at one time she had been an excellent skater . . . at one time she had been young. But now she was thirty. Yet the master had looked at her as if she were still young. . . . Slowly she left the window and returned to the table.

It was around eleven o'clock when the first squeals of delight floated faintly up from the far hall to the nursery and brought Barbara sitting upright in bed. Hugging her knees with her arms, she strained her ears to listen. What games were they playing to-night? Would Uncle Dick be chasing Miss Fanny along the gallery, and when he caught her would he pull her behind the curtain like she did with Connie when they were playing hide-and-seek with Mary? or would one of the ladies slide down the banister again? She had actually seen one start at the top but she had been unable to see what happened when she reached the bottom; but she had heard the squeals of laughter. Then there was the time she had seen three gentlemen in their nightshirts carrying someone shoulder high down the main staircase. She hadn't been able to see if it was a lady or a gentleman they were carrying, only that the person's feet and legs were bare up to the knees.

16

If Mr. Armstrong and his family were leaving to-morrow then Uncle Dick and his friends would leave shortly afterwards, and Uncle Thomas, too, would go about his business. From then onwards the house would become quiet again, except for the laughter of the servants, and there would only be Miss Brigmore, with Mary for light relief.

At this moment the future appeared very dull to Barbara. She looked through the dim glow of the night-light towards the other bed and saw that Connie was fast asleep. Connie had promised Mary not to go down, but she hadn't promised, had she?

Quietly she pushed back the bedclothes and got out of bed; then getting into her slippers and dressing gown she tip-toed quietly to the bedroom door which opened into the day nursery. Having groped her way across the dark room, she now gently turned the handle of the door leading on to the landing.

The landing was lit by one candle standing in a three-branch candelabrum. She peered first one way and then the other and she was tip-toeing gently to the head of the stairs when she heard the little sound. She stopped, and looked back towards the end of the landing to the door opposite where their bedroom door would have been if it had opened onto the landing instead of into the day nursery. The sound could have been a laugh, or a moan, and it had come from Miss Brigmore's bedroom which was next to her sitting room.

There it was again, a soft moaning sound not unlike the sound she herself made when she had toothache and hid her head under the bedclothes. Was Miss Brigmore ill? She did not care for Miss Brigmore but she must remember that the governess was always kind to them when they felt ill, and now she might be in need of assistance; perhaps she required some mixture out of the white bottle in the medicine cupboard, the same as she gave to them when they had stomach trouble.

She turned and tip-toed down the length of the landing until she was opposite Miss Brigmore's door. The sound was louder now but still soft. She noted that

Miss Brigmore's door was just the slightest bit ajar. Slowly her hand lifted and she pressed it open, but only wide enough to take the shape of her face and allow her to see into the room.

What she saw caused her to hold her breath for so long that she imagined she had stopped breathing altogether. Miss Brigmore was in her bed; the bedclothes were rumpled down to her waist, and the top of her body was bare, and lying by her side, and leaning over her, his clothes, too, rumpled, was her Uncle Thomas. He was supporting himself on his elbow and gazing down into Miss Brigmore's face while his hand caressed her breast. She noticed that Miss Brigmore had her eyes closed, but her mouth was open and from it were coming the soft moans that weren't really moans.

As she went to take in a deep gulp of air she became conscious of a movement behind her and she turned quickly to see Connie coming down to the landing. With swift silent steps she reached her sister and, grabbing her hand, she dragged her back into the nursery, and there in the dark she turned and closed the door, but softly. Then pushing Connie before her, she went towards the dim light coming from the night nursery.

'What is it?' Connie turned to her. 'I woke up; you weren't in bed. What . . . what is wrong? Is Miss Brigmore sick?'

Barbara shook her head violently before she could say, 'No, no.'

'There was a noise.'

'She . . . she was snoring.'

'Oh.' Constance giggled now. 'Does Miss Brigmore snore? I didn't know. Perhaps Mary doesn't know either. You must tell Mary. Does she do it like the pigs on the farm, like this?'

The snort brought a hasty 'Ssh!' from Barbara, and she pushed Constance forward as she said, 'Get back into bed.'

'Aren't you going down to the gallery?'

'No, no, I'm not. Get back into bed.'

'What's the matter, Barbie?'

"Nothing, nothing; just go to bed. Come on.' She

18

pulled her onto the bed, then tucked the clothes round her.

'You're vexed, Barbie.'

'I'm not, I'm not. Go to sleep.'

'Good-night, Barbie.'

'Good-night.'

She herself now climbed into bed and lay rigid, staring up at the rose coloured patterns on the ceiling created by the red glass vase which held the night light. Her Uncle Thomas doing that to Miss Brigmore and Miss Brigmore not stopping him. It was wicked. Miss Brigmore herself would have said it was wicked. But she had lain quite still with her eyes closed. Suddenly her body bounced in the bed and she turned onto her face and buried it in the pillow. But having blotted out her uncle and Miss Brigmore from her mind, they were now replaced by the ladies' and gentlemen's games she had watched from the gallery and the balcony and she knew there was a connection between them and the scene she had just witnessed. Her uncle was bad; Miss Brigmore was bad; all the ladies and gentlemen were bad; the only people who weren't bad were Mary Peel, Connie and herself. She wished the ice had cracked today and she had fallen through and been drowned.

THREE

'Look, boy, what the hell do you want, waking me at this ungodly hour?' Thomas Mallen heaved himself round in the bed, then pulled his nightcap from the back of his head down onto his brow as he screwed up his bleary eyes at the clock. 'Ten minutes to seven. God sakes! what's up with you?'

'I've got to talk with you, Father.' Dick Mallen hoisted himself up on to the side of the four-poster bed and, leaning forward, he said in a tense undertone, 'I'm in a fix. I . . . I need two thousand straightaway. It's imperative I have two thousand straightaway.'

'Ah!' Thomas fell back into the billowing soft pillows with a flop and, raising his arms towards the ceiling, he waved his hands at it as he addressed it, saying, 'It's imperative he has two thousand straightaway.' Then twisting on to his side he looked at his son with an alert gaze now and said soberly, 'What's come over you? What's happened?'

'I lost.'

'But you're always losing.'

'That isn't true.'

'Well, what I mean is, you've lost before and it wasn't . . . imperative you had two thousand right away.' He glanced at the clock again. 'Ten to seven in the morning and demanding two thousand! There's something more besides this.' He pulled himself upwards, very wide awake now, and stared at his son. 'Out with it.'

'I made a mistake.'

'You what?'

'I said I made a mistake.'

'You mean you cheated?'

'No, I tell you I . . .'

'You bloody well cheated! Playin' against fellows like Lennox and Weir, you had the bloody nerve to cheat. You must be mad.'

'I . . . I didn't cheat; there was a slight mistake.'

'Look. Look.' Thomas shook his fist menacingly at him. 'I'm an old bull; don't try to put the blinkers on me, boy. If you want two thousand straightaway you cheated. Who's pressing you?'

'Weir.'

'It would be, that bastard! . . . Well, what's the alternative?'

Dick hung his head. 'He'll finish me in town . . . and everywhere else for that matter.'

'Has he any proof?'

'Lennox'll stand by his word.'

'By God! boy, you do pick your friends. How much do you owe them altogether?'

'Four, four thousand. But Lennox'll wait.'

'They'll both bloody well wait. Get by and let me up out of this; I'll deal with them.'

'No! No, you won't.' Dick had his hands on his father's shoulders now pressing him back. 'See me through this and I'll promise it'll be the last. Honest to God, I promise.'

'I've heard that before. Take your hands off me.' There was a threat in the tone, and when his son quickly withdrew his hold Thomas slowly sat up and, thrusting his feet over the side of the high bed, he sat for a moment and held his face in his hand pressing one cheek in with his thumb and the other with his fingers before he said soberly, 'And now I'm going to tell you something. I've kept it from you for some time. I didn't want to spoil your fun, and wanted Bessie settled. But I, too, am in it up to the neck. At this present moment I couldn't raise four hundred let alone four thousand.'

The father and son stared at each other. It was Thomas who eventually broke the silence. Nodding slowly, he said, 'I've been banking on you fixing it up with Fanny. That settled, I gathered Frank would see me through, but not otherwise. I know she's a bit long in the tooth, but it won't be the first time a man's married a woman five years older than himself. I haven't pressed you, I thought I could see how things were going on their own. You asked her to stay on. . . .'

Dick's voice, almost like a groan, cut his off. 'Aye, I did, but for God's sake! not because I wanted to marry her, she's been laid more times than an old sow.'

Ignoring the scornful vehemence of his son's tone Thomas said quietly, 'That might be, but beggars can't be choosers. She's your only hope, and not only yours but mine an' all. I'm going to tell you something else, boy, and listen carefully, very carefully, for this means more to you in a way than it does to me an' it's just this. If you don't marry her it'll be the end of this.' He now lifted his hand and moved it slowly backwards and forwards in a wide sweep. 'Everything, every damned thing.'

There was a long pause. Then, his voice a mere whisper, Dick said, 'You can't mean it . . . everything?' His face was screwed up against the incredibility of the statement.

'That's what I said, everything. I've survived on borrowed money for the past ten years. It's only by keeping up appearances that I've swum this far. Let them think you've still got it and they'll give you credit. But now, boy'—he sighed deeply—'I'm tired of swimming against the tide. Mind you I never thought I'd confess to that, but there it is.' He now gently patted the great mound of his stomach. 'It's beginning to tell here an' all. I haven't the taste for life I used to have.'

'You don't do so badly.' There was deep bitterness in the remark, and Thomas replied slowly, 'No, I don't do so badly, true an' I'm not grumbling. I've had a great deal of experience of all kinds of things. But you know, I've learned very little, except one thing, boy, one thing, and that is, everything has to be paid for; sooner or later everything has to be paid for. . . .'

'Oh, for God's sake, shut up! Shut up!' Dick had sprung from the bed now and was holding his hand to

22

his brow. 'Don't you start preaching, you above all people, and at this time. Philosophy coming from you is a joke. It isn't philosophy I want. Don't you understand what they can do to me, those two? I won't dare show my face in any club, can't you see that?'

His arms were now hugging himself. His fists dug into his armpits, like a youth with frozen mitts trying to regain warmth, his body swayed backwards and forwards, and the action so lacking in dignity made Thomas turn his head away from the sight. After a moment he said quietly, 'If I ask Frank for it will you promise to put the question to Fanny before they leave?'

When there was no answer he rose to his feet, saying, 'Well it's up to you. That's the only way. If I lose everything I'm still not losing as much as you, so think on it.'

When he next looked at his son, Dick was standing with his head drooped on his chest, his hands hanging limp at his sides, and Thomas said, softly, 'They'll be leaving about twelve. When you see me going into the library with Frank you corner Fanny, that's if you haven't done it before. If Weir's as mean as he sounds your best policy is to get it settled as soon as possible. I don't expect there'll be any hesitation on her part, she's past the choosing stage.'

Thomas now watched his son flounce about as a woman might have done and stalk down the length of the long room and out into the corridor. Then he bent his head and his eyes came to rest on his bare stomach visible through his open nightshirt, and as if the sight sickened him he turned his head and spat into the spittoon at the side of the bed.

Thomas did not take Frank Armstrong into the study, nor did Dick at the first opportunity ask Fanny to be his wife. These arrangements were cancelled by the arrival on the drive at ten o'clock that morning of a shabby cab, from which three men slowly descended. Having mounted the steps one after the other, the first of them pulled the handle that was hanging below the

23

boar's head to the side of the great door. When the bell clanged within, the man turned and looked at his two companions, and they all waited.

The door was opened by Ord, the first footman. His gaze flicked haughtily over what he immediately stamped as the lower type of business men, and his voice portraying his feelings he said briefly, 'There is a back door.'

The first man, stepping abruptly forward, almost pushed the footman on to his back with a swift jab of his forearm, and when the three of them had entered the hall they stopped in some slight amazement, looking around them for a moment, before the first man, addressing Ord again, said, 'I wish to see your master.'

'My master is engaged. What is your business?'

'I'll tell that to your master. Now go and tell him that a representative of the Dulwich Bank would like a word with him.'

The Dulwich Bank. The very name seemed to convey trouble, and Ord, his manner no less haughty now but his feelings definitely uncertain, made his stately way towards the morning room where his master was breakfasting, and there he motioned to Waite, the second footman, who was assisting in carrying the heavy silver dishes from the kitchen, to pause a minute and he whispered in his ear, 'Tell Dunn I want him, it's very important. There's fellas here from the Bank.'

A moment later Dunn appeared outside the morning room door and he glanced across the hall towards the dark trio; then looking at Ord he said, 'What do they want?'

'The master; they're from the Bank.'

The butler looked at the men again, paused a moment, then turned and with unruffled step went back into the morning room.

It was a full five minutes later when Thomas put in an appearance. His head still maintained its jaunty angle, his shoulders were still back, his stomach still protruding, his step still firm, the only difference about him at this moment was that his colour was not as ruddy as usual, but that could have been put down to a series of late nights.

24

'Well, gentlemen!' He looked from one to the other of the men.

It was the tallest of them who again spoke. 'Mr. Thomas Richard Mallen?'

'At your service.'

'I would like a word with you in private if I may.'

'Certainly, certainly.'

The politeness seemed to disconcert the three men and they glanced at each other as they followed the portly figure across the magnificently carpeted and furnished hall. Their eyes, like those of weasels, darted around the room into which they followed the master of the house; moving from the row of chandeliers down to the furniture and furnishings.

In the middle of the room Thomas turned and, facing the men now, said, 'Well now, gentlemen, your business?'

His casual manner caused a moment's pause; then the tall man said, with some deference in his tone now, 'I represent the Dulwich Bank, Sir. I understand that a representative from there called on you some three months gone when your situation was made clear, since when they have had no further word from you.'

'Oh, that isn't right. I said I would see into the matter.'

'But you haven't done so, Sir.'

'Not yet ... no.'

'Then I'm afraid, Sir, it is my duty to hand you this.' Whereupon the man drew a long official envelope from the inside pocket of his coat and held it towards Thomas.

For a matter of seconds Thomas's arm remained by his side; then slowly he lifted it and took the envelope, and he stared down at it before opening it. Then still slowly, he withdrew and unfolded the double official paper. After his eyes had scanned the top of the first page he folded it again and replaced it in the envelope, and walking to the mantelpiece, he placed the envelope on the marble shelf before turning to the men again saying, 'Well what now?'

'We take possession, Sir.'

'Possession?' There was a crack in the coolness of Thomas's manner.

'That is the procedure, Sir. Nothing must be moved, nothing. And it . . . it tells you there'—the man motioned to the envelope on the mantelpiece—'when you'll have to appear afore the Justices. Being a private debtor, of course, you'll not be put to the indignity of going inside, Sir, as long as you're covered.'

'Oh, thank you.'

The sarcasm was not lost on the man and his chin nobbled before he said, 'I'm just explainin', Sir. Anyway if you'd taken action two years gone when you had the chance . . .'

'That's enough, my man!' Thomas's whole manner had changed completely. 'Do your business but oblige me by not offering me your advice.'

The man's jaw moved from side to side now and his eyes narrowed and it was some seconds before he spoke again, saying, 'This is Mr. Connor, and Mr. Byers, they will make an inventory. It will take some days. We will board here, you understand . . . Sir?'

Apparently Thomas hadn't understood the full significance of the presence of the three men until now, and he exclaimed stiffly, 'Board here!'

'Yes, Sir, board here, until the debts are paid or the equivalent is made in the sale. I thought you'd be aware of the procedure, Sir.'

There was a definite note of insolence in the man's voice now, and under other circumstances, and if he'd had a whip in his hand, Thomas would have brought it across the fellow's face. But he was wise enough to realize that for the next few hours he would need this man's co-operation, for he was now in a hell of a fix. It would happen that Kate Armstrong would get a belly pain in the night and was now unfit to travel until the afternoon or perhaps to-morrow.

He looked at the man again and forced a conciliatory note into his voice as he said, 'Yes, I understand. And you will be boarded and well, for as long as there is food . . . and'—he gave a weak laugh—'I should say the stocks are pretty ample. But one thing I would ask of you and that is to delay the taking of your inventory until later in the day when, I hope I'm right in saying, there will be no need for it.'

He turned now to the mantelpiece and took down the envelope again and, opening it, he read for some minutes before he said, 'I understand a sum of thirty thousand would assuage the Bank for the moment. Well, it is more than possible I shall be able to give you a note to this effect before this afternoon. . . . Will you comply, gentlemen?'

The three men looked at one another. It wasn't every day that their business settled them in a house like this where they might remain for two to three weeks. It was just as well to keep on the right side of those who were providing the victuals, and who knew, there might be some extra pickings. The place was breaking down with finery: the china and trinkets in those cabinets lining the far wall looked as if they might be worth a mint in themselves. And then there were the pictures in this one room alone. Yet, would all the stuff in the house and the estate itself clear him? They said he was up to the neck and over. He had mortgaged, and re-mortgaged for years past now, and that wasn't counting the money owing the trades folk. Why, they said, only three years ago he had carpeted and curtained the place out afresh. Ten thousand it had cost him. Well, it should have cost him that if he had paid it. Three thousand the firm had got and that, they understood, was all. The only tradesman who hadn't put in a claim apparently was the coal supplier, but then he got his coal straight from Armstrong's pit. Would it be from Armstrong he was hoping to get the loan? It would have to be some butty who would stump up thirty thousand by this afternoon.

The tall man nodded now before he said, 'Very well, Sir. But there's one thing: you'd better tell them, the servants, who we are; we want to be treated with respect, not like dirt, 'cos we have a job to do. An' tell them an' all not to try to lift anything; it's a punishable offence to lift anything, prison it is for lifting anything.'

Thomas's face had regained its colour for temper was now boiling in him, so much so that he was unable to speak. He made a motion with his head; then turning to the bell rope at the side of the fireplace he pulled it twice.

When Ord entered the room Thomas looked at him and swallowed deeply before saying, 'Take these men to the kitchen, see that they are fed. They ... they are to be treated with courtesy. They will remain there, in those quarters, until this afternoon.'

'Yes, Sir.'

Ord looked at the men and the men looked at him, then they all went out.

After staring at the closed door for some seconds, Thomas gazed slowly round the room as if he had found himself in a strange place. What was really happening was that now, on the point of losing his home, he was recognising its full splendour for the first time. His eyes finally came to rest on the portrait over the mantelpiece. It was not a portrait of his father but of his grandfather, the man who had built this house. It had been painted while he was in the prime of his life; his hair was still black and the streak flowed like molten silver from the crown of his head down to his left temple. The face below it was a good face, and yet they said it was with him the ill luck had started; yet it was with him also that the Mallen fortunes had flourished, because although they could date their family back to the sixteenth century it was only in the Industrial Revolution that the Mallens had come up from among the ordinary merchants.

Through wool, and various other activities, Wigmore Mallen had amassed a fortune. He'd had four sons and each one he provided with an education that could only be purchased with money. One of them gave him cause for great pride for he was sent to Oxford and became a scholar. But not one of his sons died in his bed, all had violent deaths.

Thomas's own father had been shot while deer-stalking in Scotland. It was an accident, they said. No one could tell how the accident had really happened. The shot could have come from any one of the dozen guests out that day, or any one of the keepers. Thomas had often wondered how he himself would die. At times he had been a little afraid but now, having passed the fifty mark and having lived vitally every day of his life since he was sixteen, the final incident that would end his existence no longer troubled him. But what was troubling him at this moment, and greatly, was that the end, when it came, might be so undignified as to take place in drastically reduced circumstances and without causing much concern among those who mattered. Such was his make-up that this thought was foremost in his mind, for being a Mallen he must not only be a man of consequence, but be seen to be such. Even the fact that he had confessed to his son that he was weary of the struggle did not alter the fact that he had no desire to end the struggle in penury.

He laid his head on his arm on the mantelshelf and ground out through clenched teeth, 'Damn and blast everything to hell's flames!' He lifted his head and his eyes focussed on the massive gilt frame of the picture. What would become of them if Frank didn't give a hand? Frank Armstrong he knew to be a close man, a canny man. He had clawed himself up from nothing, and had thrust aside his class on the way. He had kicked many a good man down, pressed faces in the mud, and stood on shoulders here and there, all to get where he was to-day. Frank, he knew, had a heart as soft as the stones he charged his miners for should they send any up from the depths in their skips of coal. Oh, he had no illusions about his friends. But there was one crack in Frank's stony heart, and it wasn't made by his wife, but by his daughter. Frank would do anything to get Fanny settled, happily settled. Fanny had flown high and fallen a number of times. Now she had pinned her sights on Dick and her father would be willing to pay a good price to secure for her, if not happiness, then respectability. But would he go as far as thirty thousand now and the same again when the knot was tied? He doubted it. And yet he just might, for he had an eye on this house and would be tempted to go to the limit in order to see his daughter mistress of it.

He straightened up, adjusted his cravat, sniffed loudly, ran his hand over his thick grey hair, then went out of the drawing room in search of Frank Armstrong.

FOUR

By dinner-time everyone in the house, with the exception of the guests, knew that the bums were in. Even the children in the nursery knew the bums were in. They had heard Mary talking to Miss Brigmore in a way they had never heard Mary talk before, nor had they witnessed such reaction from Miss Brigmore, because Miss Brigmore could only repeat, 'Oh no! Oh no!' to everything that Mary said.

Earlier, Barbara had been unable to look at Miss Brigmore, at least not at her face, for her eyes were drawn to her bust, now tightly covered. There were ten buttons on her bodice, all close together like iron locks defending her bosom against attack, but Barbara could see past the locks and through the taffeta bodice to the bare flesh as she had seen it last night.

Miss Brigmore had asked her if she wasn't well and she had just shaken her head; Connie had asked if she wasn't well, and Mary had asked her if she wasn't well. Then of a sudden they had forgotten about her, for Mary came rushing up the stairs and did the most unheard-of thing, she took Miss Brigmore by the hand and almost pulled her out of the schoolroom and into the day nursery.

She and Connie had tip-toed to the door and listened. 'It's the bums, Miss,' Mary had said, and Miss Brigmore had repeated, 'The bums?'

'Yes, bailiffs. You know, Miss, bailiffs, duns. They're in the kitchen, they're stayin' put until s'afternoon; then they'll start tabbing everything in the house. It's the end, it's the end, Miss. What's goin' to happen? What about the bairns?'

'Be quiet! Be quiet, Mary.' Miss Brigmore often told Mary to be quiet, but she very rarely used her name; and now when she did it it wasn't like a reprimand, because she added, 'Go more slowly; tell me what's happened. Has . . . has the master seen them?'

'Oh yes, Miss, yes, Miss. An' they're all nearly frantic in the kitchen. It means the end. They'll all get the push, Miss. But what about the bairns? An' where'll we all go? They say he owes a fortune, the master, thousands, tens of thousands. All the stuff in the house and the farms won't pay for it, that's what they say. Eeh! and the money that's been spent, like water it's been spent. . . .'

'Be quiet, Mary!'

In the silence that followed the children stood looking at each other, their eyes stretched, their mouths wide, until Mary's voice came to them again, saying, 'Will they be able to take the bairns' cottage, Miss?'

'The cottage? Oh no, no. Well, I don't think they can touch that. It was left to the children, together with the legacy. They can't touch that. No, they can't touch that.'

There was another silence before Miss Brigmore asked, 'The master, how does he appear?'

'Putting a face on it they say, Miss.'

There was a movement in the next room and Barbara and Constance scrambled to the window seat and sat down. But when no one came in Constance whispered, 'What does it mean, Barbie?'

'I . . . I don't rightly know except we may have to leave here.'

'Will we go and live in our cottage?'

'I . . . I don't know.'

'I'd like to live in our cottage, it's nice.'

Barbara looked out of the window. The view from this side of the house took in the kitchen gardens and the orchards and the big farm. The cottage lay beyond the big farm on the other side of the road, almost a mile along it, and situated, almost like the Hall, with its front to the moors and hills and its back to a beautiful dale. It had eight rooms, a loft and a little courtyard, which was bordered by a barn, two loose boxes and a number of outhouses, and the whole stood in one acre of land.

The cottage had been the home of Gladys Armorer who had been a second cousin to the children's mother. She had objected strongly to Thomas Mallen being given charge of the children for, as she said, she wouldn't trust him to rear a pig correctly, and she would have fought him for charge of the children had it not been she was crippled with arthritis. Yet up to a year ago when she died she had shown little interest in the children themselves, never remembering their birthdays, and only twice inviting them to take tea with her.

So it came as something of a surprise when she left to them her house and her small fortune, in trust, a hundred pounds a year to be allotted to each during their lifetime, with further stipulations which took into account their marriages, also their deaths.

The house stood to-day as when Gladys Armorer had left it, plainly but comfortably furnished. Two servants from the Hall were sent down now and again to air and clean it, and a gardener to see to the ground.

Gladys Armorer had not made Thomas Mallen a trustee for despite his evident wealth she still had no faith in him, but had left the business in the hands of a Newcastle solicitor, which, as things had turned out, was just as well.

'Barbie!' Constance was shaking Barbara's arm now. 'But wouldn't you really like to live in the cottage? I'd love to live there, just you and Mary and Uncle and cook and . . . and Waite, I like Waite.'

'It's a very small cottage. There are only eight rooms, it would only house three people at the most, well perhaps four.'

'Yes.' Constance nodded her head sagely as if to say, 'You're quite right.'

It was at this point that Miss Brigmore and Mary came into the room. They came in like friends might, and Mary, after looking at the children, lowered her head and bit on her lip and began to cry, then turned hastily about and ran from the room.

32

Miss Brigmore now went to the table and began moving the books about as if she were dealing out cards. 'Coming along, children, come along,' she said gently. And they came to the table, and Barbara looked fully at Miss Brigmore for the first time that day and was most surprised to see that she actually had tears in her eyes.

The gallery of the Hall had always caused controversial comment, some saying it was in Italian style, some saying it was after the French. The knowledgeable ones stated it was a hideous mixture of neither. But Thomas always had the last word on the period the gallery represented, saying it was pure pretentious Mallen, for he knew that, even among his best friends, not only the gallery, but the whole Hall was considered too pretentious by far.

The gallery was the place Dick Mallen chose in which to propose marriage to Fanny Armstrong. However distasteful the union with her might appear to him, and the thought of it brought his stomach muscles tensing, he knew that life was a game that had to be played, and with a certain amount of panache, and he needed all the help he could get at the moment, so he picked on the romantic atmosphere prevalent in the gallery.

He opened the arched doorway into the long green and gold room and, bowing slightly, waited for her to pass; then together they walked slowly down the broad strip of red carpet that was laid on the mosaic floor.

There were six windows along each side of the gallery and each had at its base a deep cushioned window seat wide enough to seat two comfortable. The walls between the windows were papered or rather clothed with an embossed green velvet covering, and each afforded room for two large gilt-framed pictures, one placed above the other. In the centre of the gallery ceiling was a great star, and from it gold rays extended in all directions.

It was in the middle of the gallery that Fanny Armstrong stopped, and after looking to where two servants were entering by the far door, she turned her small green eyes to the side where another was in the act of opening or closing a window and she said, 'Is anything amiss?'

'Amiss? What do you mean?'

'I seem to detect an uneasiness in the house . . . in the servants. When I came out of my room a short while ago two maids had their heads together and they scurried away on sight of me as if in alarm.'

He swallowed deeply before he said, 'You're imagining things.'

'I may be'—she was walking on again—'but I also have a keen perception for the unusual, for the out of pattern, and when servants step out of pattern . . . well! Servants are barometers, you know!' She smiled coyly at him now, but he didn't look at her, he was looking ahead as he said, 'Fanny, I would like to ask you something.'

'You would? Well, I'm listening.' Again the coy glance.

He still kept his eyes from her face as he went on, 'What I have to ask you needs a time and a place. This is the place I had chosen, but the time, because of the'—he paused now and smiled weakly at her as he repeated her words, ' "scurry of the servants" is inappropriate. Do you think you could brave the weather with me?'

Her coyness was replaced now by an amused, cynical look which made him uneasy. He knew well enough that once married to her life would become a battle of wills; for underneath her skittish exterior was a woman who would have her own way, and if thwarted all hell would be let loose.

'Why so ceremonious all of a sudden?' She was looking him full in the face. 'If I could follow the dogs and your father through slush and mud for hours then I can risk the slightly inclement weather of to-day, don't you think?' She made a slight move with her lips.

'Good! We'll go to the summerhouse then.' With well-simulated eagerness he caught hold of her hand and drew it through his arm. 'We'll go down the back
34

way; I'll get you a cloak from the gun room.' There was a conspiratorial note in his voice now.

Like two children in step they ran through the door that the servant held open for them, then across a landing towards a green-baized door, and so into a passage, where to the right stairs led up to the nursery, and to the left down to the gun room.

The gun room was at the end of a long wide passage, from which doors led to the housekeeper's sitting room and upper staff dining room, the servants' hall, the butler's pantry; also the door to the cellars, and, at the extreme end, the door to the kitchen.

At the foot of the stairs a maid was kneeling on the flagstone passage with a wooden bucket by her side, and the expanse of stone from wall to wall in front of her was covered in soapy suds.

It was as Dick held out his hand to Fanny, with exaggerated courtesy, in order to assist her to jump prettily over the wet flags while she, with skirts slightly raised, was coyly desisting, that the voice from the butler's pantry came clearly into the corridor, saying, 'I'm sorry for the master, but not for that young skit. Now he'll likely have to do some graft and know what it is to earn his livin', but he won't have the guts for that. By! it's made me stomach sick these last few days to see the carry-on here, the Delavals of Seaton Sluice were nothin' to it. It was them he was trying to ape with his practical jokes, and show off afore his London friends. The Delavals might have been mad with their pranks but at bottom they were class, not a get-up like him.'

The girl had risen from her knees, her face showing her fear, but when furtively she made to go towards the open door Dick Mallen's hand gripped her arm fiercely and held her back. Fanny was still standing at the far side of the soapy patch and he had apparently forgotten her presence for the moment, for his infuriated gaze was fixed on the open door a little to the side of him. The voice coming from there was saying now, 'Those three in the kitchen, bums or bailiffs, call them what you like, they won't wait any longer than s'afternoon, an' they must have had their palms well greased to wait that long. But the old man thinks that by then the young upstart'll have popped the question, 'cos old Armstrong won't stump up any other way. And oh, by God! I hope he gets her. By God! I do, I hope he does, for she'll sort his canister for him, will Miss Fanny Armstrong, if I know anything. Mr. Brown tells me that the old man had to kick his arse this morning to get him up to scratch, 'cos he played up like hell. She was all right for a roll in the feather tick, but marriage, no. Still, beggars can't be choosers, not when the bums are in, and it means the end of Master Big Head Dick if she doesn't. . . .'

When Waite was dragged by the collar of his tight-necked braided uniform coat and flung against the wall of the corridor he was dazed for a moment, but only for a moment, because the next thing he knew was that he was struggling with the young master, and fighting as if for his life.

When he again hit the wall it was Ord's arm this time that had thrust him there, and he slumped for a moment until he heard Dick Mallen yell at him, 'Out! Out! you swine. Do you hear? Out! You're dismissed. If you're not out off the grounds within half an hour . . .'

Waite pulled himself upright from the wall, but he didn't slink away under the fury of the young master as many another servant would have done, for there was in him a stubbornness born of a long line of protesting peasants; his grandparents and great-grandparents had originally worked on the land, but his father had been forced into the pit at the age of seven and when his first child was born he had stated bitterly and firmly, 'This is one who won't have chains atween his legs an' be pulling a bogie when he's seven. My God! no, I'll see to that.' And he had seen to it, for he had put the boy into service.

Harry Waite had started first as a stable lad but soon, the ambitions of his father prompting him, he had turned his eyes towards the house, for promotion was quicker there and the work was easier and you weren't out in all weathers. He had been in two situations before coming to the Hall five years ago, and since then he had married and his wife had given him

36

two children and was on the point of being delivered of a third.

This morning the fortunes of the house had worried him almost as much as they were worrying his master. Positions were difficult to get, particularly if you had to ask for a house in which to house a wife and three children; but being suspended because of the fortunes of the house was one thing, being thrown out without a reference was entirely another, and something to be fought against. And now the resilience of his father, and his father's father against injustice came spurting up in protest, and he dared to face the young upstart, as he thought of him, and say in no deferential term, 'Oh no, I don't; I don't go out of here by your orders, Sir, 'cos I wasn't bonded by you; if anybody's tellin' me to go it'll be the master, not you.'

Even Ord was aghast; as for Dunn, who had just come through the green-baized door and was staring with an incredulous expression at the scene, he was too overcome by the enormity of what he was witnessing to utter a word. Then, his training coming to the fore, he regained his composure and was about to step forward when he was startled by the young master leaping past him and almost overbalancing him as he rushed towards the gun room door.

His intention was so plain to everyone that pandemonium, or something near to it, took place, for now Dunn and Ord almost leapt on Waite and dragged him along the passage and into the kitchen, there to be confronted by the startled staff and three sombre-faced men.

As the butler, releasing Waite, pushed him forward, hissing, 'Get yourself away out, man,' Fanny Armstrong's voice came from the corridor, crying, 'No! No!' Then the kitchen door burst open again and Dick Mallen stood there with a long barrelled gun in his hand. Lifting it to his shoulder, he pointed it to where Waite, who was actually on his way to the far door, had stopped and turned, scarcely believing that the young master could mean to shoot him, yet at the same time knowing that he would.

'Ten seconds . . . I give you ten seconds!'

Whether it was that Waite couldn't quite take in the situation as real, or that his innate stubbornness was preventing him from obeying the command, he did not turn towards the door and run; not even when the kitchen maids screamed and huddled into a corner with the cook, while Dunn and Ord protested loudly, 'Master Dick! Master Dick!' but keeping their distance the while.

The three bailiffs too stood where they were; that is, until Dick Mallen, narrowing his eyes, looked along the barrel of the gun. Then the one who had done the talking so far said in a voice that held authority, 'Put that gun down, Sir, or else you'll do somebody an injury.'

Dick Mallen's eyes flickered for a moment from the gun to the bailiff, and now his hatred of him and all his breed came over in his words as he growled, 'Mind it isn't you.'

When the bailiff sprang forward and gripped the gun there was a moment's struggle in which no one interfered. Then, as Dick Mallen had thrust Waite against the wall only a few minutes previously, now he found himself pushed backwards against the long dresser with the gun across his chest. The indignity was not to be borne. Lifting his knee up he thrust it into the bailiff's belly, then rotating the gun, he brought the butt across the side of the man's head. The bailiff heeled over and hit the stone floor with a dull thud.

There followed a moment of concerted stunned silence, then the women's screams not only filled the kitchen but vibrated through the house.

Only one woman hadn't screamed. Fanny Armstrong had just gasped before turning and fleeing along the corridor, through the green-baized door into the hall, calling, 'Father! Father! Father! Father!'

Like the rest of the household, Frank Armstrong was making his way into the hall, Thomas by his side. They had both been in the library, where Thomas had tactfully touched on the subject of a substantial loan, and Frank Armstrong after humming and hahing had then come into the open and said, 'Well, it's up to the youngsters, Turk. You know what I want in that direction; if my girl's happy, I'm happy and I'm willin' to

38

pay for it.' It was at the exact moment when Thomas was exhaling one long drawn breath of relief that the screams rang through the house. Now as he watched Fanny Armstrong throw herself into her father's arms, he cried, 'What is it? what is it?' But he received no answer, until Dunn, bursting through the door into the hall, came to his side, then was unable to get his words out.

'What is it, man? What is it, those women screaming?'

'Sir . . . Sir, an . . . an accident.' The imperturbable butler was visibly shaking. 'M . . . Master Dick, the bailiff, he . . . the bailiff, he's, he's injured. Master Dick used his gun on him.'

Thomas glared at the man as if he were about to accuse him of being drunk which he knew he could have done any night after the man's duties were over. Then he bounded across the hall, banging wide the green-baized door, down the corridor and into the kitchen. But he stopped dead just within the doorway. The expression on his face was much the same as had been on his butler's when he had come upon the scene in the corridor not more than five minutes earlier.

Thomas now walked slowly towards the man lying on the floor and looked down at him. His companions had opened his coat, his vest, and his shirt, and one of them had placed his hand on the man's heart, the other was attempting to staunch the blood pouring from the side of his head and face.

'Is . . . is he bad?' Thomas's words were thin and scarcely audible. One of the two men turned a sickly white face up to him and said, 'Seems so, Sir; but he's still breathin'.'

Thomas now swept his glance around the kitchen. Everyone, including his son, seemed fixed as in a tableau. The screaming had stopped; the only sounds came from the girls huddled in the corner of the room.

Thomas's gaze turned on his son. He was standing by a side table, on which the gun now lay; he had one hand still on the barrel, the other was hanging limply by his side; his face, which had been red with fury, now looked ashen. He gazed at his father, wetted his

39

lips, then muttered low, 'Twas an accident. An accident
... I was out to frighten that'—he lifted a trembling
finger and pointed to where Waite was standing utterly
immobile looking like a mummy which had been taken
from its long rest. No muscle of his face moved; he was
not even blinking.

Thomas now let out a bellow and, turning to the
doorway where Frank Armstrong was standing side by
side with the butler, he yelled at Dunn, 'Send the
coach! Get a doctor, quick! Clear those women out.'
He swept his arm towards the corner of the kitchen.
'Get them to bring a door and bring the man upstairs
.... See to it, Ord. You!'—he was pointing at the cook
now—'get hot water. Move! Move yourself.'

The kitchen came to life, scurrying, firghtened, apprehensive life.

Frank Armstrong now moved slowly forward and
stood at Thomas's side and looked down at the man for
a moment before slanting his narrowed gaze towards
where Dick was standing, his hand still on the gun.
Then without a word, he turned and walked out of the
kitchen and back into the hall, where Fanny was supporting herself against the balustrade at the bottom of
the stairs. Without a word he took her arm and together they went up the stairs and into her room, and
there, facing her, he said, 'How did it come about?'

Fanny Armstrong stared at her father. She was not
an emotional type of woman, she was not given to
tears, Frank Armstrong couldn't remember when he
last saw her cry, but now as he watched the tears
slowly well into her eyes and fall down her cheeks he
put his arm about her and, leading her to a chair, said,
'Tell me.'

And she told him.

She began by saying, 'It was because he heard a servant, the footman, speaking the truth about him,' and,
her lips trembling, she ended with deep bitterness, 'The
whole house knows he was being forced into asking me
and that he hated the very idea of it. You know something? I hope the man dies, and he dies too for what
he's done because I hate him. I hate him. I hate him.

Oh Father, let us get out of here, now, now.' The next minute her face was buried against his waistcoat and he had to press her tight into him to stifle the sound of her sobbing.

FIVE

There were four people in the house still unaware of what had taken place during the last hour. They were Miss Brigmore, Mary Peel and the children.

Miss Brigmore, Mary thought, had turned almost human during the last few hours. She told herself that never in her life had she seen anyone change so quickly, and when Miss Brigmore, taking her aside, told her of what she planned to do that very day, well, she couldn't believe her ears, she just couldn't.

And this is what Miss Brigmore had worked out. She, Mary, was to go down into the drawing room, or the dining room, whichever room she found empty, and unbeknown to anyone, she was to pick up small pieces of silver, such as silver napkin rings and a Georgian cruet. One wouldn't be missed as there were three of them on the table most days. Then there was the small Georgian silver tea service that was in the cabinet in the drawing room, there were six pieces and a tray. She was to take large pins and pin anything with handles to her petticoats—did you ever hear anything like it? And Miss Brigmore had even demonstrated how she was to do it. Then, when she had got as much small silver as possible, she was to take from here and there, in the display cabinets, cameos and snuff boxes. She had really gaped at Miss Brigmore when she had told her the exact positions of the pieces; she herself had been in this house almost three times as long as Miss Brigmore and she couldn't have told what was in the cabinets, let alone just where each piece was placed. When she had got her breath back she had asked, 'But what'll we do with all that stuff? They'll take account of up here an' all.'

'Don't be stupid, Mary,' Miss Brigmore had said, reverting to her usual tone; 'they won't remain long up here.'

'But how will we get them out, an' where will we put them?'

'Mary'—Miss Brigmore's voice had been slow and patient—'the children will be going to live at the cottage, won't they? I shall most certainly be accompanying them, very likely you too, and I should not be surprised if the master doesn't reside there for a time. . . .'

'The master at the cottage!'

'Yes,' said Miss Brigmore, 'the master at the cottage, Mary. Now these men start taking an inventory the moment they enter a room, they take mental stock of almost everything they see, bailiffs have eyes like lynxes, nothing escapes them, so it would be foolish, very foolish don't you think, if after collecting the articles we were to leave them up here, or that we should leave the collecting until later for that matter?'

'Yes, Miss,' Mary had answered.

'So you will take the children for their airing as you do every day, but today I shall accompany you, and we shall carry as many things as possible on our persons. What can't be pinned or sewn on we must insert in our bodices. The children will help. We can fasten their cloaks with cameos. . . . Now, listen carefully. . . .'

Miss Brigmore then told Mary where the articles in question were placed, and she ended, 'Go to the drawing room first and if you find it empty, collect the miniatures and snuff boxes, and should anyone ask you what you are about refer them to me; just tell them to come to the nursery and see Miss Brigmore.'

And Mary did exactly as she was told. She had even enjoyed doing it, getting one over on them bums, who were spoiling everything, finishing the Hall off, an' the master an' all. But eeh! wasn't that Miss Brigmore a surprise? Who would have thought it? She was acting like she was almost human.

Mary made four journeys from the nursery to the

ground floor and only one person had asked her what she was about. This was Waite. 'What you up to there, Mary?' he said. 'You can't get away with that. You want to end up along the line?'

'I'm doin' what I'm told, Harry,' she answered tartly. 'You go and see Miss Brigmore.'

'So that's it,' he said.

'That's it,' she answered.

'That one knows what she's about. What's she going to do with them?' said Waite.

'Take them to the cottage for the master.'

'Well, he's likely to need what they'll bring afore he's finished, I suppose. Here, I'll give you a hand,' he said.

But to his proposal she answered, 'No, I know what I'm to get, but you could keep the coast clear outside and if anybody makes for here or the dining room, cough.'

So Miss Brigmore and her charges and Mary Peel went out for a walk before noon. They walked slowly until they were out of sight of the house and then they walked more quickly through the gardens. But their pace was controlled by the weight of their petticoats. They went out through the main gates and along the coach road to the cottage, where, there being no cellar, Miss Brigmore ordered Mary to look in the outhouses for a hammer and chisel. When these were found Miss Brigmore pushed the dining room carpet back until it touched the stout, claw-footed let of the table, then using the hammer and chisel as if so doing were an everyday occurrence to her, she prised up the nine-inch floor board.

After thrusting her hand down into the dark depths, she said, 'This'll do nicely; there's a draught of air passing through and the bottom is rough stone. Now Mary, and you, children, hand me the pieces, carefully, one after the other. There is no need to wrap them as they won't rest here long.'

Constance giggled as she passed her pieces to Miss Brigmore. She was finding the business exciting, whereas Barbara on the other hand showed no outward sign of feeling at all.

Although Miss Brigmore had tried to turn the whole

44

episode into a game Barbara knew it had a very serious side. She was overwhelmed by a sense of insecurity and she remembered this feeling from as far back as the time when her Uncle Thomas had first brought her to the Hall.

Miss Brigmore sensed the feeling in her charge, and after she had replaced the floor board and the carpet was rolled back and the house door closed, she took Barbara's hand and said, 'Come, you and I shall race Mary and Constance to the main road.'

Barbara, too, saw that Miss Brigmore had changed, but in spite of this and the new softness in her, she was still seeing her as she had done the previous night, lying on the bed moaning; and she knew she was wicked.

It was with a certain sense of triumph that Miss Brigmore finally marshalled her pirate company through the main gates after their second visit to the cottage. The day was closing in, it was bitterly cold and raining, but the weather didn't trouble her. The last time she had been engaged in such a manoeuvre she had failed, at least her mother had, and it was only the timely assistance of a friend that had prevented her mother being taken before the justices. But this time she had succeeded. At a rough estimate she guessed they had retrieved some thousand pounds' worth of objects, the minatures being the most valuable. Of course, she admitted to herself, she might have been precipitate in her action, for the master had a good friend in Mr. Armstrong. Morcover, if the match between Miss Fanny and Master Dick were to be arranged, then the problem would be solved, and indeed her action might be frowned upon—or laughed at, which would be harder to bear. But as Mr. Brown had confided in her only yesterday he had his grave doubts concerning Master Dick's intentions. To quote his own words, Master Dick was a bit of an unruly stallion, and he couldn't see Miss Fanny Armstrong breaking him in. In Mr. Brown's opinion, apart from her being much too old for him, she wasn't his type; some stallions, for all their temper and show of strength, had tender mouths, and his guess was that Miss Fanny would pull too hard on the bit.

Mr. Brown's similes always favoured the stables. She sometimes wondered how he had chosen the profession of valet, seeing his knowledge, and apparently his sympathies, lay so much with the four-footed creatures. Nevertheless she was inclined to take Mr. Brown's opinion with some seriousness for he had proved himself to be right on other occasions with regards both to the master and Master Dick.

It was as she was crossing the drive, ushering the children and Mary quickly before her out of the rain, that she had a mental picture of herself explaining her actions to the master, at the opportune moment of course, and the opportune moment, as seen in her mind, brought a warm, exciting glow to her body, for now she could see no end to the opportune moments. If the master's affairs were in order such moments would continue at intervals; if he were forced through circumstances to retire to the cottage they would most certainly continue, and more frequently. Whichever way things went she felt that for once she couldn't lose. Her cloistered, nun-like days were over. She had never been cut out for celibate life. Yet her early upbringing had made it impossible for her to find bodily expression with those males who, in the hierarchy of the staff, were classed as fitting mates for a governess, such as valets and house stewards.

She did not guide her charges towards the front door, nor yet round the corner into the courtyard to the back door, but going in the opposite direction she marshalled them round the side of the house and along the whole length of the back terrace until she entered the courtyard from the stable end; then opening a narrow door, she pushed the children into the passage, followed them and was in turn followed by Mary.

Mr. Tweedy, the steward, Mr. Dunn, the butler, and the housekeeper, Mrs. Brydon, who had all been in deep conversation, turned startled faces towards her, and such were their expressions that she was brought to a halt and enquired, 'What is it? What has happened?'

It was Mrs. Brydon who spoke. 'A dreadful thing, a dreadful thing, Miss Brigmore. You wouldn't believe it; none of us can believe it. Master Dick ... Master Dick attacked one of the bailiffs, the head one. He was going to shoot Waite, I mean Master Dick was, and the bailiff went to stop him. It's all through Waite, he started the trouble. They've sent for the doctor. He's bad, the bailiff, very bad. He could go like that, just like that.' She made a soundless snap with her fingers.

It was Mr. Dunn who said in a very low voice, 'If he does, Master Dick could swing for it seeing it's a bailiff.'

'Quiet! That is enough.' Miss Brigmore's voice thundered over them, then she turned from them and pushed the gasping children along the passage and up the stairs, leaving Mary behind.

Mary stood and gaped at her superiors, then she muttered, 'Waite? What's happened to him?'

The steward's voice was the voice of authority now, head of the household under the master. 'He is packing his belongings and going this very hour. . . now.'

'But . . . but Daisy; she's on her time, they can't . . .'

'Peel!' Mrs. Brydon checked Mary's further protest. 'Enough. It's none of your business. What is your business is to see to the nursery, and get you gone there this instant.'

After a moment's hesitation Mary went, but slowly, not thinking now of the master or of Master Dick, or even of the bailiff, but of Daisy Waite and her trouble. The bairn could come any day, she was over her time; and look at the weather. She paused at a window on the first landing and looked out. Through the blur of rain she could see the family cottages, as they were called. They were allotted to those of the staff who had children yet were in indoor service. The three houses were attached to the end of the stables. As she stared the door of the middle cottage opened and a man came out and although she couldn't identify the figure through the rain she knew it was Harry Waite, for he was lifting a box on to a flat handcart that stood outside the door.

The handcart, which was nothing but a glorified barrow, had caused a great deal of laughter when he had arrived with his belongings on it five years ago. No one had ever heard of a footman coming to take up a position pushing a handcart. But he had withstood the laughter, for apparently his father had made the handcart for him when he first went into service, with the words 'When you've got enough luggage to cover that, lad, you'll be all right.' And now, thought Mary tearfully, he had more than enough luggage, he had two children and a wife ready for her bed. What would happen to them? Where would they go? She wanted to run out and say good-bye to them because Daisy was her friend. But Mrs. Brydon was still in the passage, she could hear her voice.

She went heavily up the remaining stairs shaking her head as she said to herself, 'Eeh! the things that have happened this day; it's like the end of the world, it is that.'

SIX

The house was quiet. It was like the quiet that follows a hurricane; it was so peaceful that if it wasn't for the debris no one would believe that a storm had recently passed that way.

The quiet hit Thomas with the force of deep resonant sound as he entered the Hall. Dunn had not met him at the outer door as was usual—Dunn hadn't time these days to listen for the carriage and be there to take his hat, coat and stick, for Dunn was now doing the work of a number of men—and so as he came hurrying from the direction of the study and towards Thomas he said, 'I'm sorry, Sir.'

Thomas waved his hand. He had helped himself off with his coat, which he now handed to Dunn, saying, 'Has anyone called?'

'Mr. Ferrier's man brought a letter, Sir; it's in the study.'

He walked quickly across the hall now and into the study. A letter was propped against a paper-weight on the only clear space on his desk. He did not take up the slender hoof-handled paperknife to open it, but inserted his finger under the flap and whipped it across the top.

He stood while reading the letter. It was short. 'Dear Thomas, You know without me saying that I sympathise deeply with you in your trouble, and if it were possible for me to help you to any great extent you know I would do so, but things are at a critical stage in the works at present. As I told you when I saw you last, I'm having to close down the factory at Shields. However, if a couple of hundred would be of any use you're very welcome, but I'm sorry I can't rise to a thousand. Drop in any time you feel like it, you'll always be welcome, you know that.' It was signed simply, 'John.'

'You'll always be welcome.' The words came like grit through his teeth. He couldn't believe it. He just couldn't believe it. He crushed the letter in his hand and, putting it on the desk, he beat it flat with his fist. After a moment he sat down in the highbacked leather chair behind the desk and drooped his head onto his chest. Armstrong, Headley, and now Ferrier, men he'd have sworn would have stood by him to the death, for they were his three best friends; moreover they were men on whom he had lavished the best of his house. Why, when John Ferrier's eldest son, Patrick, was married he bought the pair silver plate to the value of more than six hundred pounds; and when their first child was born his christening mug, plate and spoon had cost something, and now here was John, his very good friend, saying he could manage a couple of hundred. It would have been better if he had done what Frank Armstrong had done and ignored his plea altogether. His appeal to Frank had been returned, saying that Mr. Armstrong, his wife and daughter had gone to London, and their stay would be indefinite. . . . And Ralph Headley? He had pushed business his way when he was a struggling nobody, he could almost say he had made him. What was more, for years he had supplemented his income with money he had lost to him in gambling. In his young days he would bet on a fly crawling up the window, and he had done just that a hundred pounds at a time, and had paid up smiling because it was to Ralph, and Ralph needed a hand.

And because he knew just how much he had helped Ralph he had asked him for the loan of three thousand: enough to cover Dick's bail and to clear the servants' wages and see him over the next few months. But what had Ralph sent? a cheque for three hundred pounds. Margaret's wedding was going to cost him something, he said, and the young devil, George, had been spending money like water. Later on perhaps, when he knew how he stood after the wedding, he'd likely be able to help him further.

The condescension that had emanated from that particular letter, and something more, something that had come over in the refusal of his friends to stand by him in this terrible moment of his life had hit him like a blow between the eyes and blurred for a time the knowledge that was pressing against his pride and self-esteem. But now that knowledge had forced its way into the open and could be described by one word, dislike. At one time he would have put the term, jealousy, to it, but not anymore. He knew now what he had really known for years; he had no friends. These men had really disliked him, as many such had disliked his father before him. He was a Mallen; 'Turk' Mallen his supposed friends called him, because his misdeeds had left their mark on the heads of his flyblows. All men whored, but the results of his whoring had a brand on them. He was Turk Mallen, 'the man with a harem in the hills,' as one wit had said. All right, he had made cuckolds out of many men, but he had never let a friend down, nor taken a liberty with his wife, nor shied a gambling debt, and no child born of him had ever gone hungry, not to his knowledge.

A knock came on the door and Dunn entered bearing a tray.

'I thought you might like something hot, Sir.'

'Oh, yes, yes, Dunn.' Thomas looked down into the steaming mug that held hot rum, and he sniffed and gave a wry smile as he said, 'This must be running short by now.'

'I've managed to secure a certain number of bottles, Sir.'

'Ah! well now, that was good thinking.' Again the wry smile. 'They'll be a comfort, in more ways than one.'

'Is there anything more you need, Sir?'

Thomas sipped at the rum, then said, 'How many of you are left?'

Dunn moved one lip over the other before he replied, Besides Mr. Brown and Mr. Tweedy, there is

51

Mrs. Brydon and, of course, Miss Brigmore and Mary Peel.'

'Six'

'Yes, six, Sir, indoors, but there are two still in the stables. They . . . they will have to remain there until . . .' His voice trailed off.

'Yes, yes, of course. Where is Mr. Tweedy now?'

'Visiting the farms, Sir. As you ordered, leaving just the bare staff.'

Thomas now looked down at the desk, his eyes sweeping over the mass of papers and bills arrayed there; then he took another sip from the tankard before looking up at Dunn again and saying, 'You'll be all right, Dunn; I'll give you a good reference. Just . . . just tell me when you want to go. There are a number of houses that'll jump at you.'

'There's no hurry, Sir, none whatever.'

'Well, you can't live on air, Dunn, no more than any of us. I won't be able to pay you after this week.'

'I'm fully aware of that, Sir. Still, there's no hurry. Mrs. Brydon is of the same opinion; as is Mr. Tweedy; and I'm sure you can rely on Mr. Brown.'

Thomas now lowered his head. Forty staff he'd employed in the house and the farms, and six were quite willing to stay with him until such times as they were all turfed out. You could say it was a good percentage. Strange where one found one's friends. He looked up at Dunn and said, 'Thank them for me, will you? I'll . . . I'll see them personally later.'

'Yes, Sir.'

As Dunn was about to turn away he stopped and said, 'May I enquire how Master Dick is, Sir?'

Thomas stretched his thick neck up out of his collar before saying, 'Putting as good a face on it as he can, Dunn. I . . . I had hopes of being able to bail him out but'—he tapped the crumpled letter that was lying to his hand now and said, 'I'm afraid I haven't succeeded.' Strange how one could talk like this to one's butler, and in an ordinary tone, without any command or condescension on the one hand or false hee-hawing on the other, as one was apt to do with one's friends.

'I'm sorry, Sir.'

'So am I, Dunn, so am I. By the way, where are the men?' He did not call them bailiffs.

'Two are in the library, Sir, cataloguing the books, the other is up in the west wing doing the bedrooms.'

'How much longer are they likely to take, do you think?'

'Two days, three at the most I should say, Sir.'

Thomas now narrowed his eyes and thought for a moment before he said, 'By the way, cook went three days ago, didn't she? Who's doing the cooking now?'

'Well, Sir'—Dunn inclined his head slightly towards him—'Mrs. Brydon and myself are managing quite well, and Miss Brigmore has been of some assistance. She has seen to the children's meals and to her own and Peel's.'

'Thank you, Dunn.'

'Thank you, Sir.'

Alone once more, Thomas sat back in the chair and, stretching one hand, he pressed his first finger and thumb tightly on to his eyeballs. He had forgotten about the children because he hadn't seen them for days, she had kept them out of his way. Funny, he thought of her as 'she.' Why? It was much too personal a tag to attach to her prim, frozen little packet of flesh. Yet she had thawed. Yes, she had indeed. Anyway, he was glad the children had her, and that they had a home to go to, and two hundred a year between them. But could they exist on two hundred a year? Well, they would have to. What did she get? He opened a drawer to the side of him and took out a long ledger and, turning the pages, he brought his finger down to the name. Brigmore . . . Brigmore Anna, employed as governess from the first of September, 1844 at a salary of forty-five pounds per annum. He noted that there was no mention against this for an allowance of beer, tea or sugar.

Forty-five pounds, that would make a big hole in the two hundred. Then there must be someone to do the work. The Peel girl, how much was she getting? He turned back the pages. Mary Peel, bonded, third kitchen maid, two pounds twelve shillings per annum, extra beer, sugar and tea allowed; promoted second kitchen maid at five pounds per annum; promoted first kitchen maid at seven pounds ten shillings per annum; promoted nursery maid 1844 at twelve pounds per annum, extra beer, tea and sugar allowed.

Well, that was another twelve pounds. That would hardly leave three pounds a week to feed them all. Could it be done? He doubted it. What could one get for three pounds a week? What could four people get for three pounds a week?

. . . . And what are you going to do?

It was as if someone were asking the question of him, and he shook his head slowly from side to side. If it wasn't for Dick he knew what he would do, and this very night, for here he was without a penny to his name and no prospect of having one in the future. Even if the estate sold well, and the contents of the house also, he knew it would not give his creditors twenty shillings in the pound.

But damn his creditors, damn them to hell's flames, each and every one of them, for almost without exception they had overcharged him for years. Why, he asked himself now as he stared at the row of sporting prints hanging above the mantelpiece opposite to him, why hadn't he been like others under similar circumstances and made a haul while the going was good? Even Dunn had had the foresight to look to himself and secure some bottles and he would like to bet that there wasn't a servant in the house but had helped himself to something. But he, what had he done? Well, what had he done? Could he, when the house was in an uproar, when his son had gone to pieces, when the place was swarming with officers of the law, deliberating whether it might be manslaughter or excusable homicide if the man were to die, and seeming to infer that the eventual penalty would be severe because the victim happened to be a law man, could he then have gone round surreptitiously acquiring his own valuables? Yet there was not one of his so-called friends who would believe that he hadn't done so, either before or after the bailiff incident. No one but a fool, they would say, would let bums have it all their own way, and Turk Mallen was no fool. . . . Yet Thomas Mallen, the

Thomas Mallen he knew himself to be, was a fool and always had been.

But now it was Dick he must think about; he must get him bailed out of there or by the time the trial came up he would be a gibbering idiot. Thank God it looked as if the man was going to survive, otherwise there would have been no question of bail. As it was, they had made it stiff, a thousand pounds.

He had never expected Dick to break as he had done. He had imagined, up till recently, there was a tough side to him, or had he just hoped there was? His own father used to say, a man can be fearless when cornered by a rutting stag as long as he's on a horse and has a gun to hand. But meet up with the stag when on his feet and empty-handed, and who do you think will run first?

Dick had met the stag in the form of the law and he had neither gun nor horse. As he had looked on him to-day in that stark, bare room he had felt both pity and scorn for him, aye, yes, and a touch of loathing, because it was he, this son of his, and he alone, who had brought them all to such a pass. But for the false pride that had made him turn on that bloody ingrate of a footman everything would have been settled between him and Fanny Armstrong and no doubt at this very moment the whole Hall would have been in a frenzy of preparations for the engagement banquet; whereas he would now be lucky to have one course for a meal to-night.

He sat with his head bowed until his thoughts touched on the children again; he must see to them, get them out of this and to the cottage, the atmosphere of the house wasn't good for anyone anymore. Slowly he reached out and rang the bell, thinking as he did so what it would be like to ring a bell and have no one answer it—well, he would soon know, that was certain.

It was some minutes before Dunn made his appearance and then, deferential as ever, he stood just within the door and said, 'Yes, Sir?'

'Tell Miss Brigmore I'd like to see her for a moment ... please.' Again he felt a tightness in his collar and he ran his finger around the edge of it. That was the first time he could ever remember saying please to his butler. Sometimes he had given him a perfunctory thanks, but that was all. Had one to be destitute before becoming aware of good manners? Strange that he should learn something at this time of trial. . . .

When Miss Brigmore knocked on the study door she was immediately bidden to enter. After closing the door quietly behind her, she walked slowly up to the desk and looked at her master. Her look was open and held no trace of embarrassment. She was grateful to him for ending her years of virginity, her years of personal torment. She had never been able to see any virtue in chastity, and had questioned the right of a piece of paper which legalised a natural desire, a desire which, indulged in before the signing of the paper, earned for the female the title of wanton or whore, while it was considered the natural procedure for a male, even making him into a dashing fellow, a real man, and a character. She had strong secret views on the rights of the individual—the female individual in particular, and it was only the necessity to earn her livelihood that had kept them secret, and herself untouched, this far.

Still she knew that had Thomas Mallen never taken her, she would still have cared for him, looked up to him, and feared him a little. Now she no longer looked up to him nor feared him, but she loved him.

'Sit down'—he paused—'Anna.'

'Thank you.' She did not add 'Sir.' He had used her Christian name, there was no need now for titles.

'It's about the children. I . . . I don't know whether you are aware'—he knew she was aware all right, every servant in the house was aware of everything appertaining to his business—'but the children jointly own the cottage and have an income of two hundred pounds a year between them. Now'—he paused and ran his tongue round his lips—'if you'll still consent to take charge of them, they could afford to pay you your salary, also perhaps Peel's too, though it would not leave much for living. I'm afraid your fare would be rather scanty, as would other amenities, so I . . . I shall not take it amiss if you decide to terminate your agreement.'

56

Anna Brigmore would have liked to retort at this moment 'Don't be silly!'

What she said was, 'I have already arranged to go to the cottage with the children; everything is in order, the rooms are ready . . . yours too.' She paused here, then added 'Sir,' for it seemed at this point a title was called for. 'That is, if you wish for a temporary dwelling before you make other arrangements. The house appears small at first, but it is really quite roomy. I've had the furniture re-arranged and fresh drapes hung; the place is quite comfortable. What is more, I took the liberty of transferring some of your belongings . . . objects, of the smaller type, to the cottage. Certain pieces which I think are of some considerable value, and which . . .'

'You what?' He had jerked himself forward in his chair and now, with his forearm on the desk, he was leaning towards her and he repeated, 'You what?'

'I arranged for some objects from the cases in the drawing room to be transferred and . . . and with the assistance of Mary Peel and the children they are now safely hidden in the cottage.'

'An-na.' A smile was spreading over his face and he shook his head as he looked at the prim figure sitting before him, prim but pretty. He had noticed her prettiness six years ago when he had first met her, and had remarked laughingly to himself, 'This one's chastity belt's secured all right.' It was strange, he thought now, that she should be the first indoor servant he had taken. He had made a rule never to tamper with indoor servants. His father had put him up to this. 'It's always embarrassing,' he had said, 'to see bellies swelling inside the house and you having to deny claim for your own handiwork. Keep your sporting well outside; your own farms if you must, but further afield is always safer.' But there had been something about Miss Anna Brigmore, something that appealed to him; not only had he wanted to end her virginity but he'd had the desire to strip the primness from her and expose the prettiness. Well, he had taken her virginity, but he hadn't managed to strip the primness from her. She was still

Miss Brigmore, softer in a way, yes, but nevertheless Miss Brigmore, even when he addressed her as Anna.

But Miss Brigmore had had the sense to do what he should have done, or at least have ordered someone to do on the side. He could have said to Brown, 'See that my personal belongings are put in a safe place.' How many sets of gold cuff links and odds and ends had Brown tucked away in his own valise? He wasn't blaming Brown, he wasn't blaming any of them, let them get what they could while the going was good. But Miss Brigmore hadn't thought of herself, she had thought of him and his future needs. Strange . . . strange the quarters from which help came.

'What did you take?' he asked quietly.

'I should imagine about fifty pieces in all.'

'FIFTY PIECES!' He grimaced in disbelief.

'Some I should imagine more valuable than others, such as the pair of Swiss snuff boxes and the Louis XVI enamelled one.'

His eyes crinkled at the corners and he said softly, 'Fifty! and the Louis snuff box among them?'

'Yes.'

'How did you know what to take?'

Her chin moved slightly upwards before she said, 'I've read a great deal about such things. What is more, my parents found themselves in a similar situation to yourself when I was sixteen.'

His mouth was open, and his head nodded twice before he said, 'They did?'

'Yes.'

'And . . . and you managed to secure some trinkets of your own before? . . .'

'No; we weren't successful. The articles were discovered for the simple reason that there were in no way as many pieces to choose from. The result was very trying.'

He nodded again, saying, 'Yes, it would be.' Then going on, he added, 'Yet knowing it could be very trying here too, you transferred fifty pieces to the cottage? How did you do it?'

'I . . . I selected certain things, and ordered Mary Peel to bring them up to the nursery; then I pinned or

58

sewed what could be pinned or sewed to ... to our under-garments; the other pieces we managed to secrete on our persons.'

In blank silence he stared at her. . . . 'You must have done all this before ... before the accident, and made several journeys—it's some distance to the cottage.'

'Only two journeys, and the children looked upon it as a game. If ... if you would care to come to the cottage you will be able to judge for yourself as to the value of what is there. I would have informed you sooner but there has not been the opportunity.'

Slowly he rose from the chair and came round the desk and, standing over her, he put out his hand and when she had placed hers in it he pressed it tightly, saying, 'Whatever they're worth, tuppence or ten thousand, Anna, thank you, thank you.'

Her eyes blinked, her mouth pursed; then, her face suddenly relaxing, she smiled up at him softly as she said, 'I only wish I'd had more time.'

Drawing her to her feet he gazed at her for a moment before saying, 'We will go now to the cottage. Bring the children. It will appear as if we are taking a stroll.'

She looked at him as if he were proposing just that, a stroll with him along a country lane. . . .

Half an hour later they walked down the long drive and through the lodge gates, which Thomas opened himself and found it a strange experience, for he hadn't realized how heavy they were. They walked briskly for it was a cold, raw day. The sky was lying low and heavy on the hills and promised snow. After a short while Thomas's step slowed considerably for he found he was out of breath, and he lightly chided the children, saying, 'If you want to gallop, you gallop, but let me trot.' And the children ran on ahead, but Miss Brigmore suited her step to his.

When at last they reached the gate of the cottage he leaned on it and stood looking at the house before him. It was built of grey granite stone; it had been built to withstand wind and weather, but no softness had been incorporated into its erection. He followed Miss

Brigmore up the narrow winding path and watched her insert the key in the lock, then they all went inside.

'Well, well!' Thomas stood in the small hall and looked about him. It wasn't the first time he had been in the cottage but he remembered it as a dull characterless place; now, even this little hall looked different.

There were five doors leading out of the hall and they were all open. He walked towards the first one to the left of him; it led into a sitting room, tiny by the standards of the Hall, being only fifteen by twenty feet in length, he imagined. Yet it looked a comfortable room, solidly comfortable, although at a glance he would say there wasn't one piece of furniture of any value in it.

He turned and smiled at Miss Brigmore, and when Constance grabbed his hand and cried, 'Come on and see the dining room, Uncle,' he allowed himself to be tugged into the next room. Here he stood nodding his head as he looked about him, saying, 'Very, very nice, very nice. You should be quite happy here.' He looked down at Constance and then at Barbara. Barbara wasn't smiling. That was the difference in these two little sisters, Constance always appeared happy, whereas you could never tell whether Barbara was happy or not. He said to her now, 'Do you like the cottage, Barbara?'

'Yes, Uncle.'

'You'd like living here?'

She paused for a moment before saying again, 'Yes, Uncle.'

'I'll love living here, Uncle.' Constance was tugging at his hand again, crying now, 'Come and see your study.'

'My . . . ?' He did not look at the child but turned and looked towards where Miss Brigmore was walking into the hall, and again he allowed himself to be tugged out of the room and through another doorway into a smaller room. He looked at the long narrow table that served as a desk, at the leather chair, the leather couch, and at the end of the room the two glass doors opening out on to a small terrace.

'This is your room, Uncle, your study.'

He turned to face Miss Brigmore, but Miss Brigmore was not in the room. He could see her now ascending the bare oak staircase.

'Come and see your bedroom, Uncle.' As Constance led him towards the stairs she pointed to the other two doors leading from the hall, saying, 'That one is the morning room and that one leads to the kitchen,' and she added to this, 'The kitchen requires a lot of seeing to; the stove smokes.'

He was on the landing now and being tugged towards a second door that led off from it. 'This is your bedroom, Uncle.'

The room was of a fair size, almost as large he imagined as the sitting room. It held a four-poster bed, a stout wardrobe and dressing table, but its most significant feature was the unusually large window that gave a view of the foothills and the mountains beyond.

Thomas turned now to where Miss Brigmore was standing in the doorway. Constance was still hanging on to his hand, and the look in his eyes spoke a different language from his words as he said, 'You have transformed the place; I remember it as a very dismal dwelling.'

'There is a toilet room, Uncle, next door, too, and you won't have to go out in the ...'

'Constance!'

'Yes, Miss Brigmore.' Constance hung her head, knowing that she had touched on a delicate and unmentionable subject.

Miss Brigmore now said hastily as she pushed open another door, 'This is ... is a spare room for anyone you might wish to stay'—she did not say 'Master Dick'—'and this'—she opened yet another door—'is the children's room.'

'Isn't it pretty, Uncle? and the desk-bed in the corner is for Mary, she doesn't want to sleep in the attic. But isn't it pretty, Uncle?'

'Yes, my dear, it's very pretty.' He patted Constance's head.

Miss Brigmore did not open the fourth door, she merely said, 'That is my room. Then leading the way down the stairs again, she added, 'If we can dispense with the morning room I would like to turn it into a schoolroom.'

'Do as you wish, Miss Brigmore, do as you wish.' He was nodding down to the back of her head.

In the hall Miss Brigmore looked at Barbara and said, 'Would you like to gather some wood for the fire? It would be nice if we had a fire, wouldn't it? And then we could have a cup of tea.'

'Yes, Miss Brigmore. Come, Connie.' Barbara held out her hand and took Constance's and forced her now to walk out of the room, not run as she was inclined to.

Miss Brigmore looked at Thomas and said quietly, 'They're in here.'

He followed her into the dining room, and watched with amazement as she knelt down and rolled back the carpet and prised up the floor boards with a chisel. When she put her arm down into the hole and began handing him articles of silver, cameos, and trinket boxes he did not utter a word, he just kept shaking his head.

At last the collection was arrayed on the top of the sideboard and the round table, and he stood gazing at it in amazement. Picking up a small Chelsea porcelain figure of a mandarin, he fingered it gently, almost lovingly; when he looked at her he found he was still unable to speak. This one piece alone would be worth five hundred, if not more, and then there were the snuff boxes; three of them, no, four. He put out his hand and stroked the Louis XVI gold enamelled box, his fingers tracing the minute necklace that graced the slender neck of the lady depicted in the middle of it.

One after the other he handled the pieces: a pair of George I sugar dredgers; a set of three George I casters; and when he came to the Chinoiserie tankard he cupped it in both his hands, then as if it were a child he had lost and found again he held it tight against his waistcoat while he looked at her. And now he asked quietly, 'What can I say to you, Anna?'

She stared back into his eyes but did not answer.

'An hour ago I was a desperate man; now I'm no longer desperate, you have given me new life.'

There was another silence before she asked in a

practical manner, 'Will you be able to sell them immediately?'

He looked away from her for a moment, bit on his lower lip as he nodded his head, and said, 'Yes, yes, Anna, I'll be able to sell them immediately. I know of a gentleman in Newcastle who is of great assistance to people like us.'

Her eyes were unblinking as she kept them fixed on him. He had said us.

'Not that he'll give me half what they're worth; but as long as it's enough to get Dick out of that place.'

Miss Brigmore suddenly gasped as she felt herself almost lifted from the ground and pulled into his embrace. He kissed her, his mouth big, warm and soft covering hers entirely. When he at last let her go she experienced a strange feeling; for the first time in her life she knew what it was to feel like a woman, a mature fulfilled woman. She hadn't experienced this when he came to her room because then he had merely given her his body. Now he had given her something from his heart.

SEVEN

For five weeks now Thomas had been living in the cottage, and he had taken his change of circumstances with good grace, hiding the feeling of claustrophobia that the rooms gave him, hiding the feeling of despair when he thought of the future, and hiding the disturbing feeling of disdain whenever he looked at his son. For Dick Mallen had not taken the change with good grace.

To Dick Mallen the cottage appeared merely as an extension of prison. As for thanking the governess for being the means of his temporary liberation, when his father had suggested that he afford Miss Brigmore this courtesy he had looked at him as if he thought his father were mad. Thank the governess for giving them what was theirs! Very likely they had only received half of what she had taken.

Thomas, who up to that moment had kept his temper, had sworn at his son, saying, 'You're an ungrateful sod, Dick, that's what you are, an ungrateful sod.'

After his release Dick Mallen had visited the Hall, but had returned empty-handed. He had been informed, and in no subservient manner, by the bailiff that his strictly personal belongings, which meant his clothes only, had been sent to the cottage; as for the remainder, they had been tabulated against the day of the sale.

He knew that his man Taylor would surely have lined his pockets with cuff links, scarf pins, cravat rings and the like, and he wished he could get his hands on him, but the beggar had gone long since, and he couldn't find out if he had become established in another position.

When he thought of the attitudes of their various friends he just couldn't believe it. He could understand Armstrong's reaction but not that of old Headley and Ferrier. Yet he had to admit that Pat Ferrier had turned up trumps. Then, of course, he should, he would have been damn well amazed if he hadn't, for Pat had cleaned him out time and again over the past three years; and after all, what was a few hundred compared to what he had lost to him.

He had said nothing to his father about Pat Ferrier's help. He said little to his father at all these days; the old man, he considered, had gone soft in the head. The way he treated that governess made him sick, for he constantly deferred to her as if she were an equal. One thing he was certain of, her stay would be short once the trial was over. . . . The trial! It was that word that had the power to take the bombast out of him. He was fearing the trial for although the man had recovered they said he was badly scarred; moreover he knew that public opinion would be against him. If only there were some way out. . . .

Thomas too kept thinking, if only there were some way out, but his thoughts did not run along the same channels as his son's. His idea of a way out was to beat the law by engaging one of the finest barristers and to do this he needed money, big money, and all he could call upon was the refund of the bail money and the little that was left over from the sale of Anna's haul, as he came to think of the pieces she had retrieved.

With the exception of two miniatures and a snuff box he had disposed of all the pieces to the gentleman in Newcastle. With regard to these three pieces he had private thoughts concerning them, but had decided he would do nothing about them until the sale was over.

It was on Monday the fourteenth of April that the sale of the contents of the ground floor of High Banks Hall began. It was well attended, and the auctioneer was more than pleased with the result at the end of the day.

On Tuesday, the fifteenth, the contents of the first floor were sold; again the result was favourable. On the morning of Wednesday, the sixteenth, the auctioneer dealt with the contents of the nursery floor, the attics and the kitchens. In the afternoon he sold off the contents of the coach-house, the harness rooms, and the servants' quarters. The livestock, such as the coach horses and the four hunters, had been sent to the West Farm, where the sale of all livestock would take place on the Tuesday following Easter Monday.

But it was Thursday, the seventeenth, the day before Good Friday, that was the important day of the sale, for on this day the Hall and the estate, together with its two farms, was put up for auction. The carriages came from Durham County, Cumberland, Westmoreland and Yorkshire. There were gathered in the library quite a number of men bearing names that spelt money. Then there were those others who held themselves apart. These men had names that didn't only spell money but distinction of class. Yet at the end of the day the Hall had gone neither to a self-made man nor yet to one of title.

The Bank had put a reserve price on the estate and no bidder had touched anywhere near it. The auctioneer had at one time become impatient, and as he looked at the men he would have liked, very much, to say, 'Gentlemen, I know why you hesitate. On such occasions of distraint on property, beggars can't be choosers, you're thinking. But you are mistaken in this case. The Bank wants its money and it means to have it, and it is prepared to wait. Oh I know you gentlemen of old, you think if the estate doesn't go to-day you will to-morrow put in an offer and we will gladly take it. Oh, I know you of old, gentlemen.'

What he did say was, 'Gentlemen, this is a very fine estate and I've no need to remind you what it contains, you have it all there in your catalogues; five hundred acres of land containing two productive farms, and then this house, this beautiful, and I will add, grand house, you could not build this house for sixty thou-
66

sand to-day, and gentlemen, what are you offering? Twenty thousand below the asking price. We're wasting each other's time, gentlemen. I'll ask you again: what am I bid over the last bidder of thirty thousand? . . . Well now, well, come, come gentlemen. . . . No? Then, I'm afraid that to-day's business is at an end, gentlemen.'

Thomas Mallen took the news with a deep sigh, but Dick stormed and ranted until his father turned on him angrily, saying, 'Stop it! stop it! Anyway, what good would it do you if they had bid twenty thousand over the asking price?'

'None. I'm well aware of that, none, but it riles me to think they're harping over a few bloody thousand. Pat tells me the Hamiltons were there from Edinburgh; also the Rosses from Glasgow; they're weighed down with it, but both as mean as skilly bowls. . . . And God Almighty, how you can sit there and take it calmly! . . .'

'Blast you to hell's flames, boy. Stop your stupid ranting, and don't say again I'm taking it calmly. Let me tell you this, I'm neither taking the loss of my house calmly, nor yet the way my son has conducted himself in this predicament. And I will say it, although I told myself I never would; but for your trying to play the injured master we wouldn't be in this position to-day. You're weak gutted underneath all your bombast, boy, you're weak gutted. Only the thought of penury prodded you; but too late as it turned out, to ask Fanny Armstrong, whereas if you'd had any spunk you'd have clinched the matter a year ago, for you were up to your neck then. . . .'

The altercation had taken place in the study on Thursday evening, and Thomas's roar had easily penetrated into the children's bedroom above, where Anna was putting them to bed.

'Uncle's vexed,' said Constance; 'perhaps he didn't like his supper. I didn't like it much. We don't have nice meals now, do we, Miss Brigmore?'

'You have good plain food, that is all you require. Now lie down and go to sleep and no more talking. Good-night.'

'Good-night, Miss Brigmore.'

Anna turned and looked down at Barbara; then she put her hand out and pulled the sheets over the child's shoulder. 'Good-night, Barbara,' she said softly.

'Good-night, Miss Brigmore.'

Anna looked down for a moment longer on the child. There was something on her mind; she had changed of late, perhaps she was missing the house. She had never been gay like Constance, she was of a more serious turn of mind, but lately there had been an extra restraint in her manner. She must give her more attention; one was apt to talk more to Constance because Constance was more responsive. Yes, she must pay her more attention.

She left the night light burning and, lifting up the lamp, went out and into her own room, and there, taking the coverlet from the bed, she put it around her and sat down in a chair.

Things had not turned out as she had imagined they would. There had been no cosy nights sitting before the fire in the drawing room, Thomas Mallen on one side of the hearth, herself on the other, she doing her embroidery, he reading; or she had seen them talking; or again laughing down on the children playing on the hearth rug before the fire.

The hour that held the picture would always be the hour between six and seven o'clock in the evening. It was an hour that in most cases was lost in those preceding it, and those following it, an hour before dinner or supper according to the household; or yet again the hour after the main meal of the day as in some poorer establishments; the hour before children retired, the hour when the day was not yet ended and the night not yet begun.

But she had never visualised herself sitting huddled in a bed cover in a cold room during any part of that hour. Yet that is what was happening night after night. However, she made use of this time to collect her thoughts, trying to see the outcome of this terrible business. One outcome that didn't please her at all was the possibility that Master Dick might be found guiltless at his trial, for this would mean that he would take up his

68

abode here permanently, until such time when he should perhaps find something better. She had asked herself if she could put up with such a situation, for Master Dick's manner to her was most uncivil. But she never answered this question because she knew that as long as Thomas Mallen needed her she would stay, and she had the firm conviction inside herself that she was the one person he would need most from now on.

Life could be so pleasant here, so happy, so homely. The children would thrive better here than they had at the Hall. They had lived as much in the open air these past weeks as they had done indoors and it hadn't troubled them, much the reverse. And the food, as Constance had so recently complained, was very plain, which in a way was all to the good of one's health. It had already shown to good effect on the master, for he had laughingly said his breeches were slack. Also he walked without coughing so much. But no doubt this had been aided by his drinking less wine.

It was strange, she thought, how wine was considered a natural necessity in the lives of some people. The master had had two visitors over the past weeks who had brought him a case of wine; one was the young Mr. Ferrier, the other was Mr. Cardbridge. The Cardbridges came from Hexham. They weren't monied people, more poor upper class, she would say, and Mr. Cardbridge was merely an acquaintance of the master, but she knew that his visit had given the master pleasure solely because he had brought with him a case of wine. In her estimation the money that the wine had cost would have been much more acceptable; but that, of course, was out of the question. The master would have taken a small gift of money as an insult, but the equivalent in wine he had accepted with outstretched hands.

The question of values, she considered, would make a very interesting topic of conversation one of these nights when she conversed with him; if she were able to converse with him, for this would only come about if Master Dick got his deserts, and she prayed he would. . . .

After supper Thomas went to bed with a glass of hot

rum and sugar. He had courteously excused himself to her, saying his head was aching, but she knew that it wasn't his head that was troubling him but his temper. During supper his face had retained a purple hue. He had not spoken to her, nor had Master Dick, but then Master Dick never addressed himself to her at the table, or anywhere else, unless it was to give an order.

She was relieved when Master Dick too retired early to bed. While Mary washed the dishes and tidied the kitchen, she herself put the dining room to rights and laid the breakfast for the following morning. She also put the covers straight in the sitting room, adjusted the rugs and damped down the fire.

She was still in the sitting room when Mary opened the door and said, 'I'm away up then, Miss Brigmore.'

'Very well, Mary. Good-night.'

'Good-night, Miss Brigmore.'

As Mary went to close the door she stopped and added, 'Is it me or is it getting colder?'

'I think it's getting colder, Mary.'

'You know I had the feeling last night I could smell snow.'

'I shouldn't be surprised, Mary.'

'Nor me. I remember me mam tellin' me that one Easter they were snowed up right to the window sill; they didn't roll any of their paste eggs down the hill that year.'

Anna smiled slightly before she said, 'Put another blanket on.'

'I will. Yes, I will, Miss. I was froze last night. Will I put one out for you an' all?'

'Yes, yes, you could do, thank you. Good-night.'

'Good-night, Miss.'

When Mary had closed the door Anna looked down at the fire. The top of it was black where she had covered it with the slack coal, but in between the bars it still showed red. Slowly she lowered herself down on to the rug and, her feet half tucked under her, she sat staring at the glow. Mary had said would she put another blanket on her bed. Another blanket wouldn't warm her; once you had been warmed by a man there was no substitute.

70

This was a cold house. It was still an old maid's house, from its previous owner. Strangely, up till a few weeks ago this title could have been applied to herself but now she no longer considered she qualified for it. Given a chance she could make this house warm, happy and warm. She could act as a salve to Thomas Mallen's wounds. She could fill his later years with contentment. If never given a child herself, and oh, how she longed for a child of her own, she could find satisfaction playing mother to the children and turning them into young ladies; and who knew, some friend might present them at Court, as Miss Bessie had been, and they would make good matches. Yet under the present circumstances it was all too much like a fairy tale, something from Mr. Hans Christian Andersen or the Grimm Brothers.

She leant sideways and supported herself on her elbow and drooped her head on her hand. Still staring at the red bars she felt her body relaxing. She knew that she was in a most un-Miss Brigmore pose; she hadn't sat on a rug like this since she was a very young girl, because since she was a very young girl she hadn't known what it was to have a fire in her room—part of a governess's training was austerity and fresh air.

When her elbow became cramped she put her forearm on the floor and laid her head on it. What did it matter? Everyone in the house was asleep. If she wasn't careful she'd fall asleep here herself, it was so warm, so comfortable, even though the floor was hard. Should she lie on the couch? She could pull it up to the fire and sleep here all night, no one would know; and she was usually up as early as Mary in the mornings.

She didn't know how long she had been asleep, but being a light sleeper the opening of the door roused her. She lay still, blinking towards the faint glow between the bars which told her that her dozing hadn't been a matter of minutes but an hour or more.

She felt the pressure of the footsteps on the carpet rather than heard their tread. The person who had entered the room was either the master or Master Dick. Her mind told her that if she were discovered she must pretend to be asleep, it would be most embarrassing to

71

explain her position to either of them; especially as she realized she was lying flat on her back.

When a light spread over the ceiling her eyes opened wide; then turning her head to the side, she saw a pair of booted feet walking on the other side of the couch towards the davenport in the corner of the room near the window. She did not hear the lid of the davenport being lifted, but she did hear the slight squeak of a drawer being opened and something scraping against the wood. The feet now came down the room again; they didn't pause, but went straight to the door.

She counted up to sixty before she moved; then rising, she silently groped her way up the room to the davenport. And now she lifted the lid and opened the drawer. It was empty; the Louis miniatures and the snuff box were gone. She stood for a moment, a hand gripping her throat. If she were to call out instantly she could raise the master. Master Dick would have a horse and carriage waiting, but it would likely be some distance away and he would have to get to it. There was still time to stop him.

Of all the pieces she had brought from the house she knew that Thomas Mallen treasured most the three articles he had placed in that drawer. He hadn't locked them away, or hidden them underneath the floor boards again, there was no need; if the bailiffs had suspected anything was missing they would have searched the cottage long before this. The three pieces, she knew, would have brought another thousand pounds, enough to ease his way of living for a year or two until he became quite used to the change; enough to get him a case of wine now and again, a few choice cigars and some delicacies for high days and holidays. She had seen those three pieces as an insurance against his despair.

But she did not shout and raise the house; instead, she groped her way back to the couch and, sitting on it, she stared at the dim embers as she thought, this is the answer to my prayers. By the time Thomas gets up tomorrow morning—in this moment she thought of him quite naturally as Thomas—his son will be miles away, and by the time the authorities find he is missing he will no doubt be across some water, either to France or to Norway.

To get to France he would have to ride the length of the country southwards; on the other hand he would have no distance to go in order to catch a boat to Norway. And yet the seaways to Norway might still be too rough and dangerous. Anyway, whichever way he had chosen, and he must have had it well planned and had help, he was gone, and at last now there would come the time when she would sit by one side of this fire and Thomas at the other. And better still, she would be warm at night.

If he had raved and shouted she knew that in time he would recover from the blow, but on the discovery that his son had gone, and that the miniatures and snuff box had gone with him, he did not even raise his voice.

He had been cheery at breakfast. 'Good Friday, Anna,' he said, 'and a sprinkling of snow.' He always addressed her as Anna when they were alone together. 'I remember one year when ...ey had to dig a pathway up the drive on an Easter Monday for the carriages.'

'Really!' she said, as she wondered if it was the same time as Mary's mother had been snowed up to the window sill.

'You look tired,' he said.

'I am not at all,' she replied.

'You are,' he said. 'It's all too much, teaching, housekeeping and playing housemaid, butler and nurse-maid to a doddery old man.'

When she had not denied any of this jocular remark, and in particular did not contradict his last statement, he stopped eating and asked quietly, 'What is the matter? Something is wrong with you. It's odd, but I'm more aware of your feelings than of anyone else's I can remember. Sit down and stop fidgeting,' he commanded her now.

She sat down opposite to him at the table, and her hands folded in her lap, her back very straight, she looked at him as she said, 'Master Dick has gone.'

He did not say 'What!' He made no comment at all.

73

All he did was sit back in his chair, jerk his chin upwards, and wipe the grease from it with a napkin.

After he had placed the napkin on the table he asked quietly, 'When?'

'Last night.'

'Why . . . why didn't you let me know?'

'Because'—now her lids veiled her eyes for a moment and she directed her gaze towards the table as she replied, 'You couldn't have stopped him; he must have had a horse or carriage waiting.'

'What time was this?'

'I . . . I don't know, not rightly. I . . . I had been asleep, I was awakened, I heard a movement on the stairs. I thought it was Mary going down because of something connected with the children. Then I saw him leave stealthily. He had a valise with him.'

How easily one lied. But she could not admit to the fact that she had seen his son stealing from him and had done nothing about it. He might have understood the reason for her silence because he was very much a man of the world and of the flesh; but at the same time he might have considered the price he was being called upon to pay for their companionship together as much too costly.

At least this is what she thought until, rising from the chair, he walked slowly out of the room. It was some seconds before she followed him into the sitting room. He was standing at the davenport. The drawer was open and he was staring down into it, and when he turned and looked at her she felt the urge to run to him and fling her arms about him. But all she did was to walk sedately up to him and say, 'I'm sorry. So very sorry.'

'I too am sorry, very sorry.'

He suddenly sat down on a chair near the window and she knew a moment of anguish as she thought he was going to weep; his head was bowed, his lips were trembling. She watched him pass a hand over his face, drawing the loose skin downwards, then nip the jowl below his left cheek until the surrounding skin was drained of its blood.

It was a full minute before he looked up at her, and

74

then his voice had a croaking, throaty sound as he said, 'I'm sorry for many things at this moment, but mostly for the loss of the miniatures. I had the idea that one day, in the near future, I would hand them to you as a token of my thanks for all you have done for me and mine during this very trying time. The snuff box I intended to keep for myself, merely as a matter of pride. But now, well now'—he spread his hands outwards and in this moment he looked old, helpless, and beaten.

He had meant her to have the miniatures! Really, really. The kindness of him, the thoughtfulness of him! He was a self-indulgent man, she knew this only too well; he was flamboyant, bombastic, and few people had a good word for him, even his friends had proved to be his worst critics in this time of trial; yet there was another side to him. This she had sensed right from their first meeting. A few others knew of this side too. Dunn, she suspected, had been one of them, and Brown, his valet. Yet she wasn't sure about Brown. Brown should have stayed with him, put up with the inconveniences; he could have slept on a make-shift bed in the loft. She'd had it in her mind to contrive something like this when he had informed her that he had a new position. She had been vexed and disappointed with him, but her common sense had told her it would be one less to feed—and anyway how would he have been paid? Her mind was galloping about irrelevant items. She felt upset, so upset.

'Don't cry, don't cry.' He took her hand and gently drew her towards his side.

After a time he said, 'Another scandal to be faced. They won't believe that I was ignorant of this, will they?'

She shook her head.

. . . . 'Was . . . was there anything in his room, a letter?'

'No; I . . . I searched.'

He now released her hand and running his fingers through his grey hair he muttered thickly. 'God Almighty!' It did not, as usual, sound like blasphemy but more like a prayer. Then looking up at her he asked, 'How am I going to get through these coming weeks?'

75

For answer she moved closer to him and, holding his head in her hands, she brought it to her breast and pressed it there, and she said, 'You'll come through them, and then you'll forget them. I'll ... I'll see to it that you forget them.'

EIGHT

It was a Wednesday, June the eighteenth, the day on which the Battle of Waterloo had been fought thirty-six years earlier. Constance had got the date wrong in her exercise that morning and Miss Brigmore had chastised her firmly. But then Constance thought she understood the reason for Miss Brigmore's harshness; she was always short tempered when Uncle was out of sorts, and he had been out of sorts for some days now. That was the term Mary used. Miss Brigmore's term was lackadaisical. So, between out of sorts and lackadaisical, Constance reasoned it meant that Uncle Thomas couldn't be bothered to take his daily walk any longer. Uncle Thomas sat in the study for hours by himself, and now even his glass of wine at dinner didn't cheer him up. Of course, she supposed, one glass of wine wasn't very much for a man like Uncle Thomas because his big stomach was made to hold so much more.

The wine from the house was finished long ago, and when Mary and Miss Brigmore went into the town for the shopping they only brought one bottle back with them. She had asked Mary why they didn't bring Uncle Thomas more wine and Mary said it was because they couldn't carry any more. Constance knew this was not the right answer, the right answer was they didn't want to spend money on the wine. And this seemed rather mean, especially as she and Barbara had two hundred pounds every year to spend. She had put this to Barbara and to her surprise Barbara had snapped at her, saying, 'Don't be so silly, two hundred pounds is nothing to keep a household on. We're very poor, very, very poor. We are lucky we eat as we do. If it wasn't for Miss Brigmore's management 'we wouldn't fare so well.'

Constance accepted the rebuff. She supposed she was stupid. She supposed the reason for her stupidity was that she was three years younger than Barbara. When she was Barbara's age she supposed she'd be very wise, but already she was finding that as one grew older one became more puzzled by people. She was puzzled by Barbara's attitude to Miss Brigmore, for sometimes Barbara's manner towards Miss Brigmore wasn't courteous, yet she always spoke well of her behind her back. And then there was that odd time when she found Barbara crying and Miss Brigmore kneeling on the floor in front of her holding her hands and talking rapidly. Since then she had noticed that Barbara had defended Miss Brigmore on a number of occasions, as about the wine.

She was walking by Barbara's side now along the road towards the old house as she thought of the Hall. Miss Brigmore was walking behind her with Mary. They were all carrying baskets. She turned impulsively and asked, 'May we run, Miss Brigmore?' and Miss Brigmore said, 'Yes, you may. But don't go out of sight for there might be a carriage on the road. If you should meet one on a corner jump straight into the ditch.'

Before Miss Brigmore had finished speaking Constance had grabbed Barbara's hand and they were running along the road until, hot and panting, they stopped within sight of the iron gates of the Hall.

The Hall still remained unsold. No one as yet had come forward with a suitable offer. The Bank had kept on a skeleton staff to see to the crops on the farms and the fruit and vegetables in the Hall gardens and greenhouses.

Twice a week, for some time now; Miss Brigmore had taken her party through the gardens and there, Grayson, who had been head gardener, filled their baskets with vegetables and fruit in season. Over the past two weeks she and Mary, between them, had made
78

over forty pounds of strawberry preserve. There was an ample supply of spring onions and new carrots in the cottage stable and they had a barrel ready in the wash-house in which to salt the beans.

As Miss Brigmore remarked to Mary, Grayson was being very co-operative, and she calculated that by the time the potatoes were up they'd have enough fruit and vegetables stored to last them the entire winter, by which time they'd have their own plot of land under cultivation. This was, if she could induce some boy from the village to till the ground. In the long nights ahead a boy could do three hours of an evening and earn threepence, and there was many a one would be glad of it. . . . But the village was three miles away.

There was no need to go near the house. When they entered the gates, they could turn to the right and cut through the shrubbery, along the cypress drive, skirt the lake and the rose walk and so come to the domestic gardens; but the children always wanted to see the house. It was strange, she thought, that they saw more of the lower rooms now than they had ever done when they lived in the house. Their favourite game was to run along the balcony peering through one window after another, and to-day was no exception.

She followed them at some distance, having left Mary sitting on the house steps. Mary was having trouble with her right leg, her veins were enlarged and very painful. Barbara called to her now, saying, 'Look, Miss Brigmore, there's more soot down in the dining room, it's spilled over on to the floor boards.'

'Yes, indeed there is, Barbara.' She stood looking over the child's head, her face close to the glass. 'The climbing boys didn't do their work thoroughly there; all the chimneys were cleaned at the beginning of the year following the big Christmas fires; of course it could be the damp. There must be big pockets of soot in the bends which the boys couldn't get at, and these have come away with the damp. Some boys are not so particular as others.' She gave this information as if it were a lesson, and it was a lesson; everything she said to them, except at very rare moments, was in the form of a lesson.

'Let's go round to the stables!' Constance was running to the end of the terrace. She had reached the corner when she stopped and exclaimed loudly, 'Oh!' Then she turned her head in the direction of Barbara and Miss Brigmore, while at the same time thrusting her arm out and pointing her finger.

Barbara reached her first, but she did not make any exclamation, she just stared in the direction that Constance was pointing. Nor did Miss Brigmore make any exclamation when she reached the corner and looked at the boy standing not three yards from them.

The boy seemed vaguely familiar yet she knew she hadn't seen him before, at least not closely. Then, her gaze moving from his dark black-lashed eyes to his tousled black hair, she saw the disordered fair streak, and then she recognised him. This was the boy who came over the hills and stood on the rock to view the house. She had caught a glimpse of him once when out walking, a matter of two years ago. He had looked very small then but now he looked tall, over five feet she would say.

'Who are you, boy?'

The boy did not answer but looked at the little girl.

'Are you from the farm?'

Miss Brigmore shook Constance gently by the shoulder, saying, 'Be quiet, Constance'; then looking at the boy she said, 'You know you are on private ground.'

'Whose?' The voice was thick, the word was thick with the Northumbrian burr, and had a demand about it; whatever home he was from, he wasn't, Miss Brigmore decided, in servitude there. She would have said by the tilt of his head and the look in his eyes that he was of an arrogant nature, as arrogant as a Mallen, or as the Mallens had once been. She gave to her own tone a like arrogance as she answered, 'This estate is the property of Mr. Thomas Mallen.'

'Until it's sold. . . . You are the gov'ness, aren't you?'

'Yes, I am the governess.'

'And your name is Brigmore. You see I know.'

'I hope your knowledge affords you some comfort.'

She saw that he was slightly nonplussed by her answer and she took advantage of it, saying, 'Now tell me what you're doing here.'

'Walking round ... looking'. . . . It's a mess isn't it? It'll soon go to rack an' ruin; all ill-gotten gains return rack an' ruin.'

'You are a very rude boy. This house was not ill-gotten, it was Uncle Thomas's. . . .'

'Barbara.' Miss Brigmore now put her hand on Barbara's arm and patted it three times, not in addition to the reprimand that her tone might have implied but rather as an indication that she was agreeing with her statement.

The boy was staring at Barbara now and she at him and after a moment he said, 'You live in the cottage at the foot of the tor, and he lives there an' all now ... Mallen.'

'Mr. Mallen, boy.'

The eyes, like black marbles, flashed towards her and the tone again was aggressive as he said, 'There's some must mister him but not me.'

'You really are very rude.' Constance's face had slid into a smile as she endorsed Barbara's words, and when the boy's attention came on her again she asked playfully, 'How old are you?'

'Thirteen.'

'Oh, you are very old. I'm only seven and Barbara'—she nodded now towards her sister—'she's ten. What do you do, do you work?'

Miss Brigmore was for sternly checking Constance but Constance had asked a question, the answer to which would likely give her the boy's background, and so she remained silent while the boy, looking down at Constance, said, 'Aye, of course I work. All men should work; if you want to eat you should work.'

'What do you work at?'

'I farm; me da has a farm.'

'Oh.'

And it's a fine farm, better'n any on here.' He flung his arms sidewards and the gesture took in the whole estate.

'Come along.' Miss Brigmore now ushered the girls forward and, looking over her shoulder at the boy, said, 'And you get about your business and don't let me catch you here again.'

'I'll come when I think fit.'

Her back stiffened but she did not turn round.

'What a strange boy. He was very rude but ... but he was nice, wasn't he?'

Barbara turned her head quickly in Constance's direction, saying, 'Don't be silly; how can you be rude and nice at the same time? He was just rude, very uncouth, wasn't he, Miss Brigmore?'

Miss Brigmore didn't look at either of the girls as she replied to the first part of the question. 'Yes, he was very rude. But now let us forget about him and get to the gardens.'

It was an hour later when the children, carrying baskets of strawberries, and Miss Brigmore and Mary Peel the heavier vegetables, were making their way to the lodge gates that they heard the voice calling 'Matthew! Matthew!'

'It's that boy again.' Constance's eyes were wide, her face bright with expectation, and Mary Peel said, 'And another along of him by the sound of it. He didn't go when you told him then.' She cast a glance towards Miss Brigmore, then added, 'He wants his face skelped; afore you know it he'll have the place cleared. I've heard of him afore, as ready with his fists as he is with his tongue I hear. Thinks he's as good as the next. Huh!'

They walked on until they came onto the drive, and there, a short distance along it, stood the boy, his two hands to his mouth calling again 'Matthew! You, Matthew!'

They all turned as one now, slightly startled by the sound of running feet approaching along the path they had just left, and the next minute there came towards them another boy. His hair was very fair, his face pale; he was shorter and younger than the boy on the drive who, ignoring the four of them completely, addressed him by demanding, 'Where d'you think you've been?

Didn't you hear me callin'? By lad! you'll do that once too offen, you will.'

The fair-haired boy too, ignoring the presence of the others and the fact that he was trespassing, answered as if they were alone together. 'I was sittin' by the river,' he said. 'It's lovely down there, man; you should have come. There was a tree hangin' over and I could see the fish in the shade. . . .'

'Shut up!' The dark boy now turned to the group who were staring at him, and by way of explanation said, 'This is me brother . . . I mean me. . . .'

Miss Brigmore interrupted him, saying, 'I told you some time ago to leave the grounds, didn't I?'

'Aye, you did, an' I gave you your answer, didn't I?'

Extraordinary boy, really extraordinary. Miss Brigmore was lost for words. There was something in him that—she wouldn't say frightened her, rather annoyed her. The next minute she started as if she had been stung by the younger boy addressing the girls in the most casual and undeferential manner. 'Hello,' he said; 'it's lovely here, isn't it?'

Both Barbara and Constance had their mouths open to reply when she shut them with, 'Come along immediately.'

As they moved away the fair boy ran before them and tugged at the iron gate, but he could open it only sufficiently for them to pass through in single file.

'Thank you.' The words coming from Miss Brigmore were a dismissal, and the boy stood still until he was pushed forward by his brother. Then they followed within a few yards of the party until the most surprising thing happened. The dark boy was suddenly at Miss Brigmore's side and, grabbing her basket, said, Here, let's take it.' And she let him take it while staring at him the while.

'Matthew, take t'other.' He was nodding towards Mary Peel now. Mary smiled at the fair boy as he took the basket from her, and said, 'Ta. Thanks, lad, thanks.'

Miss Brigmore, now turning to Constance and putting out her hand, said, 'Let me have yours, Constance; it's too heavy for you.' Whereupon she was checked by

83

the voice coming at her roughly now, stating, 'She's big enough to carry it hersel. Let her be.'

'You are a funny boy.' Constance had her head back, her mouth wide with laughter, and Miss Brigmore was too perturbed at this moment to check her, even when she went on, 'Would you like a strawberry? You can, we have plenty.'

When she held out the basket towards him he shook his head, saying roughly, 'We grow bigger'n that, and them's been left wet, they'll mould if you cook 'em no matter how much sugar you put with 'em.'

Miss Brigmore was indeed nonplussed. What were things coming to? The boy had no sense of place or class. She was all for fraternising within limits, the boundaries of which were educational, and this boy, although he undoubtedly had good stock in him as his white quiff signified, still remained a rough farm boy, and the quicker he was made aware of his position the better. So now she turned her head and said sharply, 'We do not wish to discuss the merits or demerits of strawberries, so if you will kindly give me my basket you can get on your way.'

The boy stared at her, his black eyes looking deep into hers; then he almost caused her to choke when he said, 'We are all goin' the same road, so get along; the lasses don't mind.'

The girls were staring at her, Mary Peel was staring at her; only by a struggle could she take the basket from him, and then she doubted if she would gain anything but ridicule by such an effort. Her chin high, she said, 'Are you aware that these young ladies are Mr. Mallen's nieces?'

'Aye, I know that; who doesn't?'

Really! Really! What could one say to such a person? It was evident that he took pride in his bastardy and because of it considered himself an equal of everyone. It was a good thing, she thought wryly, that all the master's dubious offspring weren't of like character and determination, or else the Hall would have been invaded before now. And she thought too it was strange that the boy, being as he was, should have kept his distance all these years, viewing the house only from the

84

rock. Not until the house and its master had fallen had he put in an appearance, and then to gloat, apparently. Well, there was one thing she must see to, and right away, he must on no account come in contact with his . . . with Thomas for his manner would undoubtedly enrage him to the extent of giving him palpitations. And so, when they rounded the next corner she would be most firm and would relieve him and his brother of the baskets and take the path across the fells to the cottage. It would be much longer this way but it would be a means of parting company with this troublesome boy.

But Miss Brigmorc's plan was shattered and her mind set in a turmoil, when, rounding the bend, she saw coming towards them no other than Thomas himself.

It was to her Thomas spoke when still some distance away, saying, 'I needed to stretch my legs, the house is as lonely as a lighthouse when you are gone. Well now, what have we here?' He had stopped before them, but was now looking past them to the two boys, and as Miss Brigmore watched him she saw his lower jaw slowly drop. The boy was staring back at him, his dark eyes half shaded by his lids, which gave a deeper concentration to his gaze.

She felt herself gabbling, 'We . . . we met these children on the road; they were kind enough to help us with the baskets. I'll take them now. . . .' She thrust her hand out but it did not reach the boy, for Thomas's voice checked it, saying, 'It's all right, it's all right.' He gently flapped his hand in her direction but didn't take his eyes from the boy's face. Then, addressing him quietly, he said, 'You've come down off your rock at last then?'

The boy made no answer, but his eyes holding an indefinable look, continued to pierce the heavy-jowled countenance before him.

'What is your name?'

Still the boy made no answer until the younger one nudged him with his elbow, while saying to Thomas, 'They call him Donald, and I'm . . .'

'I'm big enough to speak for mesel.' The younger boy was thrust angrily aside, and he would have top-

85

pled had not the hand that thrust him grabbed at him and brought him up straight again. The boy kept tight hold of the younger one now while he spoke from deep in his throat with a man's voice. 'I'm known as Donald Radlet, I'm from Wolfbur Farm an' this'—he jerked the arm in his hand—'is me brother ... half-brother ... Matthew.' There was a pause before he ended, 'An' you are Thomas Mallen.'

There was a suspicion of a smile around Thomas's lips as he answered, 'True, boy, true, I am Thomas Mallen. But tell me, why have you taken this long to introduce yourself?'

' 'Cos I do things in me own time.'

Thomas now stared at the lad long and hard, and his eyes had a steely glint to them. Then, as if considering the matter, he said, 'Yes, I suppose you would. I suppose you would.' Again he was silent, until on a somewhat lighter note he added,' Well, don't let us stand here talking like hill farmers meeting in the market, let us go. . . .'

'Don't say nowt against hill farmers, they're the best 'uns. We're hill farmers.'

Thomas's head jerked to the side, his jaws were tight. Six months earlier he would have taken his hand and skelped the mouth that dared to speak to him in that tone, but now, after a pause, he adroitly pressed the gaping children and Miss Brigmore and Mary Peel before him, and he walked in front of the two boys for quite some way before he said, 'You've got to be a good farmer to make a hill farm pay.'

'We are good farmers.'

'I'm glad to hear it.'

'Our cattle are good an' all.'

'You have cattle on a hill farm?'

'Of course we have cattle. Anyway some; we have three flat meadows. We bought two of your stock a while gone an' they were poor things; your byre-man should've been shot. Their udders were sick, full of garget; the shorthorn was half dry, only two teats workin'; an' if t'other ever gets in calf she'll be lucky. Doubt if she'll weather a service; the look of the bull'll scare her. We were done. . . .'

'I'm surprised, and you so knowledgeable! You must have got the rakings, and very cheap at that. . . .'

Miss Brigmore did not hear the boy's answer; she was hurrying the girls forward now. Such talk! Teats and calving and bulls! And she failed to understand Thomas's attitude towards the boy. He had shown no sign of palpitation at the unexpected meeting. The boy's aggressiveness seemed almost to amuse him. Could it be possible he was seeing him as his son? Because when all was said and done, that's what he was, his son. She cast a quick backward glance. Thomas was now walking alongside the boys; he seemed amused, and more alert than she had seen him for weeks. A thought entering her mind, she asked herself would she object to anything that would give him an interest in life? She was fully aware that she herself could only fill his needs in one way; or perhaps two; she saw to his comfort during the day as well as at night. But a man had to have something else, particularly a man of Thomas Mallen's stamp. Would this boy supply it? She again glanced over her shoulder, at the same time pushing the girls further forward out of earshot. Catching her glance, Thomas made a motion with his head towards her, and it was as if he were confirming her thoughts.

Thomas had guessed what his Miss Brigmore, as he playfully called her in the night, was thinking, and he was wondering at this very moment if this young, raw, vibrant, brusque individual who bore his mark on his head might not be the answer to a prayer that he hadn't known he was praying, for he was certainly no praying man.

There had, during these past weeks, been a deep void in him, a loneliness that even Anna hadn't been able to fill. It wasn't, he knew, so much the loss of his home and worldly goods and way of living—or even the loss of his son; it was the *way* in which he had lost him that had left a taint of cowardice and shame. He doubted he would ever see Dick again. And this thought brought him no great sorrow, but what did sear him, even now, was the knowledge that he had no real friends. When the hunt for Dick was at its height no one had come near him, at least no friend, but he had had enough company of officials. It wasn't until the newspapers announced that Dick Mallen must by now be well away over the sea—in what direction wasn't stated, for it wasn't known—that Pat Ferrier had paid him a call and told him that Dick was in France. A mutual friend had taken him there on his private boat. But Pat Ferrier had brought no letter from Dick, no word of regret. Nothing. The irony of it struck Thomas, when he thought that even his son could produce two good friends, at least, while he himself went barren of all but Anna.

He glanced towards the boy, walking by his side. There was a resemblance between them, a definite resemblance, and not only in the streak. He could see himself again as a young boy; perhaps his hair had not been so black, or his eyes so dark, and definitely his manner had not been so arrogant, although his upbringing could have warranted it, for the proverbial silver spoon had certainly been in his mouth all his days. Yet here was this lad, brought up on a farm, and whether good, bad or indifferent, it was still a farm, assuming the manner one might expect from someone of breeding and authority.

When the boy turned his dark, fierce gaze on him he was put at a disadvantage, until, aiming to make casual conversation, he said, 'How large is your father's farm?'

'A hundred and twenty acres, and he's not me father. I call him da; but he's *his* father.' He jerked his thumb towards the smaller boy while his gaze rested on Thomas's face. And neither of them spoke during the further twenty steps they took, but the boy's eyes were saying plainly, 'Let's have no more fiddle-faddle, you know the position as well as I do.'

It was Thomas who broke the trance-like stare, calling in a voice that was much too loud, 'What are we having for supper, Miss Brigmore?'

Miss Brigmore stopped abruptly, as did the girls and Mary, and stared at him. Then she said, 'Cold soup, ham and salad, and a strawberry pastry.'

'Have we enough for two extra?'

She could not prevent her eyes from widening and

her mouth opening and shutting once more before looking towards the boys and saying, 'They will want to get home; they have a long way to walk over the hills. Their people may be wondering.'

'They won't be wonderin'.' The boy's voice had that definite, hard, determined ring to it that seemed to be the very essence of his nature. 'Da allows us half-day a week for roamin'; we can go back anytime so long's we're up at five.'

Miss Brigmore was silenced. She seemed to have to drag her eyes from the boy, and when she looked at Thomas he smiled broadly at her and said, 'Well there, you've got your answer. We have two guests for supper.'

She turned, and they all walked on again. She should be happy that he had found a new interest, but that boy disturbed her. He was too strong, too dominant for his age. She had never encountered anyone like him before. Now if it had been the younger one, she could have taken to him, for he was much more likable, gentler, better mannered. But then, he wasn't Thomas Mallen's son.

BOOK II

DONALD RADLET
OF WOLFBUR FARM

ONE

Donald Radlet was born in the winter of 1838 when his eighteen-year-old mother, Jane Radlet, had been married about five months.

Jane Radlet had been born on the West Farm of High Banks Hall. Her father was the byre-man, her mother the dairymaid. From the time Jane was born her mother hardly left her bed until the day she died; the midwife's dirty hands had set up an internal trouble, for which there appeared no cure. Constant evacuation wore her body away, yet she lived on for twenty years.

Jane was the only child of the marriage, and she could remember back to when she was three years old, when she first visited the cesspool on her own to empty the bucket. She was about four when she began to soss the dirty sheets, and this she did every day of her life until she was eighteen years and two months old, when she left the farm and went over the hills with Michael Radlet.

On that day Michael Radlet took her past his farm without even stopping to look in, and to the church near Nine Banks and there he married her, with the gravedigger and the parson's wife for witnesses. She cried all the way back to the farm; she cried on her wedding night because she lay alone; and she had cried at intervals during the following days, because she knew that for the first time in her life she was going to be happy.

Michael Radlet was eighteen years her senior and he

was known as a good, God-fearing, hard working man, a man who had rightly prospered through his hard work, for his farm, although small, was well stocked, and his land, although on hilly ground, was utilised to the last foot by his Galloways. He worked daylight and moonlight for six days a week, but on the Sabbath he did only what was necessary for the animals; the rest of the day he read his Bible, as his father had taught him to do, and he allowed his one helper the day off to visit his people.

He first noticed Jane Collins when he took his only two Ayrshires over the hills to be serviced by the High Banks's bull. He could have taken them to Pearson's Farm, which was only three miles away, but Pearson's bull was of poor stock. Jane had been barely sixteen then, and for the next year he pondered whether he should speak to her father in case she should be snapped up. Yet he doubted if her father would allow her to be snapped up because, he understood, she was the only support in his house. She looked after his sick wife and cooked the meals and generally did the work of an adult women, and had, so he had heard, done so since she was a child. But he was quick to note that the long years of labour had not marred her beauty, for her face was round and smooth and her eyes gentle, and her hair a shining brown. Her body was good; her hips wide and her breasts promising high.

It was on the day following the Sunday when he had read and dwelt on the birth of Benjamin that he went over the hills to speak to her father, the words of the good book drifting through his mind: 'And they journeyed from Bethel; and there was but a little way to come to Ephrath: and Rachel travailed, and she had hard labour. And it came to pass, when she was in hard labour, that the midwife said unto her, Fear not; thou shalt have this son also.'

He wanted a son, badly he wanted a son. His first wife had been barren; that was God's will, but Jane Collins would not be barren. He had a feeling about Jane, a strong, urging feeling to hold her, to love her. Some of his love was threaded with pity for her plight, for it was evident she'd had a hard life.

94

John Collins was about his work in the cow-shed when he confronted him, and when he put the proposal to him he was surprised that the man should bow his head deeply on his chest. It caused him to ask, 'What is it? Is she already spoken?' John Collins had turned his head away before nodding, then looking him straight in the face he said, 'You have come too late, she has been taken down.'

Taken down! He had not spoken the words aloud but they yelled at him in his mind. He had come too late, she had been taken down. Well, it was as he thought, she could bear children. But he had imagined they would be his children, the children he needed, the son he needed. He experienced a hurt that went beyond anything he had felt before; even when his wife had died the sense of loss hadn't been so great as it was now.

His voice was hollow as he asked, 'She is to be married then?'

John Collins shook his head before raising his eyes and saying, 'No, no, she is not to be married.'

There was a silence between them, broken only by the jangle of the cows' chains and their splattering.

'You know the man?'

There was another silence before John Collins, looking into Michael Radlet's eyes, said, 'No.'

As they continued to stare at each other they both knew the answer was a lie, and John Collins knew that Michael Radlet knew it was a lie, and the denial told Michael Radlet immediately who the father of Jane's child was, and why this man couldn't speak the truth. There was only one man around these parts he would keep silent about, and that was his master, the whoring rake, Thomas Mallen. John Collins was handicapped. Should he protest to the Justices that his daughter had been raped, for raped she would have been by that sinning devil, then he would be out of a job with no roof over his head, and a wife that needed a bed more than she needed anything else, and where would he get it for her but in the workhouse? He was sorry for the man, he was sorry for the girl, and he was sorry for himself also.

When he had crossed the hills back to his farm the loneliness of the vast spaces entered into him as never before. He had lived among the hills and the mountains all his life, as had his forbears for eight generations before him. Space was in his blood, and space of the fell lands, the space of the ever rolling hills; the awe-inspiring space viewed from the peaks; the space of the sky reaching into infinity. He had always felt at home in space until that day, and on that day he had walked across the hills with his head down. . . .

It was six weeks later when he crossed the hills again, but with his head up now and his mind firm, one purpose in it: he would take Jane Collins in the condition she was. For five Sundays he had prayed and asked guidance of God, and yesterday he had received his answer. The good book falling open in his lap, his eyes saw the words, 'For I was an hungered, and ye gave me meat: I was thirsty, and ye gave me drink: I was a stranger, and ye took me in: naked, and ye clothed me: I was sick, and ye visited me: I was in prison, and ye came unto me.

'Then shall the righteous answer him, saying, Lord, when saw we thee an hungered, and fed thee? or thirsty, and gave thee drink? When saw we thee a stranger, and took thee in? or naked, and clothed thee?

'Or when saw we thee sick, or in prison, and came unto thee?

'And the King shall answer and say unto them, Verily I say unto you, Inasmuch as ye have done it unto one of the least of these my brethren, ye have done it unto me.'

He had wanted a sign, and he took it as a sign, and so the following day when he reached the West Farm he said to John Collins, 'I will marry her.' The tears had run down the old man's face and he said, 'She's a good girl.'

A week later, when Michael Radlet brought the girl over the hills and to the church, she hadn't looked at him until he put the ring on her finger, and it was then she had begun to cry. . . .

Jane Radlet had been surrounded by old people all her life. The four men on Mallen's West Farm were

96

old, their families grown up and scattered; her father was old. There were two young men on the East Farm, but they were both spoken for by maids in the house. It was on her journey to the East Farm that she had met the other old man, at least he had seemed old to her, for he was in his forties. But he was different.

Her only break in the week was on Sunday afternoon, when her father took over the household chores and she went to visit his cousin, who was wife to the shepherd on the East Farm. She did not care for her father's cousin but it was somewhere to go, a focal point, and someone to talk to. Sometimes on the road, too, she met people, who gave her a word. It was on the road she had met the man on horseback. He appeared a very hearty man, and he had stopped and talked with her, and told her that she was pretty.

It was impossible for her to believe now that she hadn't recognized the man as the master of the Hall. Yet there was an excuse for her, for she had never seen him on his visits to the farm. Their cottage stood alone and well back from the farm buildings, and such was its situation that she needn't go near the farm unless she wanted to take her father a message; yet even so, she had told herself that anyone but a fool would have recognised the master, because her father had talked of him, and her mother had talked of him. Big, dark, pot-bellied with high eating and drinking, but then, he was no worse than the rest of the gentry, and much better than some, being generous to his staff at harvest and Christmas.

Came the Sunday they had met, he had got down from his horse and walked with her through the wood, and there he had tied his horse to a tree and had laughingly pulled her down beside him on the sward. At first he just talked and made her laugh; at first she hadn't realised what was happening; when she did she struggled, but he was a big man, and heavy. When it was over and she sat numbed and dazed with her back against the bole of a tree, he dropped a gold piece down the front of her bodice and patted her cheek before he left her.

97

Weeks later, when her mother found enough strength to upbraid her, she had retorted with anger, 'Who was there to tell me? I've seen no one but you an' me da for years except for that hour once a week when I've talked with Cousin Nellie. And what does she talk about? Only the doings of her son in far away America, and how to grow pot herbs, and the like. Who was there to put me wise? Who? I had only me instinct to go by, and it didn't come to me aid, 'cos I judged him to be an old man.'

'Old!' her mother had said. 'And him only mid-forty! You're stupid, girl, men are bulls until they die, be they eighteen or eighty.... Instinct!'

When her father had told her that she was to be saved from disgrace and that Michael Radlet was going to marry her, her only reaction had been, he's old an' all, besides which he is short and thick-set, with no looks to speak of. She had felt she was merely going from one servitude to another; until, she finally reached his farm, when he told her in simple words that he would not treat her as his wife until after her child was born. Then she had looked at him fully for the first time, and seen that he was not really old, and moreover, that he was kind, and her crying had increased.

The strange thing about her crying was that she couldn't remember having cried at any time in her life before; and afterwards she realized that the constant flow of tears was a form of relief, relief from her years of servitude. Her whole life seemed to have been spent amid human excrement, washing it from linen, smelling it, emptying it. The smell had permeated the very food she ate. She had left her mother with no regret whatever. Her mother cried at her going, not so much, she knew, at the loss of her as a daughter, but because now she would be at the mercy of an old crone from the village. She was sorry though to have left her father; she liked her father, for he was of a kindly nature.

So it was that after a few days at Wolfbur Farm she knew that she was going to be happy, and that Michael Radlet was a good man. But the most surprising thing was, he was going to teach her to read the Bible.

98

Donald Radlet came into the world protesting loudly, and Jane felt he had never stopped since. As his mother, she should have loved him, but she couldn't; he had been a separate being from the moment he left her womb. She would have said that the boy himself did not know what love was, if it wasn't for the protective affection he showed for his half-brother.

He was two years old when Matthew was born, and instead of being jealous, as she thought he might become, of a new baby taking his place, he was, from the very beginning, protective towards the boy, who in colouring and character was the antithesis of himself.

Donald was nine years old when he discovered that Mike Radlet was not his father. It happened on a fair day in Hexham.

They had talked about the fair day for weeks. This day was the highlight of the year; it was the day on which the hirings took place, when farm labourer and maid were bonded into service, and there were such delights as the fair ground, inside which there was every kind of entertainment from the shuggy boats to the boxing booths. Last year they had seen a Chinese lady with stumps for feet, a child whose head was so big it had to be supported in a framework, and a fat woman with a beard down to her breasts, which you could pull—if you had the nerve, for she looked as if she would eat you whole.

As soon as they entered the town Michael let the boys go off on their own for he knew that Donald, although only nine, was to be trusted to look after both himself and Matthew as well.

The boys knew where to contact their parents. The horse and flat cart were stabled in the blacksmith's yard and their mother would be drinking tea with the blacksmith's wife, and while they were exchanging their news their husbands would be out and about in the cattle market and recalling the days of their youth together, for Michael Radlet and the blacksmith were cousins.

But it so happened that the two men and the two women were in the house around three o'clock that day when Matthew came flying in to them, the tears streaming down his face and his words incoherent.

When at last he had quietened down somewhat they understood from his gasping words that Donald had been fighting a boy in the fair ground, and another two boys had also set on him.

When Michael demanded to know why Donald was fighting, Matthew looked up at him through streaming eyes and said, ' 'Cos of you, Da.'

'Me? why me?' Michael frowned down on his son, and Matthew, after shaking his head from side to side, muttered, 'They said you weren't ... they said you weren't his da. They said because of his white streak, you weren't his da. But you are, aren't you, Da? You are his da, aren't you?'

Michael looked at Jane, and she bowed her head; the blacksmith and his wife bowed theirs also.

It was as Michael stormed towards the door that Donald entered, and as they all looked at him they voiced a long concerted 'Aw!' His lip was split, one eye was rapidly closing, there was blood running from a cut on the side of his temple. His clothes were torn and begrimed and his hands, which he held palms outwards and close to his sides gave evidence that he had been pulled over rough ash ground, for the thin rivulets of blood were streaked with cinder dust.

'Oh! boy. Oh! boy.' Jane put her hand to her face as she approached him, then said pityingly, 'Come, let me clean you up.'

He made no move either towards or away from her but stared at her fixedly, and for the first time she knew what it was to suffer his scorn and his condemnation. She had noticed before that when he was angry or deeply troubled, like the time Matthew took the fever and they thought he would die, there came into the bright blackness of his eyes a glow as if from an inner fire. You couldn't say it was a film of pink or red because his pupils still remained black, but there was this change in their gleaming that gave the impression of a light behind them, a red ominous light.

He looked past her at Michael, and he said, 'I want to go home.'

100

Without a word Michael went out and harnessed the horse to the cart, and five minutes later they set off. Donald, unrelieved of dirt and blood, did not, as was usual, mount the front seat and sit beside Michael; instead, he clambered up into the back of the cart. His feet stretched out before him, his palms still upturned resting on his thighs, his head not bowed but level, his gaze directed unseeing through the side rails of the cart; thus he sat, and didn't move except when the wheels going into a rut or jolting over a stone jerked his body, until they came to the farm.

There Michael got down from the cart and went to the back of it and, looking at the boy, to whom he had been father in every way possible, said, 'Go and wash yourself and then we will talk. And you, Matthew'—he waved the younger boy towards his brother—'go with him and handle the pump.'

Slowly Donald let himself down into the yard, and as slowly he walked to the pump.

In the kitchen Michael, putting his hand on Jane's shoulder, said kindly, 'Now don't fret yourself, it had to come. Sooner or later we knew it had to come. Perhaps we've been at fault; we should've told him and not waited for some scallywag to throw it at him.'

'He hates me.'

'Don't talk nonsense, woman.'

'I'm not talkin' nonsense, Michael, I saw it in the look he gave me back there.'

'It's the shock; he'll get over that. You are his mother and he should be grateful for it.'

He smiled at her but she didn't smile back. In some strange way she knew that her days of happiness were past; as she had been aware of the time they were beginning for her in this house, now she knew that that time had ended as abruptly as it had begun. . . .

Michael led the way into the parlour, which in itself proved that this was a very exceptional occasion, for the parlour was used only on Sundays and Christmas Day. 'Sit down, boy,' he said.

For the first time the boy disobeyed an order given him by the man he had thought of as his father and, speaking through swollen lips, he said, 'You are not me father then?' He had never used the word father before, father and da meant the same thing, yet now he was, by his very tone, inferring a difference.

Michael swallowed deeply before answering, 'No, I am not your father in that I didn't beget you, but in every other way I am your father. I have brought you up an' I have cared for you. You are to me as me eldest son.'

'But I'm not your son! I'm nobody's son. I'm what they said, a flyblow! The flyblow of a man called Mallen. One of dozens, they said; he's fathered half the county, they said.'

Michael didn't speak for a moment; then he was forced to say, 'I wouldn't know anything about that, an' people always make mountains out of molehills. There's only one thing I do know, an' I want you to know it too; your mother was not at fault. She was but a girl, an innocent, ignorant girl, when she was taken down.'

Ignoring completely the reference to his mother, Donald said now, 'Matthew, he's not me real brother?'

'He's your half-brother.'

'He's your real son; you're his father, not just his da.'

'They both mean the same thing, father an' da.'

'Not any more they don't. Not any more.'

It was as Michael stared at the boy, who was at that time almost as tall as himself, that there came into him a feeling of deep compassion, for he saw the lad was no longer a lad or a boy. True, he had never really been childish, always appearing older than his years, both in his actions and his talk, but now the very look of him had changed. He had the look of an adult man about him; it came over in the expression of his eyes. His eyes had always been his most startling feature. At odd times when some pleasant incident had softened them he had thought them beautiful, but he wondered if he would ever think them beautiful again. He said now, 'Nothing has changed; whether you think of me as your da, or your father, or whatever, I remain the same. Go on now and have your meal, an' be respectful to your mother. And hold your head up wherever you go, for no blame lies on you.'

102

Donald turned about and walked to the door, but before opening it he stopped and, looking back at Michael, he answered his last statement by saying, 'They called me a bastard.'

When, the following Sunday, Matthew came into the house, his head hanging and stated, 'Our Donald's gone over the hills an' he wouldn't let me go with him,' Jane closed her eyes and muttered to herself, 'Oh my God!' And Michael laid down the book and said, 'When was this? How long ago?'

'Just a while back. I thought he was going over to Whitfield Law but he changed his mind and went towards the Peel, and then wouldn't let me come on.'

Jane, bringing out her words between gasps, said, 'He must have started asking. What if he should go . . . I mean right . . . right to the Hall? Oh Michael, Michael, do something, stop him.'

Michael wasn't given to running. If you want to walk a long way you don't run, had always been his maxim, but on this day he ran, thinking as he did so that it had been one of his mistakes not to have brought the boy over these hills before. It was six years since he had been this way himself, for now that both Jane's parents were dead there was no need to take this road. Yet, he thought now that in denying this route to the boy when on his Sunday jaunts he must have eventually raised some suspicion in his mind.

He was blowing like a bellows before he had gone very far. He thought the boy, too, must have run, for when he reached the peak and looked down into the next valley there was no sign of him.

Michael had been on the road over an hour when at last he saw him. He stopped and stared. The boy, about a quarter of a mile distant from him, was standing on the summit of the last hill. It was the one that towered over the foothills where they spread out into the valley in which was set High Banks Hall. In the winter and the spring when the trees of the estate were bare you could get a view of the entire Hall and the terraces and sunken gardens from that point, but for the rest of the year only a gable end and the windows of the upper floor were visible.

As if he knew he was being watched Donald had turned about and looked in his direction, and then waited while Michael walked slowly towards him. When he came up with the boy he said loudly and sternly, 'You're not to go near that place, do you hear me? Anyway, you'd be thrown out on your backside an' made to look a fool.'

The boy stared at him. His face, still discoloured from the blows he had received in the fight, was tinged a deep red and he answered, 'I'm no fool.'

'I'm glad to hear it. Now come away back home. . . .'

From then on Donald went over the hills every Sunday and on special holidays, the weather permitting, and no one could do anything about it. But he went no further than the last hill, until one day in 1851 when he heard that Thomas Mallen had gone bust and that Dick Mallen had almost committed murder. That Sunday he walked along the road and stood outside the gates for the first time; but he did not venture inside until after the auction had taken place. Then he walked round the house peering in the windows, but not like the children had done, more in the manner of someone returning to his rightful home after a long absence.

The rooms were almost as he had pictured them in his mind's eye over the years. They were big and high and had coloured ceilings. Some were panelled up to the ceiling, and even in those with only skirting boards the wood was moulded three feet high from the floor. He had run his hand over the great front door, then counted the iron studs; there were ten rows of eight.

He walked through the empty stables and saw fittings that he couldn't believe any man would waste on a place where a horse was stabled. The hooks were of ornamental brass, the harness-horse was covered with leather-like doeskin, and four of the stalls each had a silver plate bearing a horse's name.

When he stood back from the house and looked up at it the most strange sensation filled his breast. It began in some region hitherto unknown to him; he felt it rising upwards and upwards until it reached his throat, and there it stuck and grew to a great hard painful
104

thing that was all set to choke him. Even when he was shaken by a violent fit of coughing it didn't entirely dissolve.

He had visited the house a number of times, alone, before the day on which he took Matthew with him; the day when he encountered Miss Brigmore and the girls, and later his father.

When they had returned home that night he had not stopped Matthew from pouring out the exciting news that they had been to supper with Mr. Mallen.

This news had actually shocked Michael, and it had not only stunned Jane but increased her fear of this son of hers. She asked herself what he expected to get out of it now, for Thomas Mallen, they said, was utterly destitute, living on the charity of his nieces.

That night, when Michael said to her, 'I suppose it's only natural that he should want to see his father,' she shook her head violently and answered, 'Nothing he does is natural, and never has been. . . .'

From that time on Jane lived in fear of the years ahead. There was a dread in her that she couldn't explain. Yet as one season passed into another and the two boys grew from youth into young men and nothing untoward happened, she looked back and felt like many another woman, saying to herself that she had been foolish in wasting her time worrying about someone over whom she knew she had no control, for she felt that she meant less to her son than did the cattle in the byres. Indeed, she had watched him show affection for them, especially when a cow was in labour. He had lost sleep to make sure that a cow was delivered of her calf and that both survived in good fettle; but for herself, she felt that if she were to drop down dead at his feet he would show very little concern, except to make sure that she was put away decently. This one trait was prominent in him; he was very concerned with doing the right thing, and this in turn warranted that he should be well put on in his dress. His taste in dress, she considered, was above that suitable to a farmer; but then she had gleaned one secret thought of his: he considered himself a cut above the ordinary run of farmer. Inside, she knew he was proud to be Thomas Mallen's son, while at the same time despising her for her part in it.

She also knew that he would never admit to this. His thoughts were locked deep within him. He never spoke his real thoughts, not even to Matthew, and if he cared for anyone it was Matthew. Not until the time came for him to act on any plan he had devised in his mind concerning the farm did he even speak of it to Michael. He rarely or never informed her of what he was about to do.

So it was on this bright autumn Sunday morning in 1861 when the four of them were seated around the breakfast table in the kitchen, and only a second after Michael had finished the grace, saying, 'We thank you, Lord, for our food which has come to us through Your charity. Amen.' that Donald said, 'I'm going straight over this morning.' They all looked at him, and each face registered reserved surprise, for they recognised by the tone of his voice and the fact that he'd altered his routine that he was about to impart something of importance.

'I'm going to ask Constance to marry me ... it's time,' he said.

Now the reserve slipped from their faces and they gaped at him, in a mixture of amazement, disapproval and even horror. On any other occasion they would have been more wary, for they never showed their true feelings to him. This attitude, which had been born of a desire never to hurt him, had developed in varying degrees in the three of them. He had to be humored as one might a sick person in order that he would not upset himself with bouts of temper or withdraw into a continued silence. There was a similarity in their attitudes towards him that was strange, for they all viewed him in different ways. But now Michael blurted out, 'You can't do that, she's near blood to you.'

'She's not near blood to me.'

'She's Mallen's niece.'

'She's not. Her mother was his step-sister, there's no blood tie atween them at all.'

Still Michael's face was grim now. 'It doesn't seem right.'

'And why not?'

'Don't shout at me, boy. Don't shout at me.'

'I'm not shoutin'. And don't forget, I'm no boy.'

'You'll always be a boy to me.' Michael thrust his chair back and stumped—for his left leg was stiff with rheumatism—from the table into the sitting room where, as was usual on a Sunday morning, he would read for half an hour from the book before attending to his Sunday duties on the farm. And even on this morning he did not side-step from his usual pattern.

Now Jane spoke. Quietly she asked, 'Does she know?'

'Know what?' He looked at her coldly.

'That . . .' she was about to say 'That you want her,' but she changed it to 'What to expect. I mean, have you given her any inkling?'

'Enough.'

She stared at him for a moment longer as she thought, that girl in this house with him for life—he'll suffocate her. Now she rose from the table and walked slowly across the stone-flagged kitchen and out through the low door that just took her height, and into the dairy. It was cool and restful in the dairy and she could ponder there, and she had much to ponder on this day, she knew.

Donald now looked at Matthew, waiting for him to speak, and as he waited his face took on a softness that slipped into a smile. After a time he asked quietly, 'Surprised?'

Matthew didn't answer, he couldn't as yet. Surprised? He was staggered; shocked, dismayed; yes, that was the word, dismayed, utterly dismayed. Dear, dear God, that this should happen, that it should be Constance he wanted! He had always thought it was Barbara, and he had the idea that Barbara thought along the same lines. Why, whenever they had been over there it wasn't to Constance he had talked, but to Barbara, and when he had seen them together he had thought, they're much alike in some ways, those two; given to silences. There are depths in both of them that were soundless, and their silences were heavy with brooding, secret brooding, lonely brooding. As his

107

thoughts were apt to do, he had dwelt on their brooding because he knew that their brooding coloured their lives. He knew that each in his way was lonely and craved something. When the craving became intense it showed, in Donald's case at least, in bursts of temper.

It was as recently as last summer that Donald had shown this side of him when, entering the cottage on one of their Sunday visits, they had found company there. There were two young men, one called Ferrier, scarcely more than a boy, and the other by the name of Will Headley about his own age, which was twenty then. It wasn't the first time he had encountered these two young men; at different times over the years they had met. He understood them to be the grandsons of Thomas Mallen's old friends and so it was natural that they should visit him.

On this particular Sunday when they entered the sitting room they were engulfed in a burst of laughter. Constance was laughing gaily; but then Constance always laughed gaily. Her beauty of face and figure was enhanced by a joyous soul, which contrasted sharply with Barbara's looks and temperament. But on this day Barbara, too was laughing unrestrainedly, and he thought that it was this that annoyed Donald, for he scarcely spoke during the whole of their visit; in fact his presence put a damper on the gathering. They had hardly left the cottage on their return journey when he burst out, 'That old witch of a Brigmore is planning to marry them off.'

He did not contradict the statement but it overwhelmed him with sickness. He'd be very sorry for Donald if Barbara did marry Will Headley; but rather that than it should be Constance. He did not take into account the Ferrier boy; he was much too young, and as he gathered from the conversation, his mind was on nothing but this Oxford place to which he was going in the autumn.

Matthew now shook his head slowly from side to side. He was shaking it at himself, at his blindness, at his lack of knowledge of this half-brother of his. He should have known that Donald never did anything the way other men did, for he wasn't like other men, he

108

had a canker inside him that gnawed at him continuously. He had been born and brought up on this farm, but from that day when he was nine years old he had disowned it while at the same time attempting to run it, even of late be master of it.

But there was one thing sure, if he didn't belong here, then he certainly' didn't belong over the hills in the house where his real father lived. For always in the company of Thomas Mallen, Donald appeared gauche and out of place, and this caused him to assume an air of condescension, as if it was only out of the goodness of his heart that he visited this old man. The butter, cheese and eggs he took over every week only emphasised this attitude. But Thomas Mallen showed plainly that he liked this son; and Donald's attitude seemed to amuse him. And the girls liked him; they, too, had been amused in those early years by his bombast. When the bombast had, with time, turned into a cautious reticence they had tried to tease him out of it, at least Constance had.

There was only one person in that household who didn't like him and who showed it, and that was Miss Brigmore. Donald, on his part, hated her. Years ago Matthew had felt he should hate her too because Donald did, but secretly he had liked her, and whenever he could he drew her into conversation because he learned from her. He knew that Miss Brigmore had something that he wanted, she had knowledge. Knowledge to give him the power to talk about things that he understood in his mind but couldn't get off his tongue; things that came into his head when he looked down into water, or watched the afterglow, or when his thoughts deprived him of his much needed sleep and he crept quietly from the pallet bed and knelt at the attic window and raced with the moon across the wild sky—Miss Brigmore had once said it wasn't the moon that raced but the clouds, and he just couldn't take that in for a long time. It was she, he knew, who could have made these things more clear to him, could have brought his feelings glowing into words; but he did not talk with her much because it would have annoyed

Donald, and he was, and had always been, secretly afraid of annoying Donald.

But oh dear, dear God! Matthew's thoughts jumped back to the present. Donald had just said he was going to ask Constance to marry him. Constance in this house every day! He wouldn't be able to bear it. He had loved Constance from the moment he saw her offering Donald a strawberry; he knew it had happened at that very moment. He also knew that it was a hopeless love, for he considered her as far above him as the princesses up there in the Palace. So much did he consider her out of his reach that he had never even thought of her and marriage in the same breath; what he had thought was, I'll never marry anyone, never. And when he thought this he always added, anyway it wouldn't be fair, not with this cough. They hadn't said he had the consumption, but he'd got the cough all right, and as time went on he became more and more tired, so much so that often he thought that it would be a poor lookout for the farm if Donald weren't as strong as two horses. And Donald delighted in being strong. Give him his due, never had he balked at the extra work. Many a day, aye, many a week he had done the work for both of them, and he had been grateful to him. But now, as he stared into the dark face whose attraction was emphasised with a rare smile, he experienced a moment of intense hate. Then he began to cough, and the cough brought the sweat pouring out of him.

'Don't let me news choke you.' Donald came round the table and thumped him on the back. 'Here, take a spoonful of honey.' He reached out for the jar, but Matthew shook his head and thrust the jar away.

When he had regained his breath, Donald asked him, 'Well now, are you going to say something?' Matthew, after a deep gulp in his throat, muttered, 'Have ... have you thought that she mightn't fit in here, in the house, I mean?'

'The house? What's wrong with the house? It's as good as the one she's in now.'

'But ... but it's different.'

'How do you mean different? It's got as many rooms,

counting the loft, an' the countryside around is bonnier.'

Matthew again shook his head. What could he say? Could he say, Yes, but it's an old house, and it's a cold bare house because it hasn't got in it the draperies and the knick-knacks, nor yet the furniture that's in the cottage? Yet, of its kind, he knew it was a substantial house, a house that many a farmer's daughter would be glad to be mistress of. But Constance was no farmer's daughter, and although she had been brought up in the cottage she had also been brought up in an atmosphere provided by Miss Brigmore, an atmosphere of refinement and learning. In short, Constance was a lady. They were all ladies over there, in spite of their poverty. Then again, their poverty was relative. He understood that they had two hundred pounds a year between them, and that to him, and thousands like him, was far from poverty. He said now, 'I thought it was Barbara.'

'Barbara! Good God, no! Never Barbara. Barbara's all right, mind, she's got a sensible head on her shoulders, but she's as far removed from Constance as night from day; sometimes I wonder at them being sisters. No, never Barbara.' He walked down the length of the kitchen now and stood looking out of the window and into the yard. A line of ducks was waddling down the central drain on their way to the pond. His eyes ranged from the stables, over the grain store and the barn, to the side wall where the cow byres began, and next to them the dairy. He now pictured Constance in the dairy. She would take it all as fun. She mightn't take to the work as quickly as another brought up on a farm, but that didn't matter. There would be no need for her to do all that much, his mother would do the rough, as usual. But Constance would transform the house; transform him, she would bring gaiety into his life. He had never experienced gaiety, only as an observer when he went on his Sunday visit across the hills. Although he rarely allowed himself to laugh, he liked laughter; he liked brightness, in another, and she was all laughter and brightness. She would rejuvenate the whole atmosphere of this place; she'd bring to it a quality it

111

had never known. It was a sombre house, and he admitted to himself that he was responsible for a great part of the feeling. It all stemmed from something in him he couldn't get rid of. Yet even before the knowledge of his parentage had been kicked into him that day at the fair he could not recall being any different. But once Constance was here, once he was married, he would feel different.

He thought wryly it was as if he were a female bastard and marriage would give him a name, a legal name. He couldn't explain the feeling even to himself; it was mixed up with his children; he knew that as each one was born his isolation would lessen. What was more, he intended to give them the name that should rightly be his. He would call his first son after Matthew because he liked Matthew—he did not use the term love—but following Matthew he would add the name Mallen. Matthew Mallen Radlet; and as time went on he could see the Radlet fading away and his children being known as Mallens; and if they bore the streak as he did, all the better.

One thing only troubled him and then but slightly, what would be the old man's reaction to him wanting Constance? He knew that the old man liked him, and he took credit for bringing a certain spice to his life. Without his weekly visits he guessed that Thomas Mallen would over the years, have been very bored indeed with his existence, for he had grown sluggish in his mind if not in his body; the latter had been kept active, no doubt, by that shrew of an old cow, who not only acted as if she were mistress of the house but to all intents and purposes was mistress of the house. He had no doubt whatever about her reactions to his wanting Constance because she would not want to lose Constance, nor the hundred pounds a year that went with her.

He himself wasn't unconscious of the hundred pounds that Constance would bring with her. He could make a lot of improvements on the farm with an extra hundred pounds a year. Oh, quite a lot.

When he turned from the window Matthew was gone, and he pursed his thin lips and pushed aside the

112

feeling of irritation that the empty kitchen aroused in him. But he could excuse Matthew for not being enthusiastic at his news; Matthew was sick, and he'd be more sick before he died. He jerked one shoulder, he didn't want to think about Matthew dying. Anyway, the consumption could linger on for years; if he was well cared for he might live till he was thirty.

He walked smartly out of the room; he must away and get changed. This was one day he'd look his best, his Mallen best.

TWO

Miss Brigmore set the bowl of porridge, the jug of hot milk and the basin of soft brown sugar at one side of the tray, and a cup and saucer and silver coffee jug at the other, and in the middle of the tray she placed a small covered dish of hot buttered toast. As she lifted up the tray from the kitchen table she looked to where Barbara was attending to her own breakfast, as she always did, and she asked, 'Did she cry in the night, do you know?'

'I didn't hear her.'

'She's taken it much better than I expected.'

'You can't tell; beneath her laughter you don't know what she is thinking; her laughter is often a cover.'

Miss Brigmore raised her eyebrows as she went towards the door which Mary was holding open for her, and she thought to herself that she was better acquainted with what went on inside Constance's head than was her sister, in fact she was well acquainted with what went on in both their heads. It would have surprised them how much she knew of their inner thoughts.

She went slowly up the narrow stairs on to the landing, turned her back to the bedroom door and pushed it open with her buttocks, then went towards the bed where Thomas Mallen was still sleeping.

'Wake up! wake up!' Her voice had a chirpy note to it. 'Your breakfast is here.'

'What! Oh! Oh yes.' Thomas pulled himself slowly up among the pillows, and when she had placed the tray on his knees he blew out his cheeks and let the air slowly pass through his pursed lips, then said, 'It looks a grand morning.'

'It's fine . . . I think you should take a walk to-day.'

'Aw, Anna.' He flapped his hand at her. 'You and your walks, you'll walk me to death.'

'You'll find yourself nearer to it if you don't walk.'

He looked towards the window, then said, 'It's Sunday,' and she repeated, 'Yes, it's Sunday.'

They both viewed Sundays with different feelings. He looked forward to Sundays; she hated them for this was the day when that upstart came over the hills and acted like the lord of the manor himself. Talk about putting a beggar on horseback and him riding to hell; if ever he got the chance there was one who would gallop all the way.

She had never liked Donald Radlet from when he was a boy; as he grew into manhood her dislike had at times touched on loathing. She, who could explain everyone else's feelings to herself, couldn't give a rational explanation for her own with regards to Thomas's natural son. It wasn't jealousy; no, because if his son had been Matthew, not only would she have liked him, she might also have come to love him. But in Donald she saw only a bigheaded, dour bumptious upstart, who made claims on this house because of his bastardy.

But perhaps, she admitted to herself, there was a touch of jealousy in her feelings towards Donald, because although the matter had never been discussed openly, she guessed that Thomas not only liked the young man, but strangely even felt a pride in him. In a way she could understand this, for not having had a sign or a word from Dick all these years, he had come to think of him as dead, and had replaced him in his affections with his flyblow, because that's all Donald Radlet was, a flyblow. She did not chastise herself for the common appellation for she considered it a true description. But for the tragedy that had befallen the Hall and its occupants those ten years ago, Donald Radlet would not have been allowed past the outer gates and Thomas, although he might have been amused by the persistency of the boy who viewed the Hall from the

115

top of the crag, would no more have publicly recognised him than he would any of his other numerous illegitimate offspring.

Thomas said now, 'How is Constance?'

'I haven't seen her this morning, but Barbara tells me she passed a good night; at least she didn't hear her crying.'

'She was disappointed.'

'More than a little, I think. It was dastardly of him to call as often as he did when all the while he was planning his engagement to another.'

'As many a man before him, he was likely astraddle two stools. If things had been as they used to be he would, I'm sure, have chosen Constance, but which man in the position the Headleys are in now could take a young woman with a hundred a year? They are almost where I was ten years ago, an' I should crow. But no; having tasted such bitterness, I wouldn't wish it on anyone.'

'Then he had no right to pay her attention.'

'He didn't pay her attention as such, he's called here for years.'

'You didn't see what I saw.'

He put his hand out towards her now and caught her arm and, gazing into her face, he said softly, 'No one sees what you see, Anna. Have I ever told you you're a wonderful woman?'

'Eat your breakfast.' Her eyes were blinking rapidly.

'Anna.'

'Yes, what is it?' She stood perfectly still returning his look now.

'I should marry you.'

The start she gave was almost imperceivable. There was a silence between them as their eyes held; then in a matter of fact way she said, 'Yes, you should, but you won't.'

'If I had put a child into you I would have.'

'It's a pity you didn't then, isn't it?'

'Yes, indeed it is; but you can't say it wasn't for trying, can you?' His voice had dropped to a low whisper and the corner of his mouth was tucked in. She now smacked at his hand playfully before saying, 'Eat
116

your breakfast, the toast will be cold, and the coffee too. And then don't linger, get up; we're going for a brisk walk through the fields.'

'We're doing no such thing.'

She reached the door and was half through it when she repeated, 'We're going for a brisk walk through the fields.' And as she closed the door she heard him laugh.

She now paused a moment before going across the narrow landing and to the door opposite, and in the pause she thought, Men are cruel. All men are cruel. Thomas was cruel; he would have married her if he had put a child into her, and how she had longed that he should. She needed children. There was a great want in her for children. That the time was almost passed for her having any of her own hadn't eased the longing, and she assuaged it at times with the thought that once Barbara and Constance were married there would be children again who would need her care; she would not recognise that marriage might move them out of her orbit.

With regard to Thomas not giving her a child, she knew that the fault did not lie with him—the proof of this came across the hills every Sunday. But over the past ten years he had not strayed, for she had served him better than any wife would have done. In serving him she had sullied her name over the county. Not that that mattered; she cared naught for people's opinion. Or did she? She held her head high now but if she had been Mrs. Mallen it would have needed no effort to keep upright.

And now here was her beloved Constance suffering at the hands of another man. Will Headley had courted Constance since she was sixteen; there was no other word for it. Before that, on his visits he had romped with her and teased her, but during the past year his manner had changed; it had been a courting manner. Then yesterday when she was expecting a visit from him, what did she receive? A beautifully worded letter to the effect that he had gone to London where his engagement to Miss Catherine Freeman was to be announced. He had thanked her for the happy days they

117

had spent together and stressed that he would never forget them, or her.

After Constance had read the letter, the bright gaiety that shone from her face, even when in repose, had seeped away. She had looked stricken, but she hadn't cried; she had folded the letter in two and, when about to return it to its envelope, she had paused and said, 'Anna,' for now she called her Anna, 'read that.'

When she had read it she, too, was stricken; but her training helped her to keep calm and say 'I am very disappointed in Mr. Headley.' Then she had taken Constance's hand and looked into her face and said, 'These things happen, they are part of your education, what matters is how you react to them. If you must cry, cry in the night, but put a brave face on during the day. You're only seventeen; the same could happen to you again before you marry.'

At this Constance had turned on her, and in the most unusual tone cried, 'It won't! it won't ever happen to me again.'

She had dismissed the outburst by saying, 'Well, we'll see, we'll see.'

Now she went across the landing and gently opened the door. She did not knock, she entered as a mother might and said, 'Oh, there you are; you're up, dear.'

It was evident that Constance was very much up. She was dressed and putting the last touches to her toilet as she sat before the small dressing table; and she looked through the mirror at Miss Brigmore while she continued to take the comb through the top of her brown hair. She did not, as usual, speak first, remarking on the weather or some other triviality; it was Miss Brigmore who, coming to her side, and smoothing an imaginary crease out of the back of her lace collar, said, 'Did you sleep well, dear?'

Constance stared at Miss Brigmore, still through the mirror, and she addressed her through the mirror as she said, flatly, 'I'm supposed to say, yes, Anna, aren't I? Well, I can't, because I didn't sleep well.' She now swung round and, gripping Miss Brigmore's hands, she whispered, 'Do you think I'll ever marry, Anna?'

'Of course you will, child. O course you will.' Miss

118

Brigmore released one hand and gently stroked the delicately tinted cheek, but her eyebrows moved up sharply as Constance jerked her head away from the embrace, saying, 'Of course you will, of course you will. . . . Of course I won't! Where are the men around here who will come flocking for my hand? Whom do we see? Let us face it, Anna, Will was my only chance.'

'Don't be silly, child.'

'I'm not silly, and don't try to hoodwink me, Anna. And I'm no longer a child. Will led me to believe . . . Oh, you don't know . . . anyway, what does it matter? As you're always saying, these are the things that make life and must be faced up to. But'—her head drooping suddenly, she ended, 'But I don't want to face up to them. I . . . I don't want to end up like Barbara, resigned. I'm . . . I'm not made like Barbara, Anna.' Once again she was gripping Miss Brigmore's hands. 'I want a home of my own, Anna; I want . . . I want to be married. Do you understand that, Anna? I want to be married.'

Miss Brigmore looked down into the soft brown eyes with pity. She was saying she wanted to be married and she was asking did Anna understand. Oh, she understood only too well; she could write volumes on the bodily torments she had endured, not only during the developing years, but in those years between twenty and thirty. She had even taken to reading the lives of the saints and martyrs in the hope of finding some way to ease her bodily cravings.

When Constance turned away from her, saying helplessly, 'Oh, you really don't understand what I mean,' she gripped her shoulders tightly and twisted her none too gently back towards her, and bending until their faces were level, she hissed at her, 'I understand. Only too well I understand. I've been through it all, only much more than you'll ever realise. Now listen to me. You'll marry; I'll see to it you'll marry. We'll make arrangements to do more visiting. We'll go over to the Browns in Hexham; there's always company coming and going there. And the Harpers in Allendale; they've invited you twice and you've never accepted.'

'Oh, the Harpers.' Constance shook her head. 'They're so vulgar; they talk nothing but horses.'

'They may be vulgar, horsey people are nearly always vulgar, but they keep an open house. We'll be going that way next week; we'll call in.'

Constance shook her head slowly from side to side. 'It all seems so ... so mercenary, so cheap, con ... conniving.'

'You have to connive in order to exist. Come on now.' Miss Brigmore straightened her back and again smoothed out the imaginary crease in Constance's lace collar. 'It's a beautiful day, and Sunday, and we're going for our walk. Now come along and put a brave face on things, and who knows, it may all have happened for the best. You know what I've always said, every step we take in life has already been planned for us. We are not free agents in spite of all this talk about free will. Have your breakfast so that Mary can get cleared away and I will get your uncle ready.' She always gave the title of Uncle to Thomas when speaking of him to them. 'And don't worry, dear.' Her voice dropping to a muted tone, she now looked lovingly at Constance. "Everything will work out to advantage, you'll see, you'll see. Don't my prophecies nearly always come true?' She lifted her chin upwards and looked down her nose in a comical fashion, and Constance smiled weakly as she said, 'Yes, Anna; yes, they do.'

'Well now, believe me when I say everything will work out for the best. Come along.'

She turned briskly about and walked out of the room, leaving the door open, and Constance rose from the dressing table and followed her, thinking with a slight touch of amusement, when Anna speaks it's like the voice of God.

THREE

It was at eleven o'clock when they were on the point of going for their ritual walk that Donald came up the path and entered the house by the front way, and without knocking. Whereas Miss Brigmore didn't knock when she entered Constance's bedroom because she felt that she had the right of a mother, Donald didn't knock at the cottage door because he felt he had the right of a son.

The girls were standing in the small hallway. Miss Brigmore was coming out of the drawing room buttoning her gloves, and behind her, protesting, as he always did on these occasions, came Thomas. When the front door opened and they saw Donald, they all exclaimed in their different ways, 'Why! we didn't expect you till this afternoon.' That is, all except Miss Brigmore, and she fumbled the last button into the buttonhole of her glove while she thought, What brings him at this time? She turned and looked at Thomas, who made a quick effort to hide his pleasure, which she knew at this time was twofold for he would see Donald Radlet's arrival as the means of getting out of taking exercise.

'Well, well! my boy, what have we? Something untoward happened? Have you closed up the farm . . . or sold it?' Thomas's deep-bellied laugh caused his flesh to shake.

'Neither.' Donald never adressed Thomas with any title, either of sir or mister. 'As to something untoward, well it all depends upon how you look at it.' He turned now and smiled at the two young women, who were

121

smiling at him, and he said to them, 'Are you off for your walk?'

'Yes, yes.' It was Barbara who spoke and Constance who nodded.

'Well, do you mind being delayed for a few minutes?'

They looked back at him and both of them said together, 'No, no,' and Barbara added, 'Of course not.'

Donald now turned to Thomas and in a manner that brought Miss Brigmore's teeth grating slightly he said, 'I want to talk to you for a minute ... all right?'

'Yes, yes, all right, all right.' Thomas was always amused by his natural son's manner, for he thought he knew the true feelings that his bumptiousness and pomposity covered. He had been a little like that himself in his young days when at times he wasn't sure of his footing, or was out to show that he was not only as good as the rest, but better. He turned to Miss Brigmore now, saying, 'You and the girls go along, go along; we'll catch up on you.'

Looking Thomas straight in the eyes, Miss Brigmore said, 'We'll wait.' Upon this she turned round and went back into the drawing room, and Constance went with her. Thomas now lumbered along the corridor towards his study, and Donald, after casting a half amused glance in Barbara's direction where she remained standing looking at him, followed Thomas.

Standing by the drawing room window, and looking towards Barbara as she entered the room, Constance said, 'I wonder what's brought him at this time, and what he wants with Uncle? Did you notice he was wearing a new suit? He can look very smart when he likes.'

Barbara didn't answer, but sitting down, she folded her hands on her lap. Yes, he could look very smart when he liked; to her he had always looked smart. But what had brought him at this time of the morning and all dressed up, and asking to speak to Uncle privately? What? Her heart suddenly jerked beneath her ribs. That look he had given her before he had gone along the corridor. Could it be possible, could it just be possible? He had always paid her attention; but really not

122

sufficient to warrant any hope that his thoughts were other than brotherly. Yet had some of her own feelings seeped through her facade and he had recognised them, and this had made him bold, and he was in there now asking for her hand? . . . Oh if it were only so. She had loved him for years, in spite of what she knew to be his failings. His weekly visits had been the only bright spot in an otherwise drab and formal existence. She had, however, kept her secret locked tight within her, the one person she would have confided in she couldn't, because Anna disliked Donald and always had done. But she didn't care who disliked him, she loved him, and if she became his wife she'd ask nothing more from life. . . .

In the study Thomas sat stiffly in the big leather chair staring at Donald. He had been utterly taken aback by the young fellow's request. Now he could have understood it if he had asked for Barbara's hand, because, over the years, it was to Barbara he had talked, and she to him. Sometimes on Sunday afternoon after they'd had dinner and he was dozing in his chair they had put him to sleep with their talking, she explaining about books and answering his questions, much as a teacher would do. She was in that way very like Anna. But he didn't want Barbara, it was Constance he was after. Well, well now, this was a strange state of affairs. And he had to ask himself a question: did he want his natural son to marry either of these girls, even if they would have him? Well, why not, why not? He had just said he would own the farm when old Radlet died. Apparently Radlet had told him this. . . . He said to him now, 'You say the farm will be yours, have you it in writing?'

'No, but I know for certain it will be.'

'What about his own son?'

'He has the consumption, he won't last for very long.'

'You never know, you never know, creaking doors. Anyway, should Radlet die, Matthew, were he alive, would inherit, and then he in turn could leave the farm to anyone he liked.'

'He wouldn't; he can't run the place, he has no
123

strength. Anyway, I'm not worried about that side of the situation. I'm putting money on the place every year with buildings and stock, and will go on doing so. It's a prosperous farm an' I'm thinking of buying more land an' all.'

The self-assurance silenced Thomas for a time. He was buying more land, he was putting in more stock, putting up more buildings, and hadn't a thing in writing. It was wonderful to have such self-confidence. This son of his knew where he was going, and Constance might do a lot worse, for now that Will Headley had failed her, he couldn't see anyone else in the running, not for the time being at any rate. Most of the young fellows to-day were on the lookout for wives who would bring with them a good dowry. It was as it had always been, if a man had to choose between his heart and hard cash, the hard cash always won. If it didn't, it was a proven fact in most cases that the heart pact soon led to disaster.

'Have you any objections?'

'Well'— Thomas let his head rest against the back of the chair, and his eyes ranged around the room before he answered, 'I don't know whether I have or not; your request has come as a surprise, and if I'm not mistaken I think it will surprise Constance too.'

'It shouldn't, she knows I like her.'

'Like her! Huh! liking and loving are two different things. Of course she knows you like her, everybody likes her.'

Thomas now got to his feet and walked with heavy tread back and forth from the desk to the door a number of times before he said, 'This'll cause talk you know, because folk don't realise that the girls have no blood connection with me. It'll be said I'm letting my niece marry my son.'

He stopped in his striding and the two stared at each other. It was the first time the relationship had been brought into the open, and the fact caused Donald to rise slowly to his feet. Eye held eye until Thomas, chewing on his lip, swung his heavy body around, saying, 'Well, you have my consent, but knowing you, you'd go ahead with or without it.'

124

When he looked at Donald over his shoulder he saw that he was smiling, and his own lips spreading slowly apart, he said on a laugh, 'You're a strange fellow, a strange fellow, and I should understand you, if anybody should I should understand you, shouldn't I? But I don't, and I doubt if anybody ever will.'

'I don't see why not; if they understand you they should understand me.'

'No, boy, no; because you know you don't take after me, not really; you take after my father's youngest brother, Rod. He too went after what he wanted and took no side roads.'

'Did he always get what he wanted?'

'I don't know; I don't know whether he wanted to be drowned at sea or not but he was drowned at sea. I don't know if he got what he wanted, but by all accounts he got what he deserved.'

The smile had left Donald's face as if it had been wiped off and, his voice stiff now, he said, 'I've been handicapped for years, an' I've risen above it. I've worked hard all my life, I've worked like two men, many a time like three; I hope I get what I deserve.'

'I meant no offence, boy, I was merely making a statement. And I say to you, I hope you get what you deserve. But ... but'—Thomas now rolled his head from side to side—'we're getting very serious and deep all of a sudden, come, we were talking of a proposal of marriage, weren't we?' He poked his head forward. 'That was the idea, wasn't it?'

'Along those lines.' The cold look still remained in Donald's eyes.

'Well then, go ahead, you have my consent; I won't say blessing because'—he now laughed a deep rumbling laugh—'a blessing from me might have little to recommend it, eh?' He thrust out his heavy arm and dug Donald in the shoulder with his fist, and they were both aware that the blow did not even stagger the thin frame.

Thomas now turned abruptly and went out of the room and made straight for the drawing room. He opened the door and said, 'Anna, spare me a minute will you?' and before she could move or answer he had turned away and gone into the dining room.

When Miss Brigmore entered the dining room she closed the door behind her, then walked slowly towards him. He did not take her hand, nor was there any placating note in his voice when he said, 'I have news for you, news that will surprise you and certainly not please you. He has asked that he may marry Constance.'

As he watched her face screw up until her eyes were almost lost from view, he waved his hand at her and turned from her, and when still she didn't speak he turned towards her again and said, 'Now it's no use, don't create a scene. I have given him my consent, and that's that. After all, he is my son, and who has a better right I ask you? And'—his voice and manner arrogant now, he went on, 'they're no blood relations, the girls, you know they're not, there's nothing against it. Except that you don't like him. All right, you don't like him, you've never liked him, but I repeat, he is my son, he is part of me.'

When she suddenly sat down in a chair he went to her, and now he did take her hands and, his voice soft, he said, 'What have you against him really? He's hard working, and as he himself has just said, he's lived under a handicap for years. You don't like his manner, he's full of the great I am. Well, in his position I likely would have been the same; I would have had to put on a front. In a way he's to be admired, not scorned.'

'You can't let it happen, Thomas, you can't.'

'Well I have, I have.' He was standing up now, his voice arrogant once again. 'And that's that. It's up to her now, and nobody's going to force her. Oh no, nobody's going to force her. It's ten to one she'll laugh at him an' that'll be the end of it.'

'It's come at the wrong time.'

'What do you mean?'

'She has been rejected. She may take him as a means of escape.'

'Don't be silly, don't be silly, woman. She has no need to escape. Escape from what?'

'You don't understand.'

126

'I don't see what there's to understand. She either takes him or she doesn't. If she takes him I'll be happy for her.'

'And I will be sad to my dying day.'

'What?'

'I said, and I shall be sad to my dying day.'

'Why, Anna, why?'

'It would be no use trying to explain to you, only time can do that.'

She rose from the chair and went out and towards the drawing room. The door was open and she stood on the threshold and, ignoring Constance and Donald, she looked at Barbara and said, 'Will you come with me for a moment, Barbara.' 'What is it, Anna?' Barbara came hurrying from the room.

'Let us go for our walk.'

They were at the front door now and Barbara turned and looked across the hall and said, 'But ... but the others.'

'We will go alone this morning.'

'Are you ill?'

'I am not ill, but I am not well.'

They had gone down the path and reached the garden gate before Miss Brigmore said, 'He has come this morning to ask Constance to be his wife, and your uncle has consented.'

She had taken three steps into the road before she stopped and looked back to where Barbara was clutching the top of the gate post, and for a moment she thought that the stricken expression on her face had been brought about by the shock of the news, but when Barbara put her hand tightly across her mouth and closed her eyes in order to suppress the tears that were attempting to gush from them she clutched at her, whispering, 'Oh no, no! Oh my dear, my dear ... you didn't expect him ... not you? You're so sensible, if only you could see through him; he cares for nobody but himself, he's a ruthless creature. Oh not you, not you, Barbara.'

When she was pushed aside she made no complaint, but walked slowly after the hurrying figure. And she

127

had thought she knew what went on in both their minds.

From the sitting room window Constance saw Barbara going down the road with Miss Brigmore following, and she turned to Donald, saying, 'They've gone, what's the matter? Where's Uncle?' She was making for the door when Donald said, 'He's in his study. Don't go for a minute, I've got something I want to say to you.'

'Oh.' She turned and looked towards him, her face straight.

He had noticed that she wasn't her merry self this morning, it was as if she'd had a quarrel with someone, but with whom he couldn't imagine, for they all adored her and she them. Even that stiff-necked old cow held her in affection.

He went past her now and closed the door. Then having walked slowly towards her again, he stood in front of her, his back very straight, his head held high, and he said, 'Your uncle has given me permission to speak to you.'

She had asked, 'What? what about?' before the meaning of the phrase struck her, and then she wanted to laugh; long, loud, and hysterically she wanted to laugh. For months she had been imagining how she would respond to Will Headley when he came from the study and said, 'Your uncle has given me permission to speak to you.' Those words could only have one meaning, and here was Donald saying them to her. It was funny, very, very funny; Donald was saying 'Your uncle has given me permission to speak to you'; he would next say, 'Will you be my wife, Constance?' But she was wrong, at least in the form of the proposal, for he did not make it as a request but as a statement. 'I want to marry you,' he said.

'Marry? Marry me? You ... you want to marry me?'

'That's what I said.' His face was straight now.

She was laughing at him; he couldn't bear to be laughed at. 'Is there anything funny about it?'

'No, no.' She closed her eyes and bowed her head and she wagged it as she said, 'No, no, Donald, there's nothing funny about it, only'—she was looking at him again—'I'm ... I'm surprised, amazed. Why ... why, you can't really be serious?'

'Why not? why shouldn't I be serious?'

'Well'—she put her fingers to her lips now and patted them. 'Well, what I mean is ... oh!' As Miss Brigmore had done a few minutes earlier, she sat down abruptly on a chair, but her manner was quite unlike that of Miss Brigmore's, for she was laughing again. 'Well, for one thing I would never make a farmer's wife, I'd be useless at milking and making butter and such, I wouldn't know how.'

'You could learn if you wanted to; but there would be no necessity for you to make butter and such.' He did not say my mother sees to that but added, 'That's already seen to. You'd be asked to do nothing you didn't want to do.'

Of a sudden she stopped laughing, she even stopped smiling, and she looked down at her hands which were now joined tightly on her lap. Yesterday the man she loved and had thought one day to marry had written her a letter, which by its very charm had seared the delicate vulnerable feelings of her first love as if she had been held over the blacksmith's fire, and definitely the letter had forged her whole conception of life into a different pattern.

'Well!'

She rose to her feet, her arms thrust out now to each side of her as if pushing away invisible objects, and, her body swaying slightly, she walked from him to the farthest corner of the room, saying, 'I ... I can't take it in, Donald. Why ... why, you've never given any sign. You've always talked to Barbara more than to me. Why should you want me?' She now turned swiftly and, all animation gone from her body, she stood still, her arms hanging by her sides, staring at him.

He didn't move from where he was nor did he speak for a time, his words seemed wedged in his throat, and when finally he uttered them they came like an echo from deep within him. 'I love you,' he said.

There was a long pause before either of them moved. During it she looked at him as if she had never seen him before. He was a man, a good looking, stern-faced young man; he was thin and tall, with jet black hair that had a white streak running down the side of it; his eyes were dark, bluey-black; he was her uncle's natural son, and because of this he had an opinion of himself. She did not blame him for that; he was hard working and had gained the title of respectability even with the stigma that lay on him. She had heard her uncle say that his judgment was respected in the cattle markets and that men did not speak lightly of him. He would, she felt, make someone a good husband—would he make her a good husband? He had said he loved her. She didn't love him, she had never thought about him in that connection; she liked him, she was amused by him. Oh yes, he amused her. His austere and bumptious manner had always amused her; she had teased him because of it. But love; could she ever grow to love anyone again? She looked him over from head to foot. He was very presentable; in a way he was much more presentable than Will Headley. Change their stations and what would have been her reactions then?

She said, 'But I don't love you, Donald. I . . . I've never thought of you in that way.'

'That will come, I'll see it comes.' He moved towards her now and he reached out and took her hand. 'Give me the chance and I'll see that it comes. You will love me, I know you will.'

She gave a small laugh as she said, 'You are as you ever were, so confident, Donald, nothing can shake your confidence in yourself and your ability, can it?'

'I know my own value.'

'And you think you can make me love you?'

'I don't think, I know I can. It may sound like bragging, and I suppose it is when I say I could have married five times over these last few years, and that's not heightening or lessening the number; five times over I say, and one the daughter of a man who has nearly enough cash stacked away here and there to buy the Hall. I'd just to lift me finger, but no, I knew who I wanted, there was only one for me, and that was you.'

'Oh Donald!' She didn't know now whether she wanted to laugh at his cock-suredness, or to cry at his devotion.

130

When he lifted her hand and rubbed it against his cheek she detected a new softness in him and she said haltingly, 'Will ... will you give me time, time to think it over?'

'All the time in the world ... a year.'

'But you said all the time in the ...'

'I know, but a year is all the time in the world that I'm going to give you. At the end of a year we'll be married, you'll see.' When he put his arms about her she remained still and stiff and something recoiled in her while she thought, Is this in the plan for me? and her mind gabbled rapidly, No, no. Yet when his mouth touched hers she did not resist him, she even experienced a shiver of excitement as she felt the strength of him and smelt the strange odour that emanated from the mixture of soap, rough tweed, and the farm smell that she always associated with him. He was a man, and he wanted her—and Will Headley didn't.

BOOK III

CONSTANCE

ONE

There were periods during the following year when Miss Brigmore's feelings towards Constance's suitor softened and she was forced, even if grudgingly, to show her admiration for him. These were the times when, although the hills and mountains were impassable with snow he would appear as usual for his Sunday visit. That he accompanied these feats with an element of bravado was visible to all, but that he accomplished them at all, she was forced to admit, was due not only to his physical strength but also to his sheer tenacity.

Of course there were other times when he had to admit defeat. On these Sundays—once there had been three in succession—she had observed Constance's reactions closely. The first Sunday she had taken as a matter of course and even shown some relief, but when he hadn't appeared on the second and third Sunday, she had shown concern, and when the day came that he finally arrived she had greeted him warmly.

Constance had been three times over the hills to the farm. Her first visit had not turned out to be a complete success. Its failure had nothing to do with the farm or its inhabitants; she had spoken highly of his parents and their reception of her, stating only that the farmhouse seemed a little bare after the cluttered homeliness of the cottage. What had actually spoilt the visit for her was the storm; she had a horror of storms. Thunder and lightning terrified her. Since she was a child she had always sought the darkest corner during a

135

storm, and its approach always made her nervy and apprehensive. On this particular occasion she was actually sick and had to delay her return until quite late in the evening; and Donald, although he couldn't understand her fear, had been concerned for her.

Constance could not herself pinpoint the time when she had specifically said to Donald that she would marry him, but the date had been fixed within six months of the particular Sunday when he amazed her with his declaration of love.

As the weeks passed her reactions had varied from excitement to fear bred of doubt. But the latter she always tried to laugh off, even as she laughed at the man who was the cause of it. The questions 'What is there to fear from Donald?' and 'And if I don't marry him, who then?' would nearly always dispel the fear.

For the past two days the weather had been sultry owing to the unusual heat that had continued daily for over a week now, and Constance had been on edge as she often was with an impending storm. Added to this, Miss Brigmore did not discount the nerves that frequently attended marriage preparations, not that the preparations for this wedding were anything elaborate, but nevertheless there were the usual things to be seen to, such as the clothes she would take with her, the linen, and what was more important and what had been causing a great deal of discussion, the amount of money she would retain.

At first Constance had insisted that she transfer her hundred pounds a year income to Barbara; for, as she stated plainly, were the house deprived of it they would find great difficulty in managing. What was more, she had insisted that Donald would confirm her opinion on the matter.

But Donald hadn't confirmed her opinion; when the question was put to him he had remained silent for a time before saying, 'It's a good thing for everyone to have a little money of their own, it makes them sort of independent.'

Thomas had wholeheartedly endorsed this, while at the same time Miss Brigmore knew that he was only too well aware that the household strings were already pulled as tight as it was possible for them to be without actual discomfort. She, herself, had taken no salary from the day they had come to the cottage in order that he might have the little luxuries of cigars and wine that made life more bearable for him. As for Mary, she was on a mere pittance; it was only her devotion to the girls that had made her suffer it all these years.

The question of the money had not, as yet, been actually resolved. Constance had said only that morning she would have none of it. She had got into a tantrum, which was unusual for her, and said that unless she could do as she pleased with her allowance she wouldn't marry at all. She had made quite a scene in front not only of Donald but of Matthew too.

It wasn't often that Matthew came to visit them now. He hadn't come more than half a dozen times during the past year. Matthew always aroused a feeling of sorrow in Miss Brigmore. Why was it, she asked herself, that a person with such a nice nature as Matthew's should suffer such a crippling disease, while Donald, with his arrogance, be given enough health for two men? Matthew's speech and manner had always pleased her, and she had thought secretly that if the step-brothers could have exchanged places she would have welcomed the match without reservation.

She looked at the young man now sitting opposite her. They had the room to themselves. Thomas had retired to the study for his after-dinner nap; Barbara was in the garden reading. Barbara read a lot these days, but now she didn't discuss what she read. Instead, she had become very withdrawn over the past year. Deep in her heart she was sorry for Barbara; and here again she wished that the roles could be changed, for she would have been less unhappy about the situation if Barbara had been marrying Donald, because there was a firm adultness in Barbara that was, as yet, lacking in her sister. Yet she felt that perhaps she was not quite right in this surmise, for Constance too had changed during the past year, only at intervals now did her gay girlish self appear; for most of the time she wore a thoughtful expression.

She brought her whole attention to Matthew as she
137

said, 'I have not had time to ask you yet, but how have you been feeling of late? We haven't seen you for such a long time.'

'Oh, about as usual, Miss Brigmore, thank you. No worse, no better.' He shrugged his thin shoulders. 'I'll be quite content if I continue like this. And I could'— he now nodded at her as he smiled—'if we had this weather through the winter.'

'Yes, indeed'—she laughed with him—'if we had this weather through the winter. It really has been remarkably warm of late, too warm some days I would have said. Yet in another month or so we shall have forgotten about it, and be shivering once again.'

He said now, 'It's very cold this side in the winter, I think we're more fortunate over our side.'

'I'm sure you are. And Constance tells me it's very pleasant in your valley.'

'You must come over and see it. Don . . . Father is going to get a horse and trap, or some such, he's going into Hexham for the sales next Friday. Me mother suggested, as we were using the horses we come over by the waggon to-day, but Donald would have none of it.' He now pulled a face at her and they both exchanged smiles. 'Besides the fact it would have to be cleaned up for the journey, it's a bit big and lumbering and has no style about it whatever.'

There was a slight mocking note to his last words, and Miss Brigmore brought her lips together tightly while her eyes smiled back at him with a knowing smile.

There followed a companionable silence between them now, as if each were waiting for the other to speak. Miss Brigmore wanted to ask so many questions. How did his mother and father view the alliance, particularly his mother? How did Donald act in his own home? Did he still keep up his authoritative manner amidst his own people? Was he kind? Of course he had shown kindness for years in bringing the commodities of the farm on his Sunday visits. But that wasn't the kindness she meant. There appeared no softness in him, no gentleness. A man could appear arrogant and bumptious in public, she knew only too well, but in private he could become a different creature. It was strange but she couldn't imagine Donald becoming a different creature in private. But there was only one person who would ever know if he changed character, and that was Constance. She had often wondered how he acted towards her when they were alone for his manner in public gave off the impression that he already possessed her. She turned her gaze towards the window from where she knew, if she rose, she'd be able to see them going towards the curve in the road, taking the same walk they did every Sunday, because Donald liked that walk, for at the end of it were the gates of the Hall. . . .

It would have surprised Miss Brigmore at this moment if she could have overheard the conversation between the two people who were deep in her thoughts for the subject was the same as that in her own mind, kindness.

Walking with a slow, almost prim step, Constance was saying, 'He appears to have such a kindly nature.'

'He has.'

'You're very fond of him.'

'Aye, I'm very fond of him. There's nobody I like better, except'—he turned his head towards her and paused before he said, 'you. If I were speaking the truth there are only two people I care about in the world, the rest could sink, burn or blow up for me.'

His words brought no change in her attitude, but she asked, 'What about Uncle?'

'Oh.' He nodded his head once or twice, then repeated, 'Uncle? Funny, but I can't explain what I think about him. Pride, hate, grudging admiration, loathing, oh, I could put a name to all the vices and very few of the virtues that go to make up my feelings with regards to him.'

She had paused for a moment in her walking and stared at him as she said, 'But I thought you liked him?'

'I do, an' I don't. I don't an' I do.' His head wagged from side to side with each word. 'Aw, don't let's talk about—Uncle, for I wouldn't be able to speak the truth about my feelings for him if I tried, 'cos I don't know them myself. There's only two things I'm sure of, as

139

I've told you, and the main one is I love you.' His voice dropped to a mere whisper as he stopped and turned towards her. 'I love you so much that I'm afraid at times, and that's proved to me the strength of my feelings, for fear and me have been strangers up till now. Now, every time I leave you I fear something'll happen to you. But once I have you safe over the hills, it'll be different. I'll know peace, an' I'll be whole. You know, that's something I've never really felt—whole; but once we're married you'll make me whole—won't you? . . . Aw Constance, Constance.'

Her lips fell slightly apart and she looked at him in something of surprise, for in this moment she was seeing him as never before, and she felt stirring in her an emotion she hadn't experienced before. It wasn't love—or was it? She couldn't tell, for it had no connection with the feeling she had felt towards Will Headley. Was it pity? But how could she pity him, h : was the last person one could pity; if he were dressed in rags and begging on the road he would not evoke pity. And yet, when she came to consider it, she could not give to this feeling any other name. She realised that he had allowed her to see beneath the surface of his arrogance, wherein she had glimpsed a depth of loneliness. She herself had no understanding of loneliness, never once having been lonely. There came into her mind the fact that she had never been alone in her life except in the privacy of the water closet; sleeping or waking there had always been someone, Barbara, Anna, Mary, or her Uncle.

When his arms went about her and pulled her fiercely to him she gasped and whispered, 'We're on the main road.'

'What of that! Have we ever met anyone on the main road at this time on a Sunday?'

His mouth was on hers, hard, searching. After a moment her stiff body relaxed against him and her lips answered his.

When he released her he stood gazing down into her face; then he cupped her chin in his hand as he said, 'A fortnight to-day we will have been married for twenty-four hours.'

She gave a nervous laugh, drew herself from his embrace and walked on, and he walked close beside her now, his bent arm pressing hers tight against his side.

A fortnight to-day at this time they would have been married for twenty-four hours.

A fortnight ago she all but decided to tell him she could not go through with the marriage, and then she had asked herself, if she did that what would life hold for her, what prospects had she of marrying if she refused this opportunity? She could see herself ending up, not only like Barbara, but like Anna, and she couldn't bear the thought. She wanted a husband and a home of her own and children, lots of children. She had read in a Ladies' Journal only recently an article that explained that the bearing of children, and the doing of good works within one's ability and the contents of one's pocket, brought to women great compensation, and contributed towards a better and longer lasting happiness than did the early experience of so-called love marriages, wherein the young bride saw life through rosy-tinted glasses.

There was another thing that was worrying her, she did not know whether she would like living in the farmhouse; it wasn't that she disliked his mother and father, nor that they disliked her, but there was a restraint in their manner towards her. They acted more like servants might be expected to do and this made her uneasy. The one comforting thought was that Matthew would be there. She got on well with Matthew, she liked Matthew, she had always liked him, he seemed to belong to another world altogether from that which had bred Donald. He was more refined, gentle. She had never teased Matthew as she had teased Donald, which was strange when she came to think of it; perhaps because Matthew had talked little and had been rather shy. He was still shy.

They had walked in silence for some time, and she didn't like long silences, she always felt bound to break silences, and now she reverted to their previous topic and said, 'I thought Matthew was looking very well to-day.'

'He's well enough considering, an' if he sticks to the

141

horse and doesn't walk too much he'll be better. If I don't keep me eye on him he's off up the hills with a book; he'll be blind afore he dies, I've told him that. Had things been different from what they are with him he would have made a good school teacher; he's learned you know.' He had turned his head towards her and there was a note of pride in his voice as if he were speaking of a son, and she nodded and said, 'Yes, yes; I think he is.'

'Think!' he repeated. 'Be sure of it; he never goes into Hexham or Allendale but he borrows a book. That reminds me. I've got to go to the sales next Friday an' that's when you were coming over to meet Uncle and Aunt, so Matthew'll come for you early on. He'll bring Ned along; Ned's back's as broad as an inglenook, and you couldn't fall off him if you tried.'

She laughed now as she said, 'I could, even without trying. You know I'm no horsewoman. It isn't that I dislike horses, I just can't ride them. Now Barbara, she sits a horse as well as any man. I always think it's a pity we weren't able to keep one; she would have loved it.'

He said abruptly, 'Barbara's grown sullen.'

'You think so?'

'I know it. It's because she doesn't want to lose you. And that's understandable.' He was nodding at her. 'They all don't want to lose you, but their loss is my gain.' He pressed her arm tighter into his side. Then, his voice unusually soft, he said, 'You know, I determined years ago to get everything I set me heart on, and I set me heart on you from the beginning. But even so, there were days and nights, long nights, when I doubted me own ability, an' now it's come about, well'—he gazed sideways at her and, his voice just above a whisper, he said, 'Have you any idea how I feel about you, Constance?' Without waiting for an answer he made a small motion with his head and went on, 'No, you never could have, for I can't explain the sense of . . . what is the word?' Again he made a motion with his head. 'Elation, aye, that's it, the sense of elation I feel every time I look at you.'

142

'Oh, Donald! don't, don't; you make me feel embarrassed, as if I were someone of importance.'

'You are. Look at me.' He jerked her arm and when, half-smiling, she looked at him he said 'You are, you are someone of great importance. Get that into your head. There's nobody more important than you, and there's only one thing I regret.'

When he paused she asked, 'And what's that?'

And now he pointed along the road towards the iron gates. 'Them,' he said.

'Them?'

'Aye, them. If I could perform a miracle I'd have them opened as we get near. The lodgekeeper would hold them wide, and we'd go up the drive sitting in a carriage behind prancing horses, an' the lackeys would run down the steps and open the house door. They'd put a foot-stool out for you, and they'd bow their heads to me, and the head lackey would say, "I hope you had a pleasant journey, Sir?" And we'd go through that hall and up the staircase and into our apartments—not rooms mind, apartments, an' I'd see you take off your hat and cloak; I'd see you change into a fine gown; then down the stairs we'd go together and into the dining room an' . . . '

They had reached the gates now and she gripped the rusty iron railings, and leaning her head against them she laughed until her body shook, and when she turned to look at him her face was wet with her laughter; but his was straight and stiff and he said, 'You think it funny?'

'Yes, yes, Donald, I do, for it would take a miracle, wouldn't it?'

He stared at her for a long moment before saying, 'If I had been brought up in that house as I should have been, as his son, we would be there today, I know it, I feel it inside.'

'Don't be silly.' Her voice held an imperious note. 'You were a boy then, only thirteen; you could no more have made a miracle then than you could now; the miracle that was needed then was the sum of thirty thousand pounds, I understand, and that would only have acted as a stopgap.' Her own face was straight

143

now, and what she said next was a statement rather than a question, 'You have always hated it, haven't you, that you weren't recognised as his son.'

When she saw his chin go into hard nodules and his cheekbones press out against the skin she said hastily, 'Oh I'm sorry, Donald, I . . . I didn't mean it in a nasty way. I'm sure you with your forethought and tenacity would have tried to do something, I'm sure you would, even as young as you were. Believe me'—she put out her hand and touched his—'I wasn't intending to hurt you in any way. You do believe me?'

He drew in a deep breath, then let it out slowly before answering, 'Aye . . . aye I believe you. And what you say is true.' He turned from her, and now he gripped the iron bars and looked through them and up the weed-covered drive and into the dark tunnel where the trees were now meeting overhead, and he said, 'It's a blasted shame.' He turned his head and glanced at her. 'I don't mean about me, but about the place. Why didn't they stay, they paid enough for it? Only three years in it and then they cleared out and didn't leave even one man to see to the grounds.'

She, too, was looking up the drive as she said, 'This part of the country accepts or rejects as it pleases. They were from Hampshire, this was another world to them; what was more, they were new to money and thought it could buy anything. If they had been disliked I think they could have understood it, but not being ignored. Uncle was disliked. Oh yes.' She nodded at him. 'He was hated by many people; but he was someone they couldn't ignore—nor can they now.' She chuckled, and he smiled as he muttered, 'No, I'll give him that, you can't ignore him.'

Once again she was looking up the drive and her voice had a sad note to it as she said, 'They'll never get the gardens back in order; it took two years before, but now the place has been deserted for almost four years. The house must be mouldering. This lock always annoys me.' She now rattled the chain attached to the huge lock. 'And that glass they had put all along the top of the walls.' She looked first to the right and then to the left of her. 'It seemed an act of spite to me. And
144

when I think of all that fruit going rotten inside, oh, I feel like knocking a hole in the wall, I do.' She nodded at him, her face straight, but when he said playfully, 'I'll do it for you if you like. Wait till I go and get a pick,' and pretended to dash away, she laughed again.

They turned from the gate, walked a little way along the road, then mounted the fells to take the roundabout way back to the cottage, and when with an impulsive movement she slipped her hand through his arm he gripped it tightly; then swiftly he caught her under the armpits and lifted her into the air and swung her round as if she were a child. When at last he stopped whirling her and put her feet on the ground she leant against him gasping and laughing and he pressed her to him as he looked away over her head towards the high mountains, and the feeling that he termed elation rose in him and burst from him and formed itself into a galloping creature, and he saw it clear the peaks one after the other until it reached the farm.

TWO

They were all standing in the roadway outside the gate seeing her off, Matthew at the head of the two horses. Mary was giggling, saying 'I don't blame you, Miss Constance; you wouldn't get me up on that, not for a thousand pounds you wouldn't't.'

'If I offered you one gold sovereign you wouldn't only be on it, but you'd jump over it this minute, woman.'

It spoke plainly for the change in the social pattern that Thomas could joke with his one and only servant and Mary answer, 'Oh, Master. Master, I'd as soon jump over the moon, I would so, as get on that animal. I don't envy you, Miss Constance, I don't that, I . . .'

'Be quiet, Mary!' At times Miss Brigmore's manner reverted to that of the Miss Brigmore that Mary remembered from years back, and on these occasions she obeyed her without murmur.

Miss Brigmore now stepped towards Constance where she was standing near the big flat-backed horse and she said, 'You have nothing to fear, he'll just amble.'

'He won't gallop?' Constance divided the question by a look between Miss Brigmore and Matthew, and Matthew, smiling, said, 'His galloping days are over, long since.'

'It's so close, you don't think there'll be a storm?'

Constance was now looking at Barbara, who, her face unsmiling but her expression pleasant and her voice consoling, said, 'No, I'm sure there'll be no
146

storm, it's passed over. Look'—she turned and pointed—'it's passing to the south of us. By the time you get on to the hills the sun will be out.'

The two sisters looked at each other. It was a long probing look as if they each had the desire to fall into the other's arms.

'It'll be to-morrow you'll get there if you don't make a start; hoist her up, Matthew, and get going.'

Matthew bent down, cupped his hands and Constance put her foot on them; the next moment she was sitting sideways in the saddle. Then without a word Matthew mounted the brown mare, and after inclining his head towards those on the road he said, 'Get up there!' and the two horses moved off simultaneously.

No one called any farewell greetings, but when Constance turned her head and looked back at them Miss Brigmore raised her hand in a final salute.

It was almost ten minutes later, after they had left the road and were beginning to mount upwards, that Matthew spoke. Looking towards her, he said, 'You all right?'

'Yes, Matthew, yes. He's . . . he's quite comfortable really.'

'Yes, he's a steady old boy, reliable.'

They exchanged glances and smiled.

A few more minutes elapsed before she said, 'It's looking dark over there; you don't think we'll ride into the storm do you, Matthew?'

Matthew did not answer immediately because he was thinking that that was exactly what they were likely to do. Barbara's statement that the storm was passing south was quite wrong, it was coming from the South-West if he knew anything, and it would likely hit them long before they reached home. He said, 'Don't worry, if it docs come we'll take shelter. There's the old house on the peak, you remember it?'

'That derelict place?'

'Yes, it's derelict, but it's been a haven to many in a storm these past years, and even before that when the Rutledges lived there.'

"I can't imagine why anyone would want to live in such an isolated spot.'

'They had their sheep and a few Galloway; and some people want to be alone.'

'Yes, I suppose so.' She nodded towards him. His face looked grave, serious. On each of the occasions she had met him over the past year his expression had been the same, grave, serious. At one time, even in spite of his shyness, he had appeared jolly. When he smiled she thought he looked beautiful, in a delicate sort of way. She had wondered often of late whether he was displeased at the prospect of her coming to live on the farm. If that was the case it would be a great pity, for she had imagined him enlivening the evenings during the long winter ahead. She had visualised them conversing about books, as he did with Anna. She knew she wouldn't be able to converse with Donald about books; she had remarked to Anna recently it was a pity that Donald wasn't a reader, and Anna had replied tersely that she had to face up to the fact that her husband-to-be was a doer rather than a dreamer. That was a very good definition of Donald, a doer rather than a dreamer. Matthew here was the opposite, he was a dreamer rather than a doer, but it was his health, she supposed, that made the latter impossible. She felt a deep pity for Matthew and a tenderness towards him. She had realised of late that she was somewhat hurt by his restrained attitude towards her.

The path was getting steeper; the land on one side of them fell sharply away to a valley bottom before rising again, but more gradually, to form distant peaks; on the other side of them it spread upwards in a curving sweep to form what from this distance looked like a plateau.

Matthew looked towards this height and calculated that before they covered the mile that would bring them to the top, and within a few minutes' ride of the old house, the storm would break. Even as he stared upwards the first deep roll of thunder vibrated over the hills, bringing a startled exclamation from Constance, and he came closer to her side, saying, 'It's all right. If it comes this way we'll take shelter.'

She was gripping the reins tightly; her face had gone pale. She looked at him and murmured hesitantly, 'I'm

... I'm sorry but ... but I'm really afraid of storms. I've tried to overcome the feeling but I can't. It ... it seems so childish ...'

'Not a bit, not a bit. There are plenty of men who are afraid of storms an' all.'

'Really!'

'Aw aye, yes. I know ... I know two.'

'Men?'

'Yes, men. There's a fellow who lives over by Slaggyford, a farmer he is.'

'And he's afraid of storms?'

'Yes; dives for the cow byre every time the sky darkens.' He hoped she never repeated this to Donald for he would laugh his head off.

'Is ... is he a grown man?'

'Yes, he's a good age. But it's got nothing to do with age. There's a young boy in the market. I see him at times, that's when there's not a storm about, for he makes for shelter when there's the first sign of thunder, mostly under a cart. So you're not the only one, you see.'

She smiled at him, and he smiled back while he congratulated himself on his ability to tell the tale.

'Get up there! Get up there!' He urged the horses forward, but Ned, having maintained one pace for many years now, refused to alter it; and the coming of a storm didn't make him uneasy, he had weathered too many. But the younger horse was uneasy. She tossed her head and neighed, and Matthew tried to calm her, saying, 'Steady now, steady,' while at the same time thinking whimsically it was no good lying to a horse.

As the first flash of lightning streaked the sky above them Constance bowed her head and smothered a scream, and Matthew, bringing his horse close to hers again, put out his hand and caught her arm, saying, 'It's all right now, it's all right. Look, we're nearly at the top; another five minutes and we'll be in shelter.'

She lifted her head and looked at him and gasped, 'Can ... can you make it hurry, the horse?'

'No, I'm afraid he'll go his own gait, come flood, storm or tempest. But don't worry, don't worry, everything'll be all right; just sit tight.'

'It's getting dark.'

Yes, it was getting dark; the valley to the left of them was blotted out; the sky in front seemed to be resting on the hills. Her face appeared whiter in the dimness, there were beads of perspiration round her mouth. He looked at her mouth and shivered. Then moving his horse forward, he gripped Ned's rein and yelled, 'Come on! Come on, Ned! Get up with you! Get up!'

The quickening of the horse's stride was not perceivable, but he kept urging him.

When the next roll of thunder came he was startled himself for he thought for a moment that Constance had fallen from the horse. He moved back to her side where she was doubled almost in two, her face resting against the horse's mane, and he leant towards her and put his hand on her shoulder and soothed her, saying, 'There now, there now, it's passed. Look, it's passed.'

As he spoke the first big drops of rain descended on them and before they had moved a hundred yards they were enveloped in a downpour, so heavy that his body too was now doubled against it.

It was more by instinct than sight that he left the road at the spot where the derelict house stood. Dismounting he made his way round to her side and, her body still bent, she fell into his arms and he guided her at a run into the dark, dank shelter. Then leaving her to support herself against the wall, he said, 'I won't be a minute, not a minute; I'll just put them under cover,' and dashing out, he led the horses into a ramshackle lean-to that had once served as a stable, where he tied them before running back to the house.

Groping his way towards her, he found that her body was no longer bent; she was standing with her back pressed tight against the wall, her hands cupping her face, and he said to her, 'Come over here, there's a bench and rough table of sorts. The road travellers use this place as a shelter; there might be some dry wood, we'll make a fire.'

When he had seated her on the form she clutched at his arm and muttered through chattering teeth, 'You're soaked. You . . . you shouldn't be soaked.' Anna had told her that people with the consumption should never get their feet wet, in fact should never be out in the rain; people with consumption should, if they could afford it, go and live in a different climate. 'Take your coat off,' she said; 'it may not have got through.'

He made a small laughing sound at her solicitude, and it held some relief with the knowledge that she had for the moment got over her fear of the storm.

'I'm all right, don't worry about me,' he said; 'you're like a wet rabbit yourself.' He pointed to her hat, where the brim was drooping down each side of her face, and he added, 'A very wet rabbit, its ears in the doldrums.'

When she lifted her hands and took her hat off he said. 'I would take off your coat an' all.'

'No,' she said as she shivered, 'I'm cold.'

He turned from her and made his way through the dimness to the far corner of the room where there was a rough open fireplace, and from there he called, 'We're in luck, there's dry wood here, quite a bit, and kindling. You'll be warm in no time.'

'Have you any matches?'

'No; but if I know anything the roadsters will have left a flint around somewhere; they look out for each other, the roadsters do. That is, the regular ones.'

There was a long pause and then his voice came again, on an excited note now, 'What did I tell you! In this niche, a box with a flint in it! Here we go.'

As Constance watched the sparks flying from the flint her agitation eased; they would soon have a fire and their clothes would dry. She wished she could stop shivering. Why did storms petrify her? She had tried, oh, she had tried to overcome her fear, but it was hopeless, she seemed to lose control the moment she heard thunder.

'There you are; look, it's alight. Come over here and get your coat dried.'

She rose from the form and was making her way towards the flickering light of the tinder when an ear-splitting burst of thunder appeared to explode over the house. When its rumblings died away she was huddled on the floor to the side of the fire, her face buried hard against Matthew's shoulder; his arms were about her

151

holding her close. When at last the only sound they could hear was the hard pinging of the rain on the slate roof and an occasional hiss as it came down the chimney and hit the burning wood, they still remained close pressed together.

The wood was well alight and sending the flames leaping upwards before she raised her head and looked into his face and whispered, 'I'm ... I'm sorry, Matthew.'

He made no answer, he was half kneeling, half sitting, as she was. Their positions were awkward and cramped but neither of them seemed to notice it. She did not withdraw from his hold but she stared into his eyes and could not help but recognise the look they held, and read there the reason for the change in him these past months.

As she watched the firelight passing shadows over his corn-coloured hair she had the greatest desire to run her fingers through it, bury her face in it, and she told herself she was a fool, a fool of a girl, not to have recognised what was in his heart, and, what was more terrifying still, in her own. She had known she held a certain special feeling for Matthew; even when she was in love with Will Headley she had still retained this feeling for Matthew, but she had looked upon it as sympathy and compassion for his ill-health. And perhaps that is how it had begun; but what it had nurtured was something much deeper.

When he whispered, 'Oh, Constance! Constance!' she answered simply, 'Matthew! Oh Matthew!'

Still with their arms about each other they slid into a sitting position now, and again they gazed at each other in silence while the fire blazed merrily to its height.

After a period he asked softly, 'Didn't you know how I felt about you?'

She shook her head, 'No; not ... not until this moment.'

'And you, Constance, you, what do you feel for me? Look at me, please ... please. Tell me.'

He had to bend his head towards her to hear what she was saying above the noise of the rain which had increased in force. 'I ... I don't know, Matthew, I really don't know. It, it can't be true, I feel it's unreal. Can one suddenly know in a moment? Things ... things like this have to grow.'

'It's been growing for years.'

She was looking at him again. 'But you never gave any sign, why?'

'How could I? And I shouldn't now, no, not at this late stage, when I'm getting ready for my grave.'

'Oh don't, don't!' She put her hand over her mouth now and her head drooped deeply on to her chest.

'Oh, don't worry, dear; don't worry. I shouldn't have said that. It sounded as if I'm sorry for myself, but nevertheless it's a fact that's got to be faced. But ... but I'm not sorry you know how I feel; no, I'm not sorry.'

'You ... you could live for years and years.'

He shook his head slowly. 'Not years and years; another winter like last and . . .'

'No, no.' She was holding his hands now. 'Don't say that.'

'But Constance'—he shook his head at her—'it's the truth. Yet you know something? I feel happier at this moment than I've ever done in me life before. I've died a number of deaths already thinking of you marrying Donald. But now it doesn't seem to matter so much and ... and I don't feel I'm betraying him by ... by telling you how I feel. When you're married . . .'

'I could never marry Donald now.'

'What! Oh! He was kneeling in front of her now, gripping her hands. 'Oh, but you must, you must. You're his life; there's no one in the world for him but you. I know him, I know him inside out. He's a strange fellow, possessive, pig-headed, and big-headed, but his feelin's are as deep as a drawn well, and all his feelin's are for you.'

As she stared up at him a flash of lightning illuminated the bizarre room and once again she flung herself against him and the impact overbalanced him. When there came the sound as if a thunderbolt had been thrown in through the open doorway she almost buried herself in him, and before the last peal of thunder had died away the inevitable was beginning.

153

On the bare floor they lay, the fire crackling to the side of them, the rain beating on the tiles and blowing through the paneless windows and the open doorway, and strangely it was he who protested, but silently, yelling at himself, 'No, no!' He could never commit this outrage against Donald. Even while his hands moved over her submissive body his mind begged him to stop before it was too late.

But it was too late, and when the lightning once again lit up the room, her crying out was not against it alone but against the ecstasy and the pain that was rending her body.

When it was over he rolled away from her for a moment and hid his face in his hands and groaned, and she lay inert, her eyes closed, her heaving breath stilled like someone who had died in her sleep.

When of a sudden she drew the breath back into her body again he turned swiftly to her and, enfolding her in his arms, cried, 'Oh Constance! Constance, me darling; me darling, me darling.'

She made no move now to put her arms about him, not even when the thunder broke over the house again did she press herself against him; she was spent and her body was no longer her own; she was in it, but not of it. A short while ago she had been a young girl, a prospective bride who was terrified of storms, now she was no longer a young girl, so different was she that she could listen to the thunder unmoved.

It was as if Matthew had read her thoughts, for now he was looking down into her face and talking rapidly, saying, 'I'm sorry. Oh God above, I'm sorry, Constance. Try to forget it, will you? Try to forget it. If Donald knew he would kill me. Oh aye, he would.' He was nodding his head at her as if refuting her denial of this. 'He would slit my throat like he does a pig's. God! if only it wasn't Donald. I don't want to hurt Donald, I wouldn't hurt him for the world.'

Gently she pressed him away from her, and as if she had performed the function a dozen times before she adjusted her clothes, her manner almost prim; then she said, ' I could never marry Donald now, but . . . but I could marry you, Matthew. And . . . and I could look

154

after you. You ... you could take your share of the farm and we could go away perhaps to a new climate.'

For answer he sat back on his hunkers and covered his face with his hands. When he looked at her again he said slowly, 'I ... I could claim no share of the farm, I have put nothing into it. What me father would give me would be of his generosity. But then, then again, were I to leave an' take you with me, Donald would leave an' all. I know this; I know it in me heart, he wouldn't be able to stand a second disgrace, a second rejection. You see, that's what he's been suffering from all his life, being rejected. He was a bastard, and all bastards know rejection. Strangely, I know how he feels, and should I take you away the second rejection would hit him worse than the first, he wouldn't be able to bear it. And what's more, it would mean the end of the farm, for me father's a sick man; you've seen yourself he's crippling with rheumatism, he depends on Donald for everything. Donald runs the farm, he is the farm.'

Slowly she rose to her feet, dusting down the back of her skirt as she did so; then, as slowly, she walked towards the form and, sitting on it, she put her joined hands on the table and bowed her head over them. And when he came and sat opposite to her and gripped her hands between his she looked at him and asked, 'Could you bear to see me married to Donald?'

He gulped in his throat twice before answering, 'I'll have to, won't I? There's nothing else for it. But now it won't be so bad, for I have part of you that I'll hold tight to until my last breath. Nothing seems to matter now, although I know it shouldn't have happened. It's my fault ... my fault ....

As she looked now at his bowed head, she knew that she was seeing not only a sick man but a weak one; he was as weak as Donald was strong. Yet the blame for what had happened was not only his. She knew in her heart that if blame, as such, was to be apportioned, then more than half of it should be put to her credit, for without her mute consent he would have got no further than kissing her. Even if he had forced himself upon her she could have resisted him, for in physical

155

strength she was the stronger; but she hadn't resisted him.

Did she love him? She stared into his flushed face, into the soft tender gaze of his eyes. She didn't know now, she thought she had before . . . before that had happened, but now she felt empty, quite empty of all physical feeling. When she returned to normal, would she know then? Only one thing she was sure of at this moment, and that was she couldn't marry Donald. Nor could she go to the farm now. It would be impossible to look Donald in the face with Matthew there.

She turned her head slowly towards the doorway. The rain was easing now; the thunder was still rumbling, but in the distance. She looked back at Matthew and said, 'I'll return home.'

'No, no'—his tone held fear—'you can't do that; he's . . . he's expecting you. If you're not there when he gets back to-night he'll be over first light in the morning.'

'Well, that's to-morrow. It'll . . . it'll give me time to think. But Matthew, can't you see. I couldn't possibly meet him to-day and, and spend the night at the farm. I couldn't. I couldn't.'

'Oh Constance.' He was gripping her forearms now, his voice trembling as he gabbled, 'Let things be as they were. What's happened atween us, let it be like a dream, a beautiful dream. If things were different I'd run off with you this minute; but as I can't support you I won't live on you, so it's no use you bringin' up your hundred a year. Anyway, we both know you'd be a widow in no time.'

'Oh Matthew! Matthew!' She screwed up her face. 'Don't keep saying that.'

'I must 'cos you've got to believe it's the truth. If it wasn't I wouldn't be sittin' here persuading you to go ahead and marry Donald.'

They were both quiet now, their heads bowed, until he began to mumble as if talking to himself, 'I feel I've done the dirty on him though, and it isn't right, for he's treated me well over the years; another one in his place, a half-brother with no claim on me father, would have taken it out on me, especially one as strong in body and mind as he is. And . . . and there's another

156

thing. I'm goin' to feel very bad about this later on, but it'll be nothing compared with my feelings if you turn from him. Do you know something, Constance? Look at me. Look at me.' He shook her arms, and when she looked at him, he said, 'He's much more in need of you than I am. God knows I need you, but his need goes deeper than mine.'

She stared at him. He was making excuses. He was a weakling in more ways than one. She turned her gaze towards the fire. The bright glow had dimmed, the thin sticks had dropped to ash leaving red stumps supporting each other. Gradually, like one awakening from a dream, she looked about the room. She could see it as a whole now, for the light was lifting outside. It was a filthy place. She noticed now that there was a smell of excrement coming from some part of it. She looked down at the floor. It was crisscrossed with filth, dried mud, pieces of straw and broken sticks. . . . Yet she had lain down there and given herself to a man. How could she! HOW COULD SHE! What had come over her? Had her terror of the storm deprived her of her wits? No, no. She had given herself to Matthew because she'd wanted to; with or without a storm she had been ready to give herself to someone. Then why hadn't she waited for just one more week? She had acted like a wanton, a street woman, giving way to the impulses inside her without thought of the consequences.

It was the thought of the consequences that brought her to her feet, and she gasped as if she had been running saying, 'I must, I mean I can't go on with you. I must go back. You . . . you can tell him that I was very frightened—and I was, I was, that is the truth—and you had to turn back. . . . I must return home, I must, I must.'

'Constance.' He had come to her side now. His hands outstretched appealingly, he said, 'Please, please.' But she shook her head and turned away from him and went towards the door, saying loudly, 'It's no use, I won't go on. I can walk back; it will be downhill all the way. That's it, I'll walk back.'

'Don't be silly.' He caught her hand, and held her

157

still as he stared hopelessly at her. Then saying gently, 'Come on,' he led her outside.

The rain had become a mere drizzle. He brought the horses from their shelter and helped her up on to Ned's back, and there were no more words between them.

They were going down the last slope and were in sight of the cottage when she drew her horse to a standstill and, looking at him, she said quietly, 'Don't come any further, Matthew. I know your clothes should be dried and you need some refreshment but I couldn't bear to give them my explanation in front of you, as ... as I'll have to lie, you understand? I'm, I'm sorry.'

He nodded at her, then got down from his horse and helped her to the ground. His hands still under her armpits, he gazed at her and asked softly, 'Can I kiss you once more?'

She said neither yes nor nay, and she did not respond when his lips touched hers gently; but when he looked at her again her eyes were full of tears and he said brokenly, 'Aw, Constance, Constance. Aw God! If only—' Then turning round abruptly, he grabbed at the horses' reins, turned them about, hoisted himself up in Daisy's saddle, and tugging at her he muttered, 'Get up there! get up!' Daisy and her companion moved off, their steps slow, steady and unruffled.

She stood on the rough road for a moment watching him, then she swung about and ran. Her skirts held above her ankles, her cloak billowing, she ran until she arrived breathless on the road leading to the cottage, and not until she had reached the gate did she pause; and then, gripping it in both hands, she leant over it.

It was like this that Miss Brigmore saw her from the bedroom window. With a smothered exclamation she hurried out of the room, down the stairs, and so out onto the pathway, saying as she met her, 'Why, Constance, my dear, my dear; what has happened?'

During the journey Constance had rehearsed what she was going to say. 'I just couldn't go on, the storm was terrifying. I made Matthew bring me back some of the way. He was very wet, so I wouldn't let him come any further than the boar rock.' But she said none of
158

this, she just flung herself against Miss Brigmore, crying, 'Anna. Oh! Anna.'

'Ssh! Ssh! What is it? Something's happened?'

They were now in the hall and Miss Brigmore looked about her. Thomas was in his study reading or dozing, Barbara was in the outhouse with Mary pickling onions and red cabbage.

Sensing that something more than ordinary was afoot, Miss Brigmore said again, 'Ssh! Ssh! Now come upstairs. Come.' Soft-footed she led the way hurriedly up the narrow stairs, and when they were in the bedroom she closed the door and, untying the strings of Constance's hat, she asked, 'What is it? What has happened? Oh my goodness!' She looked down at her skirt. 'Look at the condition of you; your dress is filthy, and your cloak too. Constance.' She backed from her just the slightest, her brow furrowed; then said sharply, 'Come, get those things off and into a clean dress. Come now, stop crying and change, and then tell me.'

A few minutes later, when she'd buttoned the dress up the back, she turned Constance about and sat her down, and sitting opposite to her she took her hands and said firmly, 'Now.'

It was an order, but Constance couldn't obey it. How could one say to the person who had been teacher and then friend since one could remember anything, how could one say, 'I have given myself to a man. The act took place on the filthy floor of a derelict house. So much for all your training . . . Miss Brigmore.'

'Something's happened to you, what is it? Tell me.' Miss Brigmore had leant forward now and was shaking Constance by the shoulders. Then as a thought came into her mind, she suddenly straightened her body, sat back in her chair, and clasping her hands tightly against her breast, murmured, 'You . . . you were attacked?'

'No, no.'

Miss Brigmore heaved a short sigh, then demanded, 'Then what?'

'I . . . I can't marry Donald, Anna.'

'You can't marry Donald, what do you mean?'

'Some . . . something's happened.'

159

Again Miss Brigmore joined her hands and pressed them to her breast. 'Then you were attacked? . . .'

'No, I wasn't attacked. . . . But Matthew, he, he loves me. It was in the storm. We were sheltering in that old house. Something happened, happened to us both. He . . . he isn't to blame.' Her head drooped now on to her breast, and then she repeated in a whisper, 'He isn't to blame.'

'Oh my God!'

Not only the words but how they were expressed brought Constance's head up. She had never heard Miss Brigmore speak in such a way; it was as a mother might, fearful for her daughter's chastity; it was too much. She flung herself forward onto her knees and buried her face in Miss Brigmore's lap.

It was a second before Miss Brigmore laid her hands on Constance's head. The consequences of the situation were looming before her, racing towards her. She was demanding that her mind think clearly, but all her mind kept saying was, She must have gone insane, she must have gone insane. And with Matthew of all people!

She said it aloud, 'You must have been insane, girl, and with Matthew of all people! He . . . Donald will kill him when he knows.'

'He . . . he needn't know. He'll never know.' Constance had lifted her tear-drenched face upwards. 'I can't marry him.'

Miss Brigmore stared down at her for a long moment, and then she repeated, 'You can't marry him? Are you going to marry Matthew then?'

'No, no. Matthew . . . ' She couldn't say 'Matthew won't marry me,' what she said was, 'Matthew can't marry me; he wants to but he can't. He's a sick man, as you know, and . . . and as you said, Donald would kill him if he knew, and I believe that.' She nodded her head now. 'He's capable of killing him even though he loves him.'

Once more Miss Brigmore took hold of Constance's shoulders; and now she was hissing at her, 'And you say you are not going to marry Donald? What of the

160

consequences of your act to-day then? What if you have a child?'

For the second time that day the breath stilled in Constance's body, and when her lips did fall apart it was to emit it in a thin whisper as she asked the question, 'It could happen after just . . . just that once?'

'Yes, yes, of course girl after just that once.' Miss Brigmore's voice was still a hiss.

They stared at each other in wide-eyed silence as if watching the consequence taking on actual shape.

It was Miss Brigmore who broke the silence, her voice weighed with sorrow now as she said, 'This morning if you had said you weren't going to marry Donald I would literally have jumped for joy, but now I'm forced to say you must marry him, and I also must add, thank God that the ceremony is but a week ahead. . . . Oh dear! Oh dear!' She put her hand to her brow now and closed her eyes and groaned. 'Constance! Constance! what possessed you? what in the name of God possessed you?'

For answer Constance turned her head slowly towards her shoulder and gazed out of the window, and when she saw that the sun was shining now she almost said, 'It was the weather, you could put it down to the weather.' And in a way that was true, because if she had not been afraid of the storm and had not taken shelter in the derelict house it certainly, certainly would never had happened. Who made the weather, God? Well, if He did He had certainly laid it as a trap for her.

She now looked towards Miss Brigmore where she was bustling about the bed, turning down the counterpane, adjusting the pillows; and when she said, 'Get your clothes off,' Constance did not say, 'But I've just changed,' but she did say, 'Why?'

'You're going to bed. Your uncle and Barbara must be given a reason for your return, and they will accept the fact that you're upset by the storm. Moreover, you must be in bed when . . . when he comes, as come he will. This will save you having to talk at length with him.'

Without a murmur she began to undress.

When at last she was in bed, Miss Brigmore said, 'Don't sit up on your pillows like that, lie down, and say little or nothing to anyone except that the storm made you ill, that you just couldn't go on, and Matthew had to bring you back. . . . Oh, and it's fortunate in a way that Pat Ferrier is calling this afternoon with a friend. Your uncle received a letter just after you left; he is going back to college at the week-end. His presence will divert Barbara's attention from you, for whatever you do you must not tell her about this. Barbara could never look lightly upon such a matter, she'd be shocked.'

She was tucking the sheet under Constance's chin when Constance, staring wide-eyed up at her, asked in a whisper, 'Are you shocked, Anna?'

In response Miss Brigmore sat down quickly on the side of the bed and, enfolding the girl in her arms, murmured, 'No child, no; for I did the same myself, didn't I? There's only one difference between us, you have the chance to cover up your mistake, and in this way you are lucky, very lucky. You can have your cake and eat it. It falls to too few of us to have our cake and eat it.'

THREE

It was over. The wedding party had been driven to the church in Donald's new acquisition; it wasn't a trap but what he called a brake, a sturdy, square vehicle on two large wheels. It seated three people at each side and another beside the driver. It looked more suited to utility than pleasure for the seats were plain unpadded wood and the back rests afforded little comfort, being but two low iron rails. Donald had explained that it wasn't exactly what he wanted, but it was the only one going at the sale and it would do in the meantime.

He had driven over the hills alone. He should have been accompanied by Matthew as his best man, but Matthew, unfortunately, as he explained, had had a bad bout of coughing last night and had shown blood for the first time. It was understood without saying that neither his mother nor his step-father would attend the wedding.

It had been anything but a merry wedding party. The only one who had shown any sign of gaiety was Thomas, and, as he commented to himself, it was getting harder going as the day wore on. What was the matter with everybody? He said this to Miss Brigmore immediately on their return. They were alone in his room. He was loosening his cravat to give himself more air, and he exclaimed impatiently, 'Wedding! I've seen happier people at a funeral. Look'—he turned to her—'is there something going on that I should know of? I've had a feeling on me these past days. She wanted to marry him, didn't she?'

'Yes, yes, she wanted to marry him.'

'Well then, why does she look as she does? In that church it could have been a funeral and she a lily on the coffin. I've never seen her looking so pale. . . . And Barbara, I can't get over Barbara, not a word out of her these days. As for you . . . now Anna'—he came towards her wagging his finger—'I know when something's amiss in your head, so come on'—his voice dropped to a whisper—'tell me. Is there something I should know?'

She stared at him for a moment while her nostrils twitched and her lips moved one over the other in an agitated fashion, and then she said, 'If there was something you should know do you think I could keep it from you? It's your imagination. It's Constance's wedding day, wedding days I'm told are a strain. Though of course I wouldn't know anything about that.'

'Aw An-na, An-na, that's hitting below the belt. Tell me'—he took her chin in his hand—'do you mind so very much, for if you did . . .'

'If I did you would still do nothing about it so it's well that I don't mind, isn't it?'

'You're a wonderful woman.'

'I'm a fool of a woman.' There was a deep sadness in the depths of her eyes as she smiled at him. Then taking his hand, she said, 'Come, we must join them now, and please me by being your entertaining self.'

At the wedding breakfast Thomas did his best to please her, as much for his own sake as for hers, for he was susceptible to atmosphere. He could never tolerate company while there was a feeling of strain. If he found it impossible to lighten it, he parted with it at the earliest opportunity. He would have liked nothing better now than to retire to his study, but as that was impossible he spread his congeniality as wide as possible, extending it to the meal and to Mary. When she almost tripped as she was carrying a dish to the table he cried to her, 'You're drunk, woman! Couldn't you wait?'

As Mary placed the dish in front of him she spluttered, 'Oh, Master, the things you say. I've never even had a drop yet; I've not even had a chance to drink

164

Miss Constance's health.' She smiled at Constance and Constance smiled back at her, a white, thin smile.

No one seemed to notice that Mary had excluded the bridegroom. Although she would have said she had nothing against him and she would have gone further and said there were things about him that she admired, the way he had got on for instance, and the way he presented himself; but she would have also said, in her opinion he wasn't the man for Miss Constance. Miss Constance should have married a gentleman, and although Donald Radlet was the master's son he was in her opinion far from being a gentleman. But anyway, it was done, and there she was, poor lamb, looking as white as a bleached sheet. Yet, she supposed, that was nothing to go by, most girls looked white on their wedding day. Now that was funny; Miss Constance had never wanted to be married in white. Months ago she had made up her mind to be married in yellow, and she had bought the material, yellow taffeta with a mauve sprig on it, and together she and Miss Barbara and Miss Brigmore had made it; and they had made a good job of it because she looked lovely in it, really lovely.

Barbara, too, thought that Constance looked lovely, and she knew in this moment that the soreness in her heart was concerned not only with the loss of Donald, because, as she had told herself, how could you lose something you had never had, but with the real loss of Constance herself for she hadn't been separated from Constance since the very day she was born. In those early days she had cared for her like a little mother, and at this moment the pain of losing her was obliterating every other feeling. She could see the winter days ahead; for her the inside of the house would be as barren as the outside. There would still be Anna and her uncle, but she must face it, they had each other. Even Mary; Mary had someone she went to see on her day off once a fortnight; they lived over near Catton. She said it was an old aunt of hers but she also mentioned that the aunt had a nephew. She had never said how old the nephew was, but it was noted that Mary always came back from Auntie's very bright-eyed and somewhat gay. For years past Mary's Auntie had been a private joke between Constance and her. Well, whoever he was, Mary had someone. They all had someone, except herself. And in another few years she'd be twenty-five. Then she would be old, and being plain, past the attractive stage unless it was to some old man who needed nursing.

But even an old man who needed nursing would be better than reading her life away in this isolated spot where a visit from an outsider was a red-letter day. And she knew now that even the red-letter days would be few and far between once Constance was gone; not even young Ferrier would come anymore.

Barbara was startled as a hand gripped her knee tightly, and she turned her head to look into Miss Brigmore's eyes. Miss Brigmore was smiling and her eyes were telling her what to do; her eyes were very expressive. She remembered the time when she had first realised that Miss Brigmore was two people; it was on the day she had told her she thought she was wicked. She had dared to tell her what she had seen, and Miss Brigmore had knelt before her and held her hands and she had talked as if she were speaking to an adult. Strangely, she had understood all Miss Brigmore had said, and when she had finished she had realised that servants, even governesses, had few privileges compared with people such as herself, and in her old, young mind she had come to the conclusion that Miss Brigmore was someone she should be sorry for. Now, Miss Brigmore, dear, dear Anna, was someone whom she envied.

The meal was almost at an end. When it was over Constance would change her dress and leave immediately. Would she be able to talk to her before she left? She had become very distant this past week, almost as reticent as she herself was; reticence was part of her own nature but it never had had any place in Constance's character. Constance was open, uninhibited, but these past few days she had scarcely opened her lips. This attitude had caused a secret hope to rise in her that perhaps Constance was going to change her mind and not marry Donald; yet at the same time she was well aware that if this should happen it would avail her nothing, because to Donald Radlet she was merely someone who read books and newspapers which gave her a knowledge of everyday matters, on which he could draw for his own information without taking the trouble or time to garner it himself.

Cynically she thought that he had used her as a form of abbreviated news-sheet, and she could imagine him repeating the information he had gathered on his sundry visits to his associates at the cattle shows, or in the market. She imagined him throwing off bits of world news with an authoritative air, which attached to him the tag of being a knowledgeable fellow. Oh, in spite of her feelings regarding him she knew him, indeed she thought she knew him better than Constance ever would.

She looked at him now and found that he was surveying her. There was a smile on his lips, a possessive, quiet, controlled smile. He looked so sure of himself, proud, as he should be for he had gained a prize in Constance, much more so than if he had married her, for she had nothing but her brains to recommend her. . . .

Donald, looking back at Barbara, thought, She really hates the idea of me having Constance. She feels as bad in a way about it as that crab across there. He turned his set smile on Miss Brigmore and let it rest there. Well, he had beaten her, well and truly he had beaten her, and she knew it. When he entered the door this morning there had been a look on her face he had never seen before, it was there still. He took it to mean defeat.

He now turned his gaze on the man who was his father and wondered how he really felt about it all. He was the only merry one present; except Mary, of course. He didn't seem to mind Constance going. But then you could never tell with the old man really; behind that boisterous laugh and his joking tongue there was a keen awareness, a cunningness that was the shield of his class and which covered his real feelings. Well, let them all react as they might; he had won Constance,

167

she was his. In one hour or less they'd be setting out over the hills. She was his wife, she was his for life. At last he had something of his own! And he would love her as a woman had never been loved before. And each year she'd give him a child, sons first, daughters later. He'd bring the colour back to her cheeks, conquer her fear of storms. By God! yes, he meant to do that after what Matthew had told him about the effect the weather had on her. He wasn't going to allow her to be fear-ridden for the rest of her life; he'd conquer her fear or he'd know the reason why.

They were drinking to them now. There they stood, the old man, and—her, and Barbara. As he gazed at them he quietly groped under the tablecloth for Constance's hand and when he found it he squeezed it tightly; but she did not turn and look at him for she was looking up at the three beloved faces that were gazing down on her. And they were beloved faces, each and every one of them was beloved. She had never imagined that leaving them would be such a wrench. She knew that she loved them all, but in different ways. She felt like flinging herself forward and embracing them all at once and crying to them 'Don't let me go. Don't let me go.' She could not believe that she was now a married woman, that the short ceremony in the bare and quiet church had given her over to Donald for life. Yet she recalled that the moment the ceremony was finished she had known a surge of relief, for now should a child be born through her madness there would be no disgrace, no life isolated in this cottage and burdened with the stigma of an unwanted child. No, the short ceremony had made her safe—but at what a price!

Donald did not stand and respond to the toast, he knew nothing of such ceremony, but he drank deeply, one, two, three glasses of wine, and all to his wife, while she still sipped at her first glass.

When Constance left the table and went upstairs both Miss Brigmore and Barbara accompanied her. Miss Brigmore did not want to leave the two sisters alone, so that there could be no private, tear-filled farewell between them. Constance's luggage was already packed, she had only to change her dress. This was quickly done, and when she was arrayed in a brown corded costume and wearing a biscuit-coloured straw hat, she stood for a moment and looked around the room. Then her eyes came to rest, first on Miss Brigmore and then on Barbara, and the next moment they were all enfolded together. But only for a moment, for Miss Brigmore, her voice breaking as she turned hastily away, said as she picked up the pair of gloves from the dressing table, 'No more now; what's done's done; it's over. Come, come.' She turned again and, spreading her arms wide, ushered them like two children through the door, and when they were on the landing she called, 'Mary! Mary! come and help with the luggage.'

But instead of Mary appearing on the stairs it was Donald who bounded up to them, saying, 'You leave that to me. What is there? where are they?' Miss Brigmore, pointing back into the room, said, 'There are three cases and four packages.'

'Three cases and four packages.' He imitated her voice, then let out a deep laugh and, going into the room, he picked up two cases in one hand and tucked a bulky package under his other arm before picking up the third case and, as Mary entered the room, he cried at her, 'I've left the rest for you.' Then in very much the manner that Thomas might have used, he poked his head forward and uttered in a stage whisper, 'How would you like to come over the hills and work for me, eh?'

'Go on with you. Go on with you.' She laughed shrilly. 'You're a funny fellow you are; you're taking enough away when you're takin' Miss Constance. Go on, get off and don't let the master hear you sayin' you want me an' all; they're losing enough the day, they are that.'

Mimicking her now, he said, 'And you've had more than a drop the day, Mary, you have that. You like your duckie, don't you?'

He was at the top of the stairs now, she behind him, and she giggled as she said, 'Eeh! the things you say. Go on with you.' He wasn't so bad after all, she thought to herself, she liked him, she did; yes, she did.

The women were outside now; only Thomas was in the hall. He was no longer smiling, his expression was sad and there was a tightness to his jaws, and when Mary, still laughing, said, 'He's a funny fellow this, Master,' he admonished her as the master of the Hall might have done at one time, saying, 'Be quiet, woman'; and she became quiet, subdued. Not until she had put the packages among the others in the back of the brake and Constance had come towards her and, putting her arms about her had kissed her did she speak again; and then her words came out on a flood of tears and she cried, 'Oh Miss Constance! Miss Constance!' and putting her white apron to her face she turned about and ran back into the house.

When Constance stood in the circle of Thomas's arms and felt his big body quiver with emotion it was too much, and she leant against him and cried, 'Uncle! Dear Uncle!' and Thomas, his own cheeks wet, looked over her head to where his son was standing near the house waiting, and he said, 'There now there now. Go on, over the hills with you.' Then he took her face in his hands and added, 'Don't forget us, my dear. Come and see us often, eh?'

She nodded at him helplessly. The next moment she was lifted bodily in Donald's arms and placed in the seat at the front of the brake, and not until he had taken his seat beside her and picked up the reins did she lift her head and look at them again. They were standing close together gazing up at her, and she spoke to them as if they were one, saying 'Good-bye, good-bye' and they all nodded their heads at her, but not one of them spoke.

Before the brake rounded the bend in the road she turned right round in her seat and waved to them, and now they waved back.

As soon as they were out of sight, Donald gathered the reins into one hand, thrust out his other arm and pulled her to his side with a jerk that caught at her breath and made her gasp, and his eyes covering her with their dark gleaming light, he muttered thickly, 'At last, at long last,' and the words brought home to her more than anything else the depths and the fierceness of his passion for her, but if it had aroused only fear in her there might have been some hope for him, but not when it also created revulsion.

FOUR

They greeted her kindly, most warmly. Both Michael and Jane Radlet came from the house into the yard as the brake drew up. It was as if they had been waiting together.

'Well, here we are then,' said Michael with a smile, and when Donald had lifted her to the ground Jane held out her two hands and Constance took them gladly. But when Jane said, 'Welcome home, my dear,' all Constance could reply, and in a stiffly polite tone, was, 'Thank you.'

Although the day was warm they had lit a fire in the sitting room. The horsehair suite had been lightened with crochet arm and head rests, a large new, hand-done proggy mat lay the length of the long stone fire-place, and the round table in the centre of the room was set for tea. On the snowy cloth lay the tea-set that had not been out of the cabinet since Matthew was christened, and the rest of the table was covered with a variety of homebaked cakes and plates of cold ham and beef, and pickles.

'Would you like to go upstairs or would you have a cup of tea first?' Jane's voice was warm, even comforting.

'I should love a cup of tea, please.' And not only one, she thought, but two, three, four, anything to delay going upstairs and being alone with him. It was no use telling herself that she had to be alone with him for the rest of her days; all she could think of at the moment was, she wanted a little breathing space.

She watched Jane bustle from the room to the kitchen back and forth several times, while Michael sat in the high-backed armchair opposite to her and nodded at her at intervals. At last he endeavoured to open a conversation.

'You've got it over then?' He still nodded at her.

'Yes, thank you.'

'How did it go?'

At this she glanced at Donald, where he was standing with his back to the fire; and he answered for her. On a laugh, he said, 'Well, it's done, signed, sealed, and I've put me brand on her.' He leant sideways and lifted up her hand, showing to Michael the ring on her finger.

'I'm sorry that Matthew couldn't get along.' Michael was still nodding.

'Yes.' She swallowed, then said again, 'Yes,' before forcing herself to ask, 'Is he any better?'

'Better than he was yesterday, but still rather poorly. We're thinkin' of sending for a doctor come Monday. He won't hear of it, as usual, can't stand doctors; but I'll have me way if he's no better come Monday.'

Jane said now, 'Will you sit up, my dear?' and Constance came to the table, and the four of them sat down. One after the other they handed her the plates, and in order not to seem impolite and ungrateful to this kind little woman she forced herself to eat, and as she ate she thought, Thank God I shall like her. That at least is one good thing. And the father too; they're good people. And she prayed, 'Please God, take this feeling that I have against Donald from me; let me at least like him, don't let me hurt him, for ... for he means well, and he cares for me.'

That was the trouble, he cared too much for her. She had not realised to the full extent the intensity of his passion; before, it had been somewhat veiled, but during the journey over the hills he had expressed his feelings, not only in words, but in looks and touch.

She now tried to delude herself into thinking that once tonight was over the fire in him would be damped a little; his intensity would relax, and they would fall into a pattern like other married couples. But what other married couples? Whom did she know who was married? She had come in contact with no young married couples, all she knew about marriage was what she had read, and most of the stories ended up with the couple getting married and living happily ever after. Those that didn't were tragedies, where the husband took a mistress or the wife took a lover. Her husband would never take a mistress, she felt sure of this. Although he was a Mallen in part, he wasn't made like that. In an odd way, he was much too proper. But she had already had a lover.

She glanced at Donald. He was sitting straight; he looked arrogant, utterly pleased with himself. He turned and looked her full in the face and jerked his chin upwards at her, and the action expressed more than any words the confidence he had in himself. And rightly, for was she not his wife and sitting, to all intents and purposes, at his table? The air of possession that emanated from him was frightening and she recalled, on a deep wave of sickness, Matthew's words. 'He would slit my throat like he does a pig's.'

It was about a quarter past seven when Jane lit the lamps. Constance stood by the table and watched her fitting on the coloured glass shades, the plain white one for the kitchen and a blue one, patterned with gold spots, for the sitting room. She remarked that the blue one was pretty and Jane replied, 'Aye, it belonged to the father's'—she always referred to her husband as the father—'it belonged to the father's grandmother and the globe hasn't got a crack in it. I get scared out of me wits every time I light it.'

Jane turned her head to the side and smiled at the girl who was to share her home, and she was surprised that her presence was creating in her a feeling of shy happiness. She told herself that if the girl settled it would be like having a daughter in the house, and somebody to talk to. That is when Donald wasn't about. But of course it all depended on her settling, and at the moment she looked as if she could take flight. She couldn't explain to herself the look on the girl's face; she didn't want to put the word fear to it be-
174

cause she couldn't see what she had to fear; she had taken Donald with her eyes open, she'd had a year to think about it, and had then gone through with it, so she couldn't imagine that it was Donald who was making her uneasy. But uneasy she was. And there was another strange thing. When they rose from the table she hadn't gone with Donald but had followed her round the house asking questions about this and that, saying she wanted to be of assistance. Only a minute ago she had smiled at her kindly and said, 'There's plenty of time. Now don't worry, I'll find you all the work you feel inclined to do; you never can be idle on a farm, you know.' And now here she was wanting to help with the lamps.

She had seen immediately the difference the girl's presence was going to make on Donald; he was like a dog with two tails, she had never seen him so amenable. He had spoken to her as he had never done before, had even made a request of her. He had come into the larder and, standing at her side, had said, 'If she wants to learn the dairy show her, will you, but don't press her. I don't want her to do anything she doesn't want to do.' And she had turned and looked at him. His expression had been soft, and for the first time in his life he looked really happy, and she had answered, 'I'll tell her anything she wants to know.'

He had nodded and stared at her silently for a moment before turning away, leaving her standing with her hands pressed flat on the cold marble slab and thinking, It's going to work out all right after all. This is what he needs, a wife such as this one, someone he can be proud of and show off, someone he could have married if he'd had his birthright. And at that moment she had understood a lot about her son she had never understood before.

When she carried the lamp in both hands held well in front of her into the sitting room she did not speak until she had placed it on the table, and then, standing back from it, she looked at Constance who was at her side and said, 'You'll find life here strange at first, because we mostly work to the light, up with the dawn, to bed with the dusk, or pretty near it. At the end of a long day we're ready for our beds, especially in the winter, 'cos that's the warmest place, bed. Of course when I say that'—she now nodded her head and smiled broadly at Constance—'I'm forgettin' about our Matthew. He'd burn oil to the dawn readin' his books. But not Donald.' She put out her hand now and indicated that Constance should sit on the couch, and as she sat down opposite to her she finished, 'Donald works very hard, very hard indeed. Since the father's had rheumatics it's been extra heavy for him. And there are times, as now, when Matthew can't do anything at all.'

Constance stared back through the lamp light into the round, homely face of this ordinary woman who in a way was on a par with Mary, but who nevertheless was her mother-in-law, and all she could do was nod. She knew already that she liked this woman. She also knew that she was going to need her in the days ahead. What she had the urge to do now was to sit close to her and hold her hands, cling to her hands. She thought too that her liking was returned. Yet what would this woman do if she knew that her new daughter-in-law had lain with one son before marrying the other? Just as Matthew had said of Donald, she would want to slit her throat. That terrible phrase was recurring to her mind more and more.

When she spoke again her question must have appeared as if she were anxious for Donald's return, for what she said was, 'Does it take long . . . I mean the last round at night?'

Jane smiled quietly as she said, 'Well, it all depends. You see, the cattle are still out, and he goes round the fields. Then sometimes the hens won't take to their roost. There's a couple in particular go clucking round in the dark; they're deranged, an' one of these mornings they'll wake up and find themselves inside the fox and that'll give them a gliff.'

She laughed, a soft gay laugh, and was herself surprised to hear it; then in a more sober tone she went on, 'Of course, in the lambing time he can be up all hours that God sends; an' then with the calfing an' all. He's very careful of the animals, very careful.' She nodded at Constance, her expression quite serious now,

176

then added, 'He's well thought of as a farmer, oh very well thought of. They take his word for lots of things roundabout.'

All Constance could say to this was 'Yes. . . .'

An hour later Jane thought to herself that she had never talked so much at one go in her life. Michael was no talker; Matthew was always in his books; and when you got a word out of Donald it was usually a comment on the animals, or a definite statement of what he was about to do. She had talked as she had done because the girl was nervous; she was all eyes. She looked a child, too young to be married, yet she was the same age as she herself had been when she was married. She recalled her own first night in this house, her fear of having to go to bed with Michael, and then her overwhelming feeling of happiness when she realised the goodness in the man she had married. But there was a great difference between Michael and Donald, and there was a greater difference between herself at that age and this girl; yet it was the first night of marriage and she was in a strange house, and they were all comparative strangers to her. She must be filled with a great unease.

She leant forward now and said gently, 'Would you like to go upstairs and see to your things and such? You must be tired; it's been a trying day for you.'

Before she had finished speaking Constance was on her feet, saying, 'Yes, I would, thank you. Thank you very much.'

'I'll light your lamp, it's up there already. I'll take the kitchen one to see us up the stairs. I'd better not take that one.' She smiled and nodded towards the blue-shaded light, and Constance said, 'No, no, of course not.'

Constance had been in the bedroom earlier. She had opened one case and hung some of her things in the old Dutch wardrobe that stood against one white wall, but she had not attempted to unpack the rest of the luggage, all she had wanted to do was to get away from the sight of the high bed covered by the patchwork quilt. Jane had pointed out to her that she had spent the winter making the quilt, and she had duly admired

177

it; she had also thanked her for decorating the room, which decoration consisted of lime-washing in between the black beams, those that strutted the walls at uneven angles and those that supported the low ceiling in three massive beetle-pierced lengths, and which gleamed dully where the linseed oil that Jane had applied so generously to them had failed to soak in.

Setting the lamp down on the round oak table to the side of the bed, Jane now turned to Constance and, her hands folded in front of her waist, she said, 'There you are then, dear. I'll leave you now and wish you good-night.' But she didn't move immediately, she stood staring at Constance and Constance at her; then, as if motivated by the same thought, they moved towards each other and their hands held and their cheeks touched; then muttering something like, 'May your life be good. God bless you, dear,' Jane hurried from the room. And Constance was alone.

She looked about the room as she had done earlier in the day, and now, although she was still filled with panic, she knew she could run no farther; she had come up against a rock face as it were, and from now on she'd have to steel herself and climb.

The room was cold, there was a dankness about it. She knelt by one of the cases on the floor and, having opened it, she took out a warm nightdress, a dressing gown and a pair of slippers from where Anna had placed them to be ready to her hand. As she laid them on the bed she hesitated whether to wash her face and hands now or to wait until she was undressed; deciding she'd be less cold doing it now, she went to the corner washhand stand at the far side of the room. The basin was set in a hole in the middle of the stand; the jug in the basin was full to the top with water—and icy cold; the towel she dried on was clean and white but rough, but all these were minor inconveniences and would, she thought, have been endured with something of amusement if only the man with whom she was to share that bed behind her was anyone but Donald. If only it had been Matthew, even a sick Matthew, she would have been happy; or at least she wouldn't have been filled with fear as she was at this moment. But let her get this one night over and she would cope. Oh yes, just let her get this one night over and she would cope.

As she was about to undress she looked at the picture that was hanging above the bed. It was one of three religious prints that Jane had hung in the room; it showed colourful even in the lamp light, the picture itself was a travesty created by an artist who had undoubtedly taken liberties with the book of Esther, for not only did it show King Ahasuerus seated in his marble pillared palace surrounded by his seven chamberlains, with Vashti, the wife he had put away, standing at a distance from him, but it also showed Esther, whom he had taken to be his Queen, seated to his side, and at her feet seven maidens, undoubtedly virgins all.

Quickly now she began to unbutton her dress. Having stepped out of it, she folded it lengthwise and laid it over the back of a chair, as of habit; then she undid the strings of her first waist petticoat and stepped out of that; and she did the same with her under petticoat. It was as she stood in her bloomers, soft, lawn, lace-trimmed bloomers, a new innovation created by an American lady—the daring pattern which she had copied from a ladies' journal—that the door opened. She did not turn her head to look towards it, but with one swift movement she gathered up her two petticoats and holding them against her neck she dropped down on to the edge of the bed and drew up her knees under their trailing cover.

Slowly and with a look of amusement on his face, Donald came towards her and, standing above her, he shook his head as he put out his hand and gently but firmly made to relieve her of her undergarments. When she resisted he closed his eyes for a moment, then said softly and as if reasoning with a child, 'Constance. Constance, you remember what happened to-day?' He now stretched his face at her in amused enquiry. 'Eh? You were married, remember? ... Look'—he now caught her hand and, holding the wedding ring between his finger and thumb, he shook it vigorously—'you were married ... we were married. Come.' With a twist of his body he was sitting beside her, one arm about

179

her, the other forcing her joined hands down over her chest.

When her protesting hands touched her lap he released them, and his fingers now moved upwards to the buttons lying between her breasts. As if she had been stung she sprang away from him and, grabbing up her nightdress, pulled it over her head, and now, half shielded by the foot of the bed and with rapid contortions, she undressed under it as she had done as a child when she shared her room with Barbara.

Miss Brigmore had early on introduced them to this pattern, reciting a little poem that went: 'Modesty becomes maidens making ready for the night.' And when alone, they had mimicked her but altered the words to: 'Modesty becomes maidens who are little mealy-mouthed mites.'

Still seated on the bed, Donald surveyed her. He was no longer smiling, no longer amused. From a deep recess in his mind a thought was oozing, like the matter from a suppurating sore. As it gained force it brought him up from the bed, and the action seemed to stem its flow; but he was still aware of it as he gripped her by the shoulders and said from low in his throat, 'Constance, you are me wife, you're no longer in the cottage with them, you've started on a different sort of life. And you're not a child, so stop acting like one.'

When he thrust her from him she fell backwards and leant against the brass rail at the foot of the bed. Her eyes were wide, her mouth open. She watched him for a moment as he turned from her and walked across the room and pulled open the top drawer of the chest; then like the child he had denied she was, she scrambled up the side of the bed, tore back the clothes and climbed in.

When she next looked at him he was undressed down to his trousers. At this point she closed her eyes. She did not open them again until she felt him moving by the side of the bed; and what she saw would, under happier circumstances, have made her laugh, for he was dressed in a nightshirt that barely reached his knees. It wasn't the first time she had seen a man dressed in a nightshirt, she had often glimpsed her uncle on his journeys back and forth to the water closet in the early morning. But then, her uncle's nightshirt reached his ankles. But Donald's nightshirt exposed his lower limbs and she saw that they were hairy, as also was his chest that she glimpsed through the open shirt; and for a reason she couldn't explain she became more fearful.

Her body stiff, she waited for him to put out the lamp; but when he clambered into the bed the lamp was still burning. Now, leaning on his elbow, he was hanging over her, looking down into her face, saying nothing, just staring at her; and as she stared back at him she saw his whole countenance alter. There came over it the softness that she had glimpsed now and again, and her thoughts, racing madly, gabbled at her. It might have been all right if that storm hadn't overtaken them. Yes, yes it might. If only she could forget what had happened in the storm, put it out of her mind, at least for to-night. But she couldn't, because Matthew was there, somewhere across the landing, coughing—and knowing, and thinking.

He still did not speak when he drew her into his arms and held her body close to his. But he did not bring his face close to hers; he kept his head well back from her and peered at her, and his whisper bore out the expression in his eyes: 'I just want to look at you,' he said; 'look and look. I've dreamt of this moment for years. Do you understand that, Constance?'

As the muscles of his arms suddenly contracted her body jerked against his, yet remained stiff. For the moment he seemed unaware of it, lost in the wonder of his own emotions and not a little blinded by his own achievement. But when his mouth dropped to hers and there was no response from her lips he brought his head up again, and now he asked, almost as a plea, 'What is it? what is it, Constance? Don't be afraid, please. Don't be afraid, I love you. I told you I love you, and I'll love you as no one has ever loved afore. I need to love you, and I need you to love me. Do you understand that?

. . . . 'Say something.' Again her body jerked within his hold.

When she did not speak, the softness seeped from his face and he said thickly, 'That damned old cow has filled your head with bloody nonsense about marriage, hasn't she?'

At this she managed to gulp and mutter, 'No, no.'

'Then what is it?'

If she had replied, 'I'm afraid, Donald, it's all so strange, everything,' he undoubtedly would have thought he understood and might even have given himself another explanation for what he was to discover within the next few minutes; but she could not put on an act for him, she was not subtle enough, sly enough, and she was aware of this.

'NO, NO! NOT YET, PLEASE, PLEASE, NOT YET.' Her voice was strangled in her throat, his mouth was eating her. His hands seemed to have multiplied like the snakes on Medusa's head and were attacking her body from all angles . . . .

It was a full three minutes after she ceased to struggle that he raised himself from her. In part she had known the man Donald Radlet five minutes earlier, but she knew nothing of the man who was gazing down at her now. The face that she was staring into had about it a stricken look; then like wind driven clouds that changed the face of the sky the expression turned into one of wild black ferocity. She held her breath and tried to press her body deeper into the feather tick in order to ward off the violence threatened by his expression, but to her relief and surprise his body moved away from hers until there was a foot of space between them, and he was sitting upright, half turned from her, but with his eyes still on her.

As if obeying a warning voice within himself, Donald moved still further towards the edge of the bed, but continued to look at her. And as he looked he knew that the pus from the secret sore in his mind was flooding his brain, and that if he didn't control it he would put out his hands and throttle the thing he loved, and wanted to go on loving. But now there was a question about that, for he knew that he had been duped; he, Donald Radlet, who was no man's fool, who was as smart as they came, who allowed no one to take the

182

rise out of him without paying for it, who knew, who had always known, that if you followed the principle of wanting a thing badly enough you would surely get it, had been made a monkey out of.

This then was the reason for her attitude. He could see it all plainly now; it was as clear as the white light that occasionally covered the hills, the light that took your gaze away into infinity. Her manner this past week, her being afraid to face him a week gone. She had taken to her bed when he had dashed over the hills to find out what the trouble was.

It was as he was leaving the cottage that he had met the Ferrier boy, because that's all he was, a smooth-chinned, weak-kneed boy. But he was going back to Oxford, he'd said, and it was doubtful if that old cow would have left him alone in the bedroom with Constance for a moment. But if not he, then who else?

There was that family in Allendale, with the two sons. Both were a deal older than she, but what did that matter? Yes, what did that matter? Look at the old man for example. Yet it must have been a month since she had visited Allendale and what had taken place had taken place within the last fortnight.

He looked into her face, beautiful, even angelic looking ... but fear-filled. Had he made a mistake? Hell's flames, no! he had made no mistake. He was no amateur coming to bed for the first time; he had been but fifteen when he took his first woman. And that was the correct term, took her; she hadn't taken him, although she had been long at the game. She had laughed at him, and liked him, and every market day in Hexham he had managed to slip up the alley. She had supplied him until he was eighteen.

One particular time when he went up the alley the door was opened by a young girl. Bella had died the previous week, she said, but would he like to come in. Her name was Nancy; she was fourteen and she was the one and only virgin he'd ever had. But if he'd never had that experience he would have known that she, lying there, his wife, on this the first night of their marriage was no virgin.

His pride was under his feet, his head was dragged

183

down, his arrogance was broken, his self-esteem was as something he had never heard of for his mind was utterly deprived of it. He was no longer a Mallen flaunting his streak, finding pride in his bastardy, and through it feeling he had the right to confer condescension on even those who considered themselves his superiors—he was nothing. He was now as he had been that day in the market place when the Scolly brothers had laughed at him and called him a bastard. Yet he was not even as he had been on that day, he was less, much less, for on that day he had become aware that there was high blood in him, gentleman's blood. On that day he found out he was the son of a man who owned a grand Hall over the hills, a man of property and substance; and on that day he had sworn that he would grow so big in all ways that nobody would dare turn a disdainful look in his direction without paying for it, and that whatever he desired from life he would get. . . .

And he had got it. She was lying there, and she was no better than any whore.

She smothered a scream as he pounced on her, his hands round her throat, his nose almost touching hers, his words like grit spitting into her face. 'Who was it? tell me! Who was it?'

When her body became limp under his hands he released the pressure of his thumbs; but now he had her by the shoulders, lifting her bodily upwards, and in a whispered hiss he demanded, 'Tell me! I'll throttle it out of you.'

When she moved her head from side to side and gasped he shook her like a dog shaking a rat, and when the tears spurted from her eyes and a cry escaped her lips he turned his head quickly and looked towards the door before thrusting her back onto the mattress.

He remained still, listening. Then satisfying himself that if her cry had carried beyond the room they would likely take it as the result of a marriage bed caper, he moved up to her again. And now leaning over her, his hands one on each side of her, he said slowly, 'You've been with somebody, haven't you?'

Her hands were holding her throat as she shook her head; then she stammered, 'N . . . n . . . no.'

'You're lying. You can't hoodwink me, not on this anyway. Who was he? I'll not keep askin' you. I'll shake it out of you. I'll beat it out of you. Do you hear, my dear Constance? I'll beat it out of you. Who was it?'

'I tell you, I tell you . . . nobody.'

He screwed up his eyes until they became mere slits, then repeated, 'Nobody? nobody you say? Then why didn't you come over as you intended last week? It must have taken some storm to have put you to bed.'

'It . . . it was . . . it was the storm.'

'You're lying.'

'I'm not.'

As she gazed into his face she realized that not only would she have to lie, but lie convincingly, for she knew that this man was capable, as Matthew had predicted, of slitting her throat as he did the pigs'.

Like an actress taking her cue she obeyed the inner voice in her and, hoisting herself away from him, she tried to assume indignation, and in no small tone she cried at him, 'You are mad. I don't know what you mean, what you suspect, and . . . and I won't stay with you to be treated in such a manner, I'll go home. . . . '

Immediately she knew she had overdone her part for he turned on her now, growling low, 'You what! you what! His lean face was purple with his anger; the fact that she could even voice such a thing showed him a new aspect of his humiliation, a public aspect, something to be avoided at all costs, especially in his case, for were she even to attempt to go back over the hills he could never outlive the humiliation. But being who he was he knew that he would never allow it to get that far, and he told her so. In a thick whisper now, leaning towards her but not touching her, he said, 'You'll go home, as you call it, when they carry you over in a box to the cemetery, but not afore, not if I know it.'

When she closed her eyes and the tears washed down her face his teeth ground into his lip, and he bowed his head for a moment and, in real agony now, he groaned, 'Oh Constance! Constance! why? why? How could you do it?'

'I didn't, I didn't. I tell you you must be mad. I don't know what you're talking about.'

He was looking at her as he said, 'Well, if you don't know what I'm talking about why do you say you didn't.'

Her head wagged on her shoulders in a desperate fashion now as she muttered, 'Because you are suggesting that I . . . I . . .'

She suddenly turned from him and rolled onto her face and pressed it into the pillow to stifle the sound of her sobbing, and he straightened his back and turned from the bed. Having crossed the room to where his clothes lay, he slowly got back into them, all except his shoes, and these he carried in his hand.

Without a backward glance towards the bed, he went to the door and, gripping it firmly so that it shouldn't creak, he opened it and closed it after him. Cautiously he crossed the landing and went down the stairs. There was no light; he didn't need one, he knew every inch of this house. Unbolting the back door, he went into the yard.

He looked up at the sky for a moment. It was high and star-studded; the air was sharp with frost, there would be rime on the walls in the morning. He crossed the yard and went through a door next to the cow byres and into the warm steamy atmosphere that came from the boiler where the pig mash was simmering. The room was part harness room, part storeroom. He pulled down a bundle of hay and brought it near to the boiler and, sitting on it, he dropped his head into his hands and for the first time in his life he cried.

Towards morning he must have dozed; but he became wide awake at the sound of the cockerel giving answer to the faint echo coming from another of his breed across the valley. He rose from the hay on which he had been lying and dusted himself down, then went out into the yard. He did not look up into the sky to see the light lifting, for his attention was caught by the gleam of the lamp coming from the kitchen. His mother must be up, but it was early for her.

When he entered the kitchen and Matthew, a teapot in his hand, swung round from the fireplace, he stopped and stared at him before saying, 'Why are you up?'

Steadying the teapot in both hands, Matthew went to the table and placed the teapot on it before he muttered, 'I . . . I needed a drink; I . . . I needed a drink; I . . . I had the shivers.'

Donald was standing at the other side of the table now and he said, 'Why didn't you knock for Mam?'

When Matthew gave no answer but reached out and drew a mug towards him Donald's eyes focused on his hand which was trembling; then they lifted to his face. His skin had not the usual transparent glow about it this morning, except for the two high spots of red on his cheekbones it looked yellow, as if it had taken the tint from his hair. His gaze was held by the odd expression in his brother's eyes; it was a startled expression holding fear. Well, he would be fearful, wouldn't he? When a man knew he was going to die it would make him fearful.

'How . . . how is Constance?'

'Look out, you're spilling the tea all over the place. Here! give it to me . . . She's all right, tired, exciting day yesterday.' He actually forced his lips into a smile; it was the first effort in the pattern he had worked out for himself last night. He would act before the others as if everything were normal, and he would see that she did the same. By God! he would. One thing he wouldn't tolerate and that was pity; even from those in this house who were near to him, for he knew that, being human, they could not help but think. And how are the mighty fallen! His da had a saying: If the eagle dies in the air it still has to fall to earth. Well, he had been an eagle and last night a vital part of him had died and he had fallen to the earth; but no one would know of his fall.

'Here, here! hold on a minute.' He could not get round the table quickly enough to save Matthew from falling backwards. When he reached him he was lying on the floor, his face now no longer yellow but deathly white.

'Matthew! Matthew!' He raised his head, then put

187

his hand on his heart; it was still beating and quite rapidly. The young fool; he shouldn't have got up it was enough to finish him off. Bending now, he picked the inert figure from the floor as if it were a child and carried it upstairs, and as he passed the first door on the landing he put out his foot and kicked it as he yelled, 'Matthew's bad, get up.'

He was lifting his foot again to thrust it out towards Matthew's bedroom door when he saw Constance standing in the open doorway of their bedroom. Her face looked almost as white as the one hanging over his arm, and he cried at her, 'Come and make yourself useful.' It was his second move in the new game, and it seemed to have an immediate effect on her, for she sprang from the doorway to his side and as he made his way towards the bed she muttered, 'What . . . what have you done? what have you done?'

He didn't answer until he had laid Matthew down and was taking off his shoes, then he looked at her from the side and said, 'What do you mean, what have I done?' His eyes followed hers to Matthew's face where the lips and chin were now covered with blood, and he thought he was the reason for her question. 'It's his lungs, he's fainted.' Then, his voice harsh, he growled at her under his breath, 'And don't you do the same, 'cos you'll witness more than a spot of blood afore you're finished.'

The words were like a threat, yet they steadied her, for she, too, had actually been on the point of fainting, and for much the same reason that had tumbled Matthew into unconsciousness; relief.

BOOK IV

BARBARA

ONE

November and December 1862 had been cruel months. Miss Brigmore had caught a severe cold through sitting on the carrier's cart, exposed to a biting wind as it travelled the hills between the cottage and the farm.

The newly married couple had visited the cottage only once, and then she'd hardly been able to have a word alone with Constance, for that man had hovered over them like a hawk. But during the short conversation she had gauged enough to gather that life was bearable during the day time but that at night it became a special kind of purgatory, became Donald was aware of her lapse; he had seemingly been aware of it from the first night of their marriage. Constance had stared at her while waiting for a clearer explanation of this, and she might have been able to satisfy her except that they had been interrupted by Donald.

Repeatedly since that visit Miss Brigmore had blamed herself for having neglected a very important part of the girls' education, yet at the same time excusing herself: should she under any circumstances have had to explain to them that they were virgins but once?

It was when the weather was about to break and there had been no further visit from the farm, that Thomas said, 'You know, I've got a feeling that everything isn't right across there; why doesn't he come like he used to? Hail, rain or snow didn't stop him this time last year, except when the roads were absolutely impassable, and they'll soon be like that again. If it wouldn't be the means of embarassing both myself and those

191

people across there'—he was referring now to Jane and Michael—'I would order a carriage and go over, I would indeed.'

He had looked at her as he finished and then had stood waiting for her response, which she knew should have been, 'And where do you think the money is coming from to provide you with a carriage?' But what she said was, 'I will go across myself; the carrier's cart will be running for a while yet.'

So, on a day when six layers of clothes were no protection against the icy wind, she crossed over the mountains to the farm, and there, at the sight of her dear Constance, she had wanted to cover her face with her hands and weep. Three months of marriage had put almost twice as many years on her. There was no spark of joy left in her; in fact the mother, who was, Miss Brigmore thought, about her own age, was much more lively than the young wife. Only one consolation did she bring back with her across the hills. The mother was kind to Constance; she evidently had a liking for her, and was glad to have her at the farm. What little she saw of the father, too, she liked. He had welcomed her quite warmly. But she had found it almost impossible to look at, much less sympathise with, Matthew where he sat huddled in blankets to the side of the roaring fire. Indeed, when their eyes had met she knew that there was no secret between them.

What she had found strange, too, was that Constance no longer wanted to be alone with her. She had not suggested taking her to her room, and when Jane had said, 'Wouldn't you like to take Miss Brigmore round the farm? Go on, wrap up well, it will do you good to get some air,' she had answered, 'Can you spare the time to come too, you can explain things better than me?' And she had turned her head in Miss Brigmore's direction but had not looked at her directly as she ended, 'I'm new to all this, you understand?'

In fact the whole being that Constance now presented to her was new to Miss Brigmore; the old Constance might never have existed; her spirit had been crushed. This wasn't altogether unexpected; for she had imagined it might happen. Nevertheless she had

192

thought it would take a number of years to come about; yet Donald had accomplished the change in the course of a few weeks.

When she had at last returned to the cottage she was cold to the very core of her being, even her mind seemed numbed, and she had not hidden all the truth from them when they asked how she had found Constance. 'She's changed,' she had said.

'Changed?' Thomas demanded, 'Changed, what do you mean?'

'She's much more quiet, sort of subdued.'

'Connie subdued? I'll never believe that, I'll have to see it first. When is she coming over?'

'I . . . I don't think she'll be over yet awhile; she's been having a rather distressing time with sickness and such.'

'Oh. Oh.' Thomas had risen from his chair, his head bobbing. He had turned and looked at her and said, 'I don't mind telling you I miss her, I miss her chatter. Do you know something?' He had poked his head forward, 'I realize I've hardly laughed since she left. Funny now that, isn't it? Barbara's different, too quiet; you could always get a laugh out of Constance.'

'No, no, it isn't funny' she had replied evenly. 'As you say, Barbara is sedate, and I cannot claim that any part of my nature tends towards provoking hilarity either.'

At this he put his head back and let out a bellow of a laugh before saying, 'I take it all back. I take it all back because there are times, my dear Anna, when you appear very, very funny.'

'Thank you.'

'Aw'—he flapped his hand at her as he turned away—'you can't put me in my place, mentally, or otherwise. Go on with you.' And he flapped his hand again as he went out, still chuckling.

Barbara had asked, 'How did you find her?' and she had answered again, 'Very changed.'

'She's not happy?'

She had stared at Barbara. Would it make her happy to know that her sister was unhappy, human nature being what it was? She didn't know.

Barbara now said, 'She's not settling?' and to this she answered, 'Yes, she's settling. But regarding happiness, no, I'd be telling a lie if I said she was happy.'

'Then why did she marry him?' The words were brought out with deep bitterness, and Miss Brigmore answered, 'There was a reason, a special reason. She had changed her mind and wasn't going to marry him. Yes'—she nodded at Barbara's surprised look—'but something happened and she was forced to marry him.'

Barbara's thin face had crinkled into deep lines of disgust as she whispered, 'She had misbehaved?'

'Yes.' Miss Brigmore nodded her head. She had decided during these last few minutes to tell Barbara the truth. Whether she would sympathise or even understand she didn't know but she felt compelled to tell her the real reason why her sister had married Donald Radlet, and so she repeated, 'Yes, she had misbehaved . . . but not with Donald.'

'Not with . . . ?' Barbara's mouth had fallen into an amazed gape.

'It happened in the storm when Matthew was taking her to the farm. You know how fearful she becomes in a storm. They took shelter in a deserted house on top of the hills. He comforted her and that was that. He told her that he had loved her as long as Donald had and she realized in that moment that she loved him too. From what little she told me I gather that she begged him to marry her but for obvious reasons he couldn't, or wouldn't. I think the main reason was he was afraid of Donald and what might happen to him if the truth were ever known.'

Barbara stood with her two hands pressed tightly over the lower part of her face; and after a time she whispered, 'And Donald, he . . . he doesn't know?'

'Yes and no. He knows that she did not come to him as a wife should but . . . but he doesn't know who was responsible.'

'Oh dear Lord! dear Lord!' Still holding her face, Barbara had paced the floor; and then much to Miss Brigmore's surprise she said with deep feeling, 'Poor Connie! poor Connie!' and she had endorsed it, saying, 'Yes, indeed Barbara, poor Connie.'

194

When, the day following her visit to the farm, Miss Brigmore had developed a cold she had treated it as an ordinary snifter—Mary's term for streaming eyes and a red nose—but on the third day when she went into a fever there was great concern in the house; and the following week when the cold developed into pneumonia and the doctor rode six miles from the town every day for four days, a pall of fear descended on them all.

What, Thomas had asked himself, would he do with his life if he lost Anna?

And what, Barbara had asked herself, would become of her if she lost Anna? She'd be left here with Uncle and Mary, Uncle who only thought of his stomach and—that unmentionable thing—and Mary, who had appeared to her as a wonderful person during her childhood, but whom she now saw as a faithful but very ordinary, even ignorant, woman. What she needed above everything now was mental companionship, so she went on her knees nightly, or whenever she gave herself time to rest, and beseeched God to spare Anna.

And Mary too, as she rushed between the cooking and the cleaning and the washing and the ironing, and lugging the coal upstairs to see that the room was kept at an even temperature twenty-four hours of the day, had also asked, what would she do if anything happened to the Miss? There had been a time when she hadn't liked Miss Brigmore, when she hadn't a good word in her mouth for her; but that was many years ago. But since they had all come to live in this house she had come to look upon her not merely as a woman of spirit, but as a sort of miracle worker. If anything went wrong Miss Brigmore would put it right; moreover she had a way of spreading out the money so that it seemed to go twice as far as it would have done in anyone else's hands, and she never went for her now as she had done in those far off days back in the nursery. Mind you, aye, she wasn't lavish with her praise, but you always knew when she was pleased. 'You've done very well, Mary,' she would say. 'I don't think you've made a better pie than that, Mary,' she would say. 'Put your feet up, Mary, and rest that leg,' she would say. The only times she showed any displeasure was when

195

she was foolish enough to take more than three glasses of her Aunt Sarah's brew on her days off, for when she came back she couldn't stop her tongue from wagging, or herself from giggling. The girls used to laugh at her, and with her, but not Miss Brigmore. A telling off would always come the next morning.

She often brought a bottle back with her. At one time, she had kept it in her room, but she had more sense now. Now she left it in a rabbit hole beyond the hedge—you couldn't see the hole from this side, and all she had to do was to go on to her knees, put her hand through the privet and pull the bottle out. She generally waited until it was dark and they'd all gone to bed, and then just before she locked up she'd slip down the garden and have a little nip. It was a great comfort, her Aunt Sarah's bottle, on cold nights.

Once, when she had taken more than the three nips and Miss Brigmore had gone for her, she had nearly turned on her and said, 'Well, I haven't got the master to keep me warm, have I?' Eeh! she was glad she hadn't let that slip out, she would never have forgiven herself. And she knew that if it would be any help to Miss Brigmore at this moment she would promise her she would never touch a drop again as long as she lived. But all she could do was to ask God to see to it.

And God saw to it, but He took His time. Miss Brigmore survived the pneumonia but it left her with an infection that the doctor could put no name to, but which, he said, would be cured with time. The infection took the form of making Miss Brigmore unable to assimilate her food. Within half an hour of eating a meal her bowel would evacuate it. Patience, said the doctor, patience. He had seen cases like this before. It might take two, or four, or six months, but it could be cured.

Up to date, Miss Brigmore had suffered the infection for four months. She was not confined wholly to bed but she was still unable to do anything other than sit in a chair by the side of the window, near enough to it to see the road, but far away enough from it to avoid a draught. . . .

It was now a March day in 1863, the sky high and clear blue. The snow had gone for the present, except from the hilltops. If you gave your imagination licence you could see spring not very far ahead. At least, this is what Barbara was saying as she bustled about the room. 'In a fortnight's time,' she said, 'three weeks at the most, we'll see the bulbs out, and the rowans too ... and with the carrier's cart to-morrow we should have a letter from Constance. I must write one to-night and have it ready for him. Do you think you can do a note to her, Anna?'

'Yes, yes, of course I'll write a note.' Miss Brigmore's tone was absentminded. 'By the way, who is that person talking to your uncle on the road?'

Barbara came to the window and, looking over the garden, she said, 'Oh, I understand her name is Moorhead, a Mrs. Moorhead. Mary refers to her as that Aggie Moorhead. She comes from somewhere near Studdon; she's working daily at the Hall doing the rough, I understand. Mary tells me they have engaged half-a-dozen such to get the place to rights before the staff arrive; but as she says, and I agree with her, it'll take six months not six weeks, and that's the time they have allowed them to clean the place down.'

'Why is your uncle talking to her?'

Barbara gave a little hunch to one shoulder as she turned from the window, saying, 'I don't suppose Uncle's talking to her, she's talking to him; to quote Mary again, she's got a loose lip.' She smiled now at Miss Brigmore, but Miss Brigmore was still looking in the direction of the road and she said, 'Your uncle's laughing.'

Barbara had been about to turn away, but she stopped and looked down at Miss Brigmore. Anna was jealous of Uncle! Well, well! It was strange, she thought, that a person could maintain jealousy into middle years. What was she now? Forty-two? No; forty-three? forty-four? Anna never talked about her age, but neverthcless she was a settled woman. She sighed heavily within herself. She wished she was over forty, for then she, too would be settled, and she was sure that by then she'd be past all feelings of jealousy and discontent—and desire. She glanced out of the window again. The Moorhead person was walking away. She was passing the lower gate and she saw that she had a jaunty walk or, what would be more expressive, a common walk; her buttocks swayed from one side to the other. As Mary had suggested, she was a very common person, low even in the working class stratum . . . .

Down on the road Thomas was thinking much the same thing. She had a lilt to her walk, that piece; she swung her hips like a cow did its udders. And she was a little cow, all right; if ever he had met one, there she went.

He had spoken to her on several occasions during the past few weeks; in fact it was she who had told him that his former home had been sold at last. After being confined to the house for days during the rough weather he had been taking the air on the road—he liked to walk on the level, he was past bobbing about on the rough fell land—and on one particular day it was she who had stopped and smiled at him as she said, 'You're Mr. Mallen, aren't you? Your old house's been sold again then.' And he had raised his brows at her and pursed his lips as he said, 'Has it indeed! has it?'

'He's a man from Manchester way they say has took it.'

'Manchester? Oh well, if he comes from there he won't stay long here. The last one came from around those parts too.'

'They say he was born this way, at least his grandparents were. Bensham they called them. He's payin' well, shillin' a day an' your grub.'

She had jerked her head at him. But her familiarity had not annoyed him, he was long past taking offence at not being given his due, because, as he so often asked himself, what, after all, was his due these days? And so with a laugh he had said, 'You are lucky then.'

'Aye,' she replied. 'Aye, I'm always lucky. Never wanted, me. Live and let live I say, an' live it well as long as you've got it 'cos you're a long time dead.'

'You've got the correct philosophy!'

'Eh?'

'You're quite right, you're a long time dead.'

'That's what I said.' She looked at him with round,
198

bright, unblinking eyes, and her lips had slowly fallen apart showing her strong white teeth, and as they, in turn, widened he had watched her tongue wobbling in her mouth. Then she gave a laugh as her head went back and in a slow movement she turned from him, saying, 'Ta-rah, then, Mister.'

He hadn't answered for a moment, but had watched her take four steps before saying, 'Good-bye.'

And she had turned her head over her shoulder and cried at him, 'An' to you.'

He had walked on down the road smiling to himself. There went a character. 'And to you,' she had said. It appertained to no part of the farewell that had passed between them, but it had sounded amusing, and meaningful. 'And to you,' she had said. She was no chicken, but what vitality! God! how he wished he were younger. No, no—he shook his head at himself—those days were gone; that past was dead and long since buried. All he wanted now was to end the time left to him quietly, with Anna herself once again. Yes, that was the important thing, Anna to be herself once again.

When he allowed himself to dwell on his past he owned that Anna was the only woman in his life who had satisfied all his needs together, for she played the roles of mistress, wife and mother to him . . . aye, and teacher, for over the past twelve years he had learned much from her, and so realised he owed her much. And at these times he asked himself why he hadn't married her. There was nothing standing in the way.

Deep within himself he knew the answer; he had been afraid that the bond of marriage would change her and he would lose the mistress and mother, and there would remain only the wife and teacher. He'd had experience of this state with his two previous wives, for they had been wives and nothing more; not that he had wanted anything more from his first marriage. It was in his second marriage that he had realised he needed something more than a bed partner, because a bed partner could be picked up any time of the night or day. Love, he had learned of recent years, had little to do with the needs of the body, yet the needs of the body were such that they couldn't be put aside. In his

199

own case he had never been able to ignore them. He considered that celibates must be a different species of man, for man, as he understood him, was born with a hunger running through his veins from the moment he felt the breast in his mouth. Here he was in his sixty-eighth year and that hunger was still on him, and of late it had become an irritation because Anna had not been strong enough to feed it. It was months since he had taken her, and it looked as though it might be as many again before she was able to come to his bed.

Of a sudden life had become full of irritations. He didn't like to admit to himself that he missed the weekly visits of his natural son, although he could admit openly that he missed the company of Constance. Yet he had never said this in Barbara's hearing, knowing that it would hurt her because Barbara was a good girl, a good woman. But she had never been a girl in the sense that Constance had been a girl. Still, she was good and kind, and Anna owed her life to her care during these past few weeks.

There was another irritation he had to suffer, and this came through Mary. Mary was a pest. He had known for a long time that the wine she drank when on her visits to her aunt was no wine at all but came from some hidden still, and although he had hinted at first, then asked her openly, but on the quiet, to bring him a bottle, she had steadfastly refused. 'Eeh! no, she had said; 'what would Miss say?' Miss would have her head. He had wanted to say, 'I'll have your head if you don't obey me,' but the days were past when he could take such a line with his one servant, for he knew that he was in her debt, and had been for years.

There was something else he had discovered about Mary that had heightened his irritation towards her. She didn't come back from her aunt's empty-handed. Coming down to the study one night not so long ago to replenish his pipe, he saw the lamp was still burning in the kitchen, and, looking in, there she was, sitting in the rocking chair before the fire, her skirts well above her knees warming her legs. Her head was lolling and she was dozing. To the side of her on the table was an empty glass. As he had lifted it from the table and
200

smelt it she had woken up, crying, 'Eeh Master! Eeh Master!', and he had nodded at her slowly as he repeated, 'Eeh Master! Eeh Master! Come on, where's the bottle? where've you got it hidden? Go and fetch it.'

She had stammered and spluttered, 'Eeh! no Master, I wouldn't. And I haven't got none hidden. I wouldn't dare bring any into the house, not a bottle I wouldn't, the Miss would be upset. I had the sniffles, I just had a drop.'

'You've got a bottle somewhere, Mary,' he said slowly. 'Come on now, where is it?'

Mary had looked at him for a moment and what she saw was a big, fat old man, with heavy jowls and a completely white head of hair, but with eyes that were still young and showing a vitality that only death would quench. With innate understanding she recognised what it must be costing this one time proud man to beg for a drink, for since Miss Brigmore had been ill there had been no hard stuff brought from the town; every spare penny was needed for extra coal to keep the house warm and a few delicacies to tempt the invalid's appetite. And all this had to be done on an income that had been cut by a quarter since Miss Constance had got married. And so she had said, as if speaking to one of her own kind, 'Well, sit you down there. Now mind, don't move, I'll be back in a minute.'

It was five minutes before she returned, and she brought him half a tumbler full of the stuff, that was all, no more, and so raw and strong it was that it seemed to rip his throat open as it went down. But it put him to sleep and gave him an easy night's rest.

And that's all she would ever give him, half a tumblerful now and again. He would go down on odd nights hoping to find her in the kitchen warming her legs, but she was crafty now, for the other would hardly retire before she went up to the attic.

And so he got into the habit of watching her whenever possible, trying to find out where she had the stuff hidden. He knew it wasn't in the house, and he had searched the outbuildings from floor to ceiling. He had an idea it was somewhere in the barn. He poked among the potatoes, the onions, the carrots and such-like in the pretence of tidying up, he poked around looking for a hole in the top of the turnip pit. There were times when his body was aching from so many needs that he pleaded with her, 'Come on, Mary, come on, just a drop,' and she would say, and truthfully, 'Master, it's all gone. Honest to God it's all gone, and there's another four days afore me leave.'

Yes, indeed, Mary was an irritation.

But over the past four weeks he had found a little diversion from the daily monotony, because when the weather was fine he'd had an exchange of words with the woman, Moorhead. That she was a trollop of the first water simply amused him; he never thought he'd have the opportunity of chatting with any of her kind ever again. Such a woman had a particular kind of dialogue, stilted, double-edged, and suggestive. He knew that this piece and himself had one thing in common, the needs of the body, and in her case she wasn't particular about who satisfied her.

When years ago he'd been able to pick and choose he would doubtless have passed her over, but now he wasn't able to pick and choose. She appeared in a way as a gift from the gods, the mountain gods, in whose fortress he was being forced to end his days. He would not allow himself to think that his thoughts were in any way disloyal to Anna; Anna was a being apart, Anna was a woman who held his life in her hands, who nourished him in all ways; at least she had up till her illness. In any case Anna had the key to his thoughts; she would have understood, for she had known what kind of man he was from the beginning; had he been made in any other but the Mallen pattern he would never have gone up to her room in the first place, and, of course, she understood this.

So gradually, over the past weeks, he had enjoyed the exchanges with the Moorhead woman, knowing exactly what they were leading to. All he needed now was a time and place. His body was too heavy to allow him to walk far; the length of the road before it bent towards the hills one way and turned towards the Hall the other was the limit of his daily exercise, so a hollow on the fells was out of the question. The only place with cover that would suit his purpose was either the stable or the barn, and both were risky; yet not so much once darkness had fallen, for neither Barbara nor Mary ventured out in the dark, except when Mary was after her bottle. But wherever the bottle was, it was certainly not in the stable or the barn, of that he had made certain.

As he now watched the buttocks wobbling away into the distance he felt his blood infusing new life into him. By God! get her on the floor and he would take some of the wobble out of her. And he could at any time from now on. She had indicated as much by the simple action of heaving up her breasts with her forearms while she looked at him with a look that did not need to be interpreted in words.

He turned about and, squaring his shoulders, walked back up the road and to the house, and he did not find it incongruous that he should immediately go upstairs to Anna.

'Ah! ah! there you are,' He almost bustled into the room. 'It's a wonderful day; pity we couldn't have got you out.'

'Did you enjoy your walk?'

'Yes and no. You know I don't like walking, but the air's good, sharp; cleans you as it goes down.'

'The woman you were talking to, who is she?'

He turned his head sharply and looked at her. 'Oh. Oh, her. You saw us? Oh, she's one of the sluts that are cleaning out the Hall; right pig-sty she says it is.'

'But I understood the new people are due in shortly.'

'Yes, yes, they are. Well'—he now nodded towards her, saying slowly, 'A right pig-sty she said it was when she first went there.' He walked to the window and looked out, and there was a silence between them for a moment until he said, 'Funny, you know, Anna, but it doesn't hurt me to know that someone is going to live there again; in fact I think I'm rather pleased. It was sad to see it dropping into decay. It's the kind of house that needs people. Some houses don't, they seem to have a self-sufficiency built into them from the beginning, but High Banks never had that quality; it was a

203

mongrel of a house, crossed by periods and giving allegiance to none, so it needed people by way of comfort.'

'You sound quite poetical, Thomas.'

He turned to her, his face bright. 'Poetical? I sound poetical? Oh, that's good coming from the teacher.' He bent over her and put his lips to her brow, then ran his forefinger through her hair, following its line behind her ears.

As she looked up at him she caught hold of his hand and pressed it against her cheek and murmured softly, 'I'll soon be myself again, have patience.'

He was now sitting in front of her, having dragged a chair quickly forward. 'Patience? Have patience? What do you mean? I've never been impatient with you.'

'I know, my dear, I know.' She bowed her head. 'But you need comfort and I'm unable to give it to you.'

'Nonsense! nonsense!' He thrust the chair back now and was on his feet again, his tone stern, even angry sounding. 'What's put such ideas into your head? You give me everything I need. Haven't I told you'—he was now bending over her—'haven't I told you that you are the only person I've really cared for in the whole of my life? God above! woman, if I've told it to you once I've told it to you a thousand times over the past years. Comfort.' His voice suddenly softened to a whisper, 'Oh, Anna, you're all the comfort I want, all the comfort I need.'

When again she brought his hand to her cheek he said in a hearty manner now, 'Another week; give yourself another week and you'll be coming down those stairs dressed in your best finery and I will have a carriage at the door and we shall drive into Hexham. Now, now, no protests.' He waved his hand before his face. 'And don't ask where the money's coming from. I've already thought up an idea that will pay for the trip. We'll take those three first editions in with us. If Barbara is right they'll be worth twenty, thirty pounds ... who knows, more. Anyway, I'm positive they'll cover our jaunt. Now what do you say?'

'I say that will be a wonderful treat, Thomas, I

should like that. And it was very thoughtful of you to think up the means whereby you could carry it out.'

He stood looking at her, his head on one side, a gentle smile on his face; and then very quietly, he said, 'You know something, Anna. You are two entirely different people; Miss Brigmore who talks like a book during the day, and Anna, the lovable woman of the night; but I love you both ... Good, good, you're blushing. Go on blushing, you look pretty when you blush.' He wagged his finger as he stepped back from her; then turning away, he went out of the room laughing.

Thomas fully intended to carry out his suggestion of taking his Anna for an outing, as also he fully intended to give the Moorhead woman a time when she could come to the barn or stable.

The following day the carrier cart brought a letter from Constance which afforded him the opportunity of bringing at least one plan to fruition.

TWO

Barbara sat next to the driver of the carrier's cart, this being the most comfortable seat. Ben Taggert had been most solicitous for her comfort; he had not only tucked a rug around her legs but had asked Mary to bring another shawl that would go over her bonnet and round her shoulders, for, as he said, you couldn't go by the weather at the foot of the hills; up there on the peaks it didn't ask any question, it just cut you in two.

And Ben Taggert's words were proved right, for as they mounted higher her breath came out of her mouth like smoke from a chimney and mingled with the steam rising from the bodies of the horses.

When they reached the edge of the plateau Ben Taggert pointed his whip, saying, 'That always amazes me, Miss, that yonder; from Lands End to John O' Groats you'll never see anything like it, nor, from what travellers tell me, in any other part of the world either. Bonnier, they'll say, prettier, but not grander. There's majesty there. Don't you think that, Miss? Majesty, that's the word. Of course there's higher ones than them hills, I admit, but it's the way they're set. And that bowl down there. One fellow I brought across here described it like this. "God," he said, "must have looked at it and thought He'd made it a little bit too rough, craggy like. And so He took His hand and smoothed out the hollow." And it was a mighty hand that did it for it's a mighty hollow. It was a good description, don't you think, Miss?'

'Very, very good, Mr. Taggert. It's a very impressive

sight; but I must admit I find it rather awe inspiring. And I shouldn't like to walk these hills alone, there's a great feeling of loneliness here.'

'Aye, there is, Miss, I'll admit that. But many do, you know. Oh aye, I see them every day. Look yonder, there's one of them.' He pointed now to the derelict house where a man was standing in the doorway, his body misshapen by his odd assortment of clothes. 'That's one of 'em.'

'What-cher there. Fine day it is.' The man's voice came to them, each word separate, sharp-edged as if it had been filed in its passage through the air.

'Aye, it's a lovely day, Charlie. But look out, it won't last; weather's changin', I saw the signs this mornin'.'

'That's right?'

'Aye, that's right, Charlie.'

Ben Taggert had not slowed the horses, the cart was still rumbling on. The man and house passed out of Barbara's vision but the memory it evoked did not leave her for some time. That was the place where it had happened! And the child that had been born last week, was it the result of that escapade or was it Donald's child? Would Constance know? She doubted it. Not until the child grew up and showed some resemblance to its male parent would the answer be given.

The letter they had received yesterday from Constance had informed them that her child had come prematurely; it had been born at three o'clock on Saturday morning. She thought that this was the result of the shock she had received when she discovered Mr. Radlet dead in the kitchen. She had come down in the night to make herself a comforting drink and she'd found him lying on the floor. The day after he was buried the child was born, a boy. She had ended her letter by saying, 'I am longing to see you, all of you, or any one of you.'

It was the 'any one of you' that was the telling phrase, and had made Miss Brigmore insist that Barbara go over the hills at the first opportunity.

She saw the farm when they were quite a distance from it; it was lying in the valley and she looked down on it. It looked like any other farm, the solid stone house, the numerous outbuildings, the walled fields surrounding it, some level over quite an area but others slopping upwards to the hills beyond.

As Ben Taggert helped her down on to the road she said to him. 'What time will you be returning?' and he replied, 'Well, I'm usually at this spot around three, but I could be a bit later the day as I've got a number of messages to do an' things to pick up. In any case it'll be well afore four o'clock 'cos I like to get clear of the hills afore dusk sets in, and home afore dark. Anyhow, Miss, I'll give you a "hello," and I won't go back without you, never fear.'

'Thank you, Mr. Taggert.'

'You're welcome, Miss.'

She took the valise from him, then turned away and walked over the rough ground to where a gateless aperture in a grey stone wall led into the farmyard. She walked slowly, looking from right to left. There was no one about. The front door to the house was away to the side; she made for the door that she guessed was most used and would lead into the kitchen. As she approached, it opened and Jane Radlet gaped at her. Then, a smile stretching her sad-looking face, she said, 'Well! well! I don't need to ask who you are, you're Barbara, aren't you?'

'Yes and you, Mrs. Radlet?'

'Yes. Come in, come in. Oh, she'll be pleased to see you. She's just gone back up the stairs this minute.'

Barbara stopped herself in the act of speaking. Constance gone back up the stairs? Constance up from her bed when the child was only seven days old? She asked hastily now, 'Is she all right?'

'Yes, yes. Weakly a bit you know, but that's to be understood; but she's all right, an' the bairn's fine. That's what she went up for, to bring him down. She'll be here in a minute. Give me your hat and coat; I'm sure you could do with a drink, it's sharp outside.'

As Barbara unpinned her bonnet and handed it to Jane she thought, What a nice woman; so thoughtful yet she must still be feeling her own sorrow.

She offered her condolences, saying, 'I was deeply sorry to hear of your loss. Mrs. Radlet.'

'Thank you. Thank you. An' it was a loss for he was a good man. But as he would have said himself, God giveth and God taketh away.' She paused before adding softly, 'I miss him.'

'I'm sure you do.'

They looked at each other for a moment; then Jane, turning abruptly away, began to bustle, saying, 'Come, sit down here, sit down by the fire.' She touched the back of the high wooden chair, and Barbara sat down. Then again they looked at each other without speaking, until Jane repeated. 'Oh, she will be pleased to see you,' and added, 'If I'd known you were comin' I would've had the fire on in the parlour.' Then looking towards the door she said, 'Where is she? Where is she? I'll go an' call her.' She nodded, smiling at Barbara, then bustled across the room and out through a door at the far end.

Barbara looked about her. Everything her eye touched on was clean and shining, showing that it had either been scoured or polished; but like the outside of the house there was a bleakness about the room. It wasn't only that the floor was made entirely of stone slabs and was sparsely covered with two clippy mats, one which lay in front of the hearth, the other placed by the side of the long wooden table that took up most of the space in the middle of the room, or that the walls were lime-washed; it was something to do with the lack of colour. The curtains on the windows flanking the door were of white Nottingham lace, and the chairs were devoid of pads or cushions; the whole room seemed dominated by a big black stove. Her eyes were brought sharply from it and towards the door as it was thrust open, and there stood Constance.

They met at the top of the table and fell into each other's arms and they held tightly, not speaking, the while Constance's body shook with her inner sobbing.

They drew apart as Jane, rocking the child gently in her arms, said, 'Here he is then. Here he is,' and Barbara turned and looked down at the swathed bundle. She stared at it for almost a minute without speaking. The child was different from what she had expected. It

209

looked all fair; it had an unusual amount of hair on its head for such a young baby, and it was fair hair. The eyes were blue, but then she understood most babies' eyes were blue to begin with, and a baby's hair often changed colour.

'He takes after his mother, he's going to be as fair as her.'

Barbara felt a little quiver inside her and she brought her eyes from the child and looked at her sister. Could it be the child was of a different fairness from Constance, a golden corn fairness such as the fairness of Matthew which would become evident later?

'How are Anna, and Uncle?'

'Oh, she's improving daily but she's still somewhat weak. But you know Anna'—she smiled—'she's made up her mind to get well, so she'll get well.'

'And Uncle?'

'Oh Uncle is still Uncle. He's had a new lease of life lately, he appears quite frisky. He's even taking exercise on his own, without being browbeaten.'

'I don't believe it.'

'Well it has to be seen to be believed, I admit.' They both gave a little laugh together, then looked towards Jane, where she was placing the child in a basket cradle, set in an alcove to the side of the fireplace, and saying as she did so, 'You must be famished, coming all this way and the wind so raw. The kettle's on the boil; I'll make you a cup of tea first and then get you a meal.'

'Oh, that's very kind of you, but a cup of tea is all I need. I'm not at all hungry, I could wait until you have your meal. Please don't put yourself out.'

'Well, you can have a griddle to put you over. But sit down, sit down and make yourself at home.' Again she motioned to a chair, and again Barbara sat down, with Constance now close to her, and like two lovers they held hands and looked at each other while Jane bustled back and forth between the table and the stove. Their silence must have told on her for she broke it by saying on a high note, 'Shall I go and tell Donald?'

'No, no.' The quick reply brought her to a standstill

and she looked at Constance, adding, 'It'll be no bother, he's up on the top field doing the wall.'

'No, no, thank you, Mam. I'll . . . we'll, we'll take a walk up there, won't we?' She turned and glanced at Barbara. 'You'd like to see round the farm, wouldn't you?'

'Yes, indeed I would.'

'That's what we'll do then, Mam. When Barbara's had her drink I'll show her round, and then we'll walk to the top field.'

'Shall I call Matthew down then?'

'I . . . I wouldn't bother. He . . . he was very tired yesterday and . . .' Her voice trailed away as the door opened and Matthew entered.

Matthew stood looking across the kitchen to where Barbara was sitting, her head turned towards him, and the high spots of colour on his cheekbones spread outwards and up on to his brow. When he came slowly across the room Barbara rose to meet him and endeavoured not to give evidence of the shock his changed appearance had on her. He had always been thin but now his body looked devoid of flesh; he had always been pale but now his skin looked transparent, his eyes had always been large but now they seemed to fill the entire bone sockets and had sunk back into his head and appeared as dark in colour as Donald's.

She was the first to speak. 'Hello, Matthew,' she said. She did not add 'How are you?'

He did not repeat her greeting but in a throaty voice said, 'This is a surprise.'

'Yes, yes; I thought I would like to come over and see the . . . the baby.' She motioned her head towards the cradle, and he turned and looked in the same direction and it was a moment before he said, 'Yes, yes.' Then he sat down on a chair near the side of the table although she was still standing; he did not, as he had been wont to do, show his manners to be those above Donald's and his own class in general, but then, of course, she thought, he was a very sick man.

'Would you like a cup of tea, Matthew?' His mother spoke to him in a gentle voice, her body bent towards him as if she were coaxing a child, and he looked at her for a moment without answering, he looked at her as if he wasn't seeing her, and then on a quick intake of breath, he said, 'Yes, yes, I'd like a cup.'

Jane poured out the tea for them all; she handed round the griddles, but only Barbara accepted one, and this out of courtesy; and it was between herself and Jane that the conversation ranged, and mostly about the weather.

'We're not finished with it yet,' Jane said, nodding her head sagely, 'not by a long chalk; there'll be another big fall, you'll see. And the wind's come up in the last hour, it's a wonder you weren't cut in two comin' over the top.'

'It was very keen.'

'Yes, I should say it was. It's years since I was up there in the winter, an' I have no desire to go, it's breezy enough in the summer. You going out now?' She turned to where Constance had risen from the chair, Constance replied, I'm . . . I'm just going to get my cloak.'

'Perhaps your sister might like to go upstairs with you, she might like to see the house, would you?'

It was evident to Barbara that this kindly woman was very proud of her house. It was all a matter of values, but then, the other rooms might show some comfort. She said quite brightly, 'Yes, yes, I would; I'm very interested in old houses.'

'There now, there now. Then take her up with you, Constance.'

The sisters looked at each other for a moment before going out of the room together like children obeying a bidding.

The hall they went into was dark, having only one small window next to the door. The oak staircase mounted steeply from opposite the door, and Constance took hold of Barbara's hand and guided her up it and on to the landing. Here it was lighter, being illuminated by a long window at the far end. She noted that there was no article of furniture on the landing, not even a table on which to place a lamp. Then Constance was opening a door, and she was in her bedroom.

She had often imagined Constance's bedroom and in the early days the thought of it had been bitter to her mind. Now that she was in the last shreds of jealousy she had felt towards Constance seeped from her, for here, and reflected deeply, she saw the same starkness as the kitchen, and part of her mind wondered why it should be so, because Constance had an artistic sense; it was she who had gone a long way towards making the rooms in the cottage not only comfortable but pretty.

Alone together now, they did not throw themselves into each other's arms once more but stood somewhat apart, each gazing at the other, waiting.

It was Barbara who spoke first. When Constance lowered her head and extended her hands towards her she gripped them, saying, 'What is it? You don't look well. What possessed you to get up so early? Shouldn't you be in bed for some days yet?'

Constance now drew Barbara to a wooden seat that was placed beneath the window and they sat down before she answered, 'One is not pampered on this side of the hills. A cow walks about immediately after calving, so what's the difference between us?'

Barbara was startled, not only by the bitterness in Constance's voice but by the context of her reply. She moved nearer to her and, putting her arms about her, she asked, 'Aren't you happy?'

'Oh Barbie!' Constance was now pressing herself tightly against her, her hands clutching at her as if she were drowning, and Barbara whispered in concern, 'What is it, what is it? Oh my dear, tell me, what is it? Tell me.'

And Constance might have told her if at that moment a voice had not risen from the yard calling loudly to a dog, saying, 'Leave it Prince. Leave it. Here! Here, I tell you.' It caused her to raise her head and look sharply towards the window. Then withdrawing herself from Barbara's hold, she got to her feet and began smoothing down her hair, then the front of her bodice, and the folds of her skirt over her slender hips; finally, she brought her hands to her waist where her fingers plucked at each other as she said, 'We'd . . .

213

we'd better go down, that's him—I mean Donald. He must have finished in the top field. It'll save us walking and . . . and you've seen the room.' She now flung one arm wide, then stopped abruptly and turned and faced Barbara again and, her voice dropping low in her throat, she repeated, 'You've seen the room. She . . . I mean Mam, she thinks it's nice, and it is to her. She' . . . she's very good to me; I don't know what I would have done without her.'

Constance was at the door, the latch in her hand, but Barbara, after standing up, hadn't moved from the window seat. She said now in a whisper, 'You're not happy, what is it?'

Constance bit on her lip, swallowed deeply, and her chin gave a nervous jerk before she said, 'Is anyone happy? Do you know of anyone who is really happy?'

'We were happy at one time.'

'At one time, yes.' Constance now nodded slowly. 'The only trouble is we never recognise real happiness when we have it.'

'But . . . but Donald, Donald loves you.' She found it surprising that it didn't pain her to say this aloud, and when she saw Constance close her eyes tightly she said again, 'What is it?' and now she moved swiftly towards her. But before she reached her Constance had opened the door; then they were on the landing, then going down the stairs, silent again.

Donald was in the kitchen when they entered and he greeted her heartily as if he were pleased to see her. 'Well, well! look what the wind's blown in,' he said, coming towards her with hand outstretched. 'What's brought you to this neck of the woods, eh, on a day like this with the wind enough to stiffen you?'

'Oh, I wanted to see the baby and find out how Constance was.'

'Oh!' The exclamation was high. 'You knew about the baby then?' He turned and glanced in Constance's direction and Barbara noticed that she didn't look at him and say, 'Yes, I wrote,' so it was left to her to explain, and she did it as casually as possible, saying, 'Yes, Constance sent me a note. And oh, by the

214

way'—she turned to Constance now who was at the table laying it for a meal—'I brought some things for the baby. Not knowing if it were going to be a boy or a girl we knitted white.' She went towards the valise where it lay just as she had left it by the side of the chair and, opening it, she drew out first a white shawl, then a variety of socks, bonnets and coats.

'Oh!' Jane exclaimed delightedly as she fingered the shawl. 'Oh, it's beautiful and so soft. This was knitted with fine wool; indeed it was. And look at the wee boots. Aw! did you ever see anything so dainty, did you now Constance?'

'No, they are lovely. Thank you, thank you, Barbara. And thank Anna for me too. What a lot of work it must have taken.'

'It was a pleasure.' Their eyes held for a moment longer! then Jane put in, 'Well, you came with a full bag an' you'll go with a full bag. You must take some butter, an' cheese, and eggs back with you.'

'Thank you. . . .'

During the next hour Barbara noticed a number of things. Matthew never uttered a word, Constance only spoke when necessary, and Jane never stopped chattering. But it was a nervous chattering. Her face sad, she kept up a constant conversation as if with herself.

When they sat down to the meal no one sat at the head of the table. Donald sat to the side with Constance opposite him; Jane sat at the bottom of the table with Matthew to her left; but although the chair at the top was empty Barbara had no doubt who was master of this house. Not only had Donald been served first but Jane ministered to him with a deference that she might have extended towards her husband, except that this deference held a nervous quality.

Barbara wondered how the farm had been divided. There would surely have been a will; she must ask Constance.

The food itself was rather tasteless. It was a stew that had been well stewed and surprisingly without herbs. But that didn't trouble her; what did was the atmosphere at the table. To say it was strained was not adequate, tense would have been a better description.

One other thing she noticed. Although Donald brought a smile to his face now and again, it never touched his eyes. When she had loved him—she noted with relief that she was using the past tense with regards to her affection towards him—she had never seen him look as he did now. His eyes were like pieces of slaty coal, their blackness was a dull blackness. She wondered now how she had allowed herself to become so attached to him. Perhaps because he had flattered her by appealing to her mind. Yes, that was it. Pride, pride.

Before the meal was over she was thinking, I could not have endured this any more than Connie is doing. Poor Connie. Poor, poor Connie.

Rising from the table, Jane said. 'I'll light a fire in the parlour.' She did not look towards Donald as she spoke, yet it was as if it were a question directed towards him, a question that required an answer, an answer giving permission, and when the answer was not forthcoming immediately Barbara put in quickly, 'Please don't trouble on my account; Mr. Taggert will be here with the cart around three he told me, and it is near two o'clock now.'

'Oh, well then, well then.' Jane nodded at her, then bustled around the table gathering up the dishes.

It was at this point that Constance went to the cradle and lifted up the baby and was moving towards the kitchen door leading into the hall when she was stopped by Donald saying, 'Where you going?'

Constance turned slowly and for the first time since coming into the room she looked straight at him, and her voice had a note of defiance in it as she answered, 'I am going to feed the child.'

'There's plenty of room here, isn't there?' He jerked his head in the direction of the empty chairs bordering the fireplace.

Their eyes held, the silence in the kitchen emphasised the sound of the wind buffeting the house, and as Constance turned about and walked out of the room Jane exclaimed loudly, 'Do you hear that? It's gettin' worse.'

Ignoring his mother's remark, Donald looked now at

Barbara and said on a thin laugh, 'You can carry modesty too far; what's more natural than feedin' a bairn, I've told her.'

Matthew seemed to have risen clumsily from the table for his chair toppled backwards and hit the stone floor, but as he went to right it Donald was there before him and, swinging it up with one hand, he stood it on its feet, saying on another thin laugh, 'You want to take more water with it, lad.'

Matthew now looked up under his lids at Barbara; then in a voice as tight as the smile on his face he said. 'I'll say good-bye. I'm glad to have seen you. Give my regards to Miss Brigmore, will you, and to your Uncle?'

'I will, Matthew, I will.' She held out her hand, and he took it. It felt like a piece of damp dough in her grasp and she was glad to relinquish it.

Donald was now standing with his back to the fire, his coat tails divided, letting the heat fan his buttocks. She had often seen her Uncle Thomas stand like that. It was the stance of the master of the house, and it was as if Donald were acting out his part for her. After a moment he asked, 'How are things across there?'

'Oh, very well. Mary and I have re-decorated the sitting room for when Anna comes downstairs. We've had a boy come all the summer in the evenings to do the garden; it's in very good shape. We had two cartloads of wood brought; and he has sawn it up. We're all prepared for an extended cold spell, should it come.'

Her answer did not seem to please him, he made no reply to it; and when there came the sound of a bucket being tumbled across the yard by the wind he made it as an excuse to take his leave, saying, 'Well, somebody's got to work round here, so I'll say good-bye to you.'

'Good-bye, Donald.' She nodded politely towards him, then added, 'Will you be bringing Constance across soon, Uncle would like to see the child?'

He had his back to her, walking towards the kitchen door as he said, 'I doubt it; she's afraid of storms, as you know.'

'But the fine weather's coming, there are periods when there won't be any sign of a storm.' She had risen to her feet.

'She's also afraid of the heights. Didn't you know?' At the door he turned and looked towards her.

'The heights?'

'Yes, the heights; terrified of heights, she tells me. Apparently there are lots of things about her you didn't know if you didn't know that.'

As she stared at him across the dim kitchen she thought, He's cruel.

'Good-bye, Barbara.'

She didn't answer, and he went out, having to pull the door closed behind him against the force of the wind.

When she sat down, Jane began to chatter again. She chatted about the cattle, the butter-making, the cheese-making; she referred to her husband as if he were still alive; and every now and again she looked towards the window and said, 'Eeh! that wind.'

It was almost twenty minutes later when Constance returned. Putting the baby once again into the cradle, she smiled at Barbara before saying to Jane, 'What will I do, the dishes, or the dairy?'

'You'll do neither, my dear, just you sit here with your sister and have a nice talk, you don't see each other that often. Now sit yourself down.'

Constance sat down at the opposite side of the fireplace to where Barbara was sitting, and they looked towards Jane, who was now standing over the shallow brown stone sink which was full of dishes; then they looked at each other again, and their eyes said, 'What shall we talk about?'

For the next half-hour they talked small talk. Barbara learned that the child was to be named Michael, after his step-grandfather. Constance learned that the Hall had been sold again, and that it was being cleaned up by a small regiment of workers, one of whom was named Aggie Moorhead, a very forward piece who wasn't above stopping Uncle and chatting with him.

By three o'clock Barbara was ready and waiting to hear Ben Taggert's call, and when a quarter of an hour had passed she said anxiously, 'I wonder if he's gone on? Perhaps we didn't hear him call because of the wind.'

'Oh, no.' Jane shook her head. 'Ben would come over an' knock you up. Ben would never go on without a passenger once he had made arrangements. Oh no, that's not Ben. . . . Listen, do you hear? There he is.'

Barbara strained her ears and heard a faint, 'Hello there. Hello there.'

Jane now grabbed up the valise and went out and for a moment Barbara and Constance were alone again. As they had done on first meeting, they enfolded each other tightly, and once again Barbara felt her sister's body tremble and she heard her murmer as if in agony of mind. 'Oh Barbie! Barbie!'

Hand in hand now they went out, their bodies bent against the wind, and when they reached the road Jane had already handed Ben Taggert the valise and he had put it in the back of the cart where there was an assortment of bundles and boxes and a bird in a cage.

'If you would like it better I could push them all asidc'—Ben nodded to the back of the cart—'you'd be more sheltered there.'

'Oh, I'll be all right riding with you, Mr. Taggert.'

'It's going to be rough, Miss, the higher we get, you know that. Still, if you change your mind we can always stop. Come on then.'

Quickly now Barbara turned again to Constance and, taking her face between her hands, she stared at her for a moment before kissing her on the lips; then she shook Jane by the hand and thanked her once more for the dairy produce she had put into the valise, and also for her hospitality.

Sitting high up in the front of the cart she looked down on Constance's upturned face. With an impulsive movement she reached down holding out her hand, and when her sister's hand gripped hers she felt such pain in her heart as she never thought to experience again. It was a more intense pain than she had known a year ago, a different pain, it could have been a pain of farewell. She made herself smile, but it was a smilc weighed with sadness, it was as if she knew she would never smile again.

The return journey was eventful with moments that created terror in her, such as the one when the wind seemed to lift the whole cart and the animals from the road and to tip them into a shallow hollow to the side of the rising hill. That they all landed the right way up seemed nothing short of a miracle to her. What had happened was that the horses and cart were blown to the side and left contact with the ground in going over the shallow ditch.

Once on the road again, Barbara, still shaking from her experience, realised that perhaps she was lucky to be able to feel the trembling of her body at all, for if they had been blown the other way then surely they would have rolled down the steeply wooded hillside to the valley below. The safety posts that were spaced at intervals along this stretch of the road and threaded by a wire would not have prevented them from being hurled over the edge to be bounced from one tree trunk to another until they reached the bottom.

Another time she found herself clinging to Mr. Taggert's arm. It was most embarrassing, at least to her. She saw his head nodding in assurance, and knew that he was yelling something at her, but she could not distinguish anything he was saying, for his words were carried away on the wind.

When, for a few minutes, there was a lull, he shouted at her, 'I've known some trips but this one'll take a beatin'. Give me snow any time. But don't you worry, don't you worry, Miss, Jake 'n' Fred'll make it; they're as sure-footed as mountain goats.' It was a pity, she thought, that she hadn't his faith in Jake and Fred.

If anything, the storm increased in violence as they descended to lower ground, and it was almost as dark as night when finally Ben Taggert helped her down from the cart and handed her the valise. She thanked him warmly and said she would never forget the journey and he laughed at her and said, 'You must try it in a blizzard, Miss; that's what you must do, try it in a blizzard. Go on now, yet yersel inside quick. Good-night to you.'

Her reply was lost to him. The cart moved past her, and holding down the shawl that covered her bonnet with one hand and carrying the valise in the other, she fought her way to the gate. But when she went to push it open she found it was held fast. In peering forward she realized that the obstacle holding it closed was a branch of the rowan tree that had stood in the front garden for years. The whole tree had been blown down.

Her body bent, she made her way to the lower gate which led into the yard. The noise of the wind was beating on her eardrums with a force almost equal to that on the heights; in fact, the wind seemed to have increased in fury, which she would have thought impossible a short while ago.

When some object rattled across the path in front of her she fell forward and would have gone on her face had not the end wall of the outbuilding saved her. She stood leaning against it for a moment, thankful that she had it as a guide for it was like night now. She decided to keep near the wall and to skirt the yard until she reached the kitchen door, for if she crossed the yard her feet would likely be whipped from beneath her.

On this side of the yard facing the house was the wood shed, stables, and lastly the barn. There was a narrow passage between the corner of the barn and the wall of the wash-house which led into the vegetable garden. The wash-house itself was connected to the scullery and larder, which were single-storey buildings, and going off at right angles from the end of these was the house proper.

She had groped her way as far as the barn when her passage was stopped abruptly by two hands grabbing her, and after the first moment of shock she sighed with relief and leant against the bulky figure of her Uncle Thomas. He held her close, protectingly, he held her so close that she dropped the valise onto the ground.

Protecting her further, he pulled her inside the barn, where the noise seemed intensified, for the old timbers were rattling like castanets. She went to shout to him,

221

'Isn't it dreadful?' but he hugged her with a compulsive movement and her breath was taken from her body by a force even stronger than the wind. What was the matter with Uncle? Was he having convulsions? Was he ill? And why . . . why was he out in the storm? It was madness for him to be out, for anyone to be out on a night like this, unless they were compelled.

'Oh, Uncle! Uncle!' She heard herself screaming, but only in her head, for her breath had been knocked out of her again as she was borne backwards. What was happening? What was the matter? It . . . it was her uncle? Of course it was her uncle. She knew by the size of his body it was her uncle. She knew by the odour of him it was her uncle. That particular odour of tobacco and rough tweed and stale wine, a not unpleasant odour and definitely peculiar to him, for no other of her acquaintances smelt like this. But he also smelt strongly of spirits.—OH MY GOD! MY GOD! SHE MUST BE GOING INSANE, IT COULDN'T BE. She began to fight him, to struggle madly, and it appeared to her that of a sudden the wind had transported her into a lunatic asylum because her uncle was also struggling with her, tearing at her undergarments, actually tearing them from her.

NO! NO! NO! OH JESUS, LORD OF ALL THE EARTH, WHAT WAS HAPPENING TO HER! The weight on her body—She couldn't breathe—She could struggle no longer—She had gone mad, for this thing could not be happening to her. She made one more effort. She dug her nails deep into the flesh of his neck, she couldn't get near his face for it was covering hers.

At the moment her body was shot through with torture, and her mind, standing apart as it were from her, told her that this was death, the death of decency, of self-respect, of love of family life—of life itself.

When the pressure on her body was released she lay still in what seemed comparative silence, for the storm seemed to have held its breath for a moment. Then as it released another blast she let out an ear-splitting scream; then another; then another; on and on and no hand came over her mouth to check her; not until a lantern swung above her did she stop. Her eyes wide, she stared up into the light. She could not see the face above it, or who else was present, not until the lamp swung to the side did she see the grey dishevelled bulk of her Uncle Thomas. His body seemed to fill the barn. He looked like a deranged giant. Then the lantern swung again, and she saw the figure of a woman running through the light and towards the open door. Then she heard Mary screaming. 'God Almighty!' was what she was screaming. She screamed it a number of times.

Then Mary, dropping onto her knees, lifted Barbara's stiff head and shoulders from the ground and, cradling her, she repeated her cry, 'Oh, God Almighty! Oh, God Almighty!' Then after a moment, her voice breaking with her sobbing, she cried, 'Come on, get up out of this, me bairn. Get up out of this. Come on, come on.' And Barbara got up and allowed herself to be led from the barn and into the house. . . .

Thomas watched them go. He was leaning against a beam to the side of the door. The lantern was still on the ground. He looked towards it. His eyes stretched wide, his mouth agape, he seemed to see himself reflected in it, an obese, dirty old man, a filthy old man. He was so repulsive in his own sight that his stomach revolted and he turned his head to the side and retched, bringing up the entire meal he had eaten only an hour before at the same table as Anna.

Anna! Anna! Anna! . . . Barbara! Oh, Christ Almighty!

His mind now went completely blank for a moment and shut off from his consciousness the act he had perpetrated. When it moved again it pulled him from the support of the beam and turned him about and he staggered from the barn out into the wind.

When he reached the kitchen door the blast almost drove him through it. There was no one in the room. He closed it, holding on first to the table and to the chairs for support; then he was in the hall, and in the lamplight he saw Anna coming down the stairs. She stopped and he stopped; they looked at each other for a long moment and the misery their eyes exchanged was unfathomable.

When he could no longer face the pain in her eyes he bowed his head and stumbled towards his study. Once inside he locked the door. Going to the wall above the fireplace he took down his gun and, placing it on the desk with the barrel pointing towards the chair, he released the safety catch, then sitting himself in the chair he leant forward, and as he did so the handle of the door was gently turned. He did not look towards it but put his finger on the trigger and pulled.

BOOK V

MATTHEW

ONE

The scandal surrounding Thomas Mallen's death would, the self-righteous in the surrounding countryside said, not die down for many a year, seeing he had left living proof of it in a young woman whom he had brought up like a daughter.

It was Aggie Moorhead who had made it impossible to put any version but the true one on Thomas's death. She had looked upon the mix-up between his niece and herself as the best joke in the world, until the girl had begun to scream. Then, when the news spread that old Mallen had shot himself the story made her the centre of attraction, not only locally but with those men who came from the newspapers.

And the newspapers didn't just deal with the incident either, they delved into Thomas Mallen's whole past and it made quite exciting reading. Even though he had been living in retirement for the past twelve years, being a Mallen, he hadn't lived alone but had taken for his mistress the governess of his two nieces, and what made things more interesting still, they stated that one of his nieces had married his natural son.

Yet even with all this, the nine-days' wonder might have died a natural death if the gardener boy hadn't observed the rising globe of Miss Barbara's stomach, and this on the first occasion he had caught sight of her in five months. This latter fact did not appear in the papers but the hill telegraph was just as efficient in spreading it around the countryside.

This particular piece of news came to Donald's ears

in the market place and he couldn't get back quickly enough to the farm to throw it at Constance.

It was three months since he had allowed her over the hills, and then he had escorted her himself on that occasion, as on the former occasion when that old cow of a Brigmore had sent him the news that Mallen was dead. He hadn't found out how he died until he had entered the cottage. He hadn't seen Barbara at all, not then, and not since.

And now he had learned that she had her belly full of the old man. The Mallen image died hard. By God! it did. And that lot in the market laughing up their sleeves at him. By Christ! he'd let them see who they were laughing at afore he was finished. He'd show them. He'd get land, and more land; he'd drag the respect out of them, then spit in their eyes.

And there was another thing he'd tell his lady wife when he got in: she was bringing that fifty pounds a year over the hills; there wasn't the old man to keep now, and he could do with another fifty a year. Yes, by God! he could. She had stood out against him on this, openly defied him, in fact. She was getting brave over certain things, but she'd better be careful. He hadn't lifted his hand to her yet but there was plenty of time for it.

Sometimes he thought he could have forgiven her the other business if she had been good to him, shown a little affection, but what she had shown him from that very first night couldn't be given any other name but scorn; at times it even overrode her fear of him. Inside her, she looked down her nose at him, and the farm and the house. She got on with his mother because she saw it as policy to keep on the right side of her. And yet that wasn't all there was to it. He suspected, and had for some time now, that there was something between them, a sort of understanding. Whatever it was, the relationship irritated him, for if there was anybody she should look down upon it was his mother who, in her turn, had been a slut. But as they said, birds of a feather, no matter from what class, recognized each other. She even turned her nose up at Matthew; she hardly opened her mouth to Matthew.

Matthew'd had a new lease of life these past few months. Perhaps it was due to the unusually dry warm weather. Netherthless his time was fast running out for he was no thicker than two laths, and though his cough had eased a bit, the blood came more often. His manner too had changed in the last year or so. He supposed it was his illness, for he could get hardly a word out of him either nowadays. There was a sullenness about him, perhaps because he knew that death was galloping on him; it wasn't good for a man to see death before it actually came.

He flapped the reins briskly and put the horse into a trot. The cart bumped over the rough road and the dust rose in clouds about him.

When he came to the junction of two roads he took the left hand one. This would mean a longer run to the farm, but it might save an axle; on the outward journey he'd had to take the cart through a new subsidence in the road and this had strained it. He'd made a note in his mind to bring a load of stone and fill in the hole.

The road he was on now was a prettier one, it wound its way through woodland and shady lanes, and the open ground was moulded into small hills where the sheep grazed, a burn ran down the valley and there was a rocky outcrop over which the water tumbled so that you could fairly give it the name of a waterfall.

He rarely came by this road, he hadn't time for scenery. All the scenery that interested him was within the stone walls of his farm. . . . And it was HIS farm.

Michael had left no will. By law the place was Matthew's, but by right of work it was his, and let anyone try to say it wasn't. It had never been a bad farm, but it was he who had made a good one into a better, and from now on he meant to turn it into a rich farm . . . and a rich man's farm.

He passed by the side of a small copse that threw the path into shadow and when he emerged he blinked into the sun for a moment, then screwed up his gaze to take in two figures sitting some distance away in the shade of a mound. With a soft word of command and a

229

tug on the reins he drew the horse to a halt, and his eyes narrowed to slits as he peered into the distance.

If he had failed to recognize the couple the sound that now came to his ears would have identified at least one of them. Not once since they were married had he heard Constance laugh, and the reason for hearing her laugh now was that the child's hands were pulling at her nose. He had seen the child doing this before, but it certainly hadn't brought any laughter from her. He had caught her smiling at it, but this would be when he happened on her unawares.

Then he witnessed something that caused a pain to rip through him, as if his body had been licked by a fierce flame. She had passed the child to Matthew and Matthew was holding him up in the air above his head and shaking him from side to side; then lowering him down, he folded him against his chest and rocked him backwards and forwards, as only a mother, or a father might do.

What he saw next was Constance hitching herself forward and soothing the child's hair back while Matthew still held it. What he was looking at was the cameo of a family.

He was numb. The pain seared all the nerves in his body. It now passed the bearing point, and for a moment he felt nothing; there followed a blessed period of time when all emotion was dead in him.

But the numbness melted, the space filled, and now there swept into him and over him with the force of a mighty wave a feeling of such hatred that if they had been within arm's length of him at that moment he would have murdered them both.

It was a gentle neigh from the horse that caused them to turn their heads in his direction, but they could not see either him or the cart. In the shadow of the trees he watched them remain still for a moment peering towards the road; then there was a quick exchange of words before they got to their feet, she carrying the child now, and they went down the field and made for the gate that led into the extreme corner of the farmland.

Not until they were out of sight did he lead the horse

forward, and then he took it from the road and tied its bridle to a tree, after which he walked a short distance and lay down in some long grass. There, at full length, he stared unblinking into the soil while he tore up handfuls of grasses and snapped them into small pieces. After a while, as if his body had suddenly been dropped from a height, he slumped into the earth and with his hand under his mouth he bit on the pad of his thumb until the blood came. . . .

Fifteen minutes later when he entered the house, the baby was in the pen outside the dairy and Jane was in the kitchen, her arms in a bowl of flour. She looked at him as if in surprise, saying, 'You're back early.'

'Where's Matthew?'

'Matthew! Oh, he's in bed. You know he always goes to bed in the afternoon.' She dusted the flour from her hands and turned her back on him and went towards the oven.

He had the urge to pick up the heavy rolling pin from the table and batter her on the head with it. She knew, she knew! They must all have been laughing up their sleeves at him all this time, the three of them. Why? Why hadn't he twigged anything before? He was seeing things now as plainly as a blind man who had been given his sight. That day Matthew had gone over the hills for her and the storm was supposed to have frightened her and he had taken her back, it had happened then. But Matthew had changed towards him lomg before that. And he could pinpoint the date. It was from the Sunday morning, in this very room, when he had told them he was going to ask her to marry him. God above! Christ Almighty! Why had he been so blind?

The answer was simple. He had trusted Matthew, because he had loved Matthew. Matthew was the only other person in the world besides her he had loved, and they had both fooled him, right up to this very day they had fooled him. If God Himself had come and told him before he had seen them together he wouldn't have believed it, because they never spoke to each other. . . . Not when he was about . . . No, that was it, not when he was about.

And his mother, that old bitch there. No wonder they were all thick. He could murder the three of them. He could take a knife and go from one to the other and slit their throats. But where would that get him? The gallows. No, there'd be no gallows for him, he had paid enough for being who he was; but by God! somebody was going to pay for this. He would play them at their own game. Christ? how he would play them. The cat and the mouse wouldn't be in it. He would make them think he knew, then make them think he didn't. He'd give them such hell on earth they'd wish they were dead, all of them. Well, one of them soon would be, but he'd make a vow this minute he wouldn't let him go until he had told him that he hadn't been so bloody clever after all. He'd see he tasted hell afore he died; he'd play him like a tiddler on a pin; he'd play them all like tiddlers on a pin, and he'd begin right now.

As if answering an order, he turned and stamped out of the kitchen, across the yard and into the dairy. She was standing at the far end with her back to him, and even at this moment the sight of her slender form made him ache. She had half turned as the door opened and then turned away again, and he came up behind her and stood close and did not speak until, pressing herself against the stone slab, she slid away from him before turning to face him, her face stiff as always when she confronted him.

'It's a grand day,' he said. 'You should be out in the sunshine with the child.'

She continued to stare at him before she answered quietly, 'You have allotted me duties; you would doubtless have something to say if I didn't carry them out.'

'Yes, yes, doubtless I would.' He nodded his head at her, then went on in a casual tone. 'I heard a bit of news in the market, caused some belly laughs it did. That's funny, belly laughs. Barbara is five months gone. The old man worked well up to the last. What do you say?'

He watched the colour drain from her cheeks, her mouth opened and shut in a fish-like gape; then he turned from her and was near the door of the dairy

232

before he looked towards her again and added, 'By the way, I was talkin' to a young doctor in the market, I was tellin' him I had a son and about my half-brother being a consumptive. I said there was none of the disease on my side, not that I knew of, and could it be caught like, and he said, aye, it was better not to let the child come in contact with anybody who has the disease, so if I was you I'd break it to Matthew, eh? You can do it better than me, put it more gently like.'

He watched her for a moment as she leaned back against the slab for support; then he went out well satisfied with the result of his new tactics. He would get something out of this, something that would be more satisfying then sticking a knife in their necks. Although one of these days, when he had her on his own, he mightn't be able to prevent himself from doing just that.

TWO

When Mary opened the door and saw a small, neatly dressed man standing there and, beyond him, on the road a hired cab with the driver slapping his arms about himself as he stamped his feet, she thought, another of them. What's this one after now?' And that is what she said to him, 'What are you after now?' She did not add. 'There's nothing new happened for you to put in your papers.'

'Is this Mr. Mallen's home, I mean the late Mr. Mallen?'

'Yes, it is; you know quite well it is.'

The small man raised his eyebrows slightly before saying, 'I should like to speak with your mistress.'

'She's not seein' nobody, neither of them."

There was a slight look of bewilderment on the man's face and he didn't speak for a moment, but surveyed Mary; then he said quietly, 'My name is Stevens, I am Chief Clerk to Maser, Boulter & Pierce, Solicitors, of Newcastle. I have some business I would like to discuss with your mistress. Please give her this.' He held out a square of card, and she took it, glanced at it, then back at him before saying in a more moderate tone. 'Well, come in then.'

In the hall she hesitated whether to leave him standing there or to show him into the breakfast room, the room that had once been the schoolroom. She decided to leave him standing there. Then giving him a look as much as to say, don't you move, she went towards a door, tapped on it, then opened it immediately.

In the room she tip-toed almost at a run across it and, coming to Miss Brigmore, where she was sitting by the fire unpicking the skirt of the last of Barbara's dresses in order to make it fit her during the late months, she whispered. 'There's a man here—not a gentleman, yet he's not one of them—he's from a solicitor's. Look.' She thrust the card at Miss Brigmore and noticed that she hesitated before taking it. She had been like that ever since . . . the business, hesitant about any contact with those outside. Well, she was like that herself; she hadn't got over the shock yet and her conscience still worried her, especially at night. She still wondered if it all would have happened if the master hadn't found her hidey-hole. He must have drunk a whole bottle, for that very night she had found it empty. Nothing worse could have happened if he had drunk the two bottles, but being the man he was he had taken only one and left her the other. Oh, the master, the poor, poor master. She was still sorry for him, she couldn't help but be sorry for him. And she was sorry for herself an' all because the business had put her off the stuff and there was no comfort anywhere, no, not anywhere, for this house that had once been merry and full of laughter, in spite of having to stretch every farthing to its utmost, was now as quiet as a cemetery.

'Show him in, Mary.'

Miss Brigmore slowly rolled up the dress and laid it in the corner of the couch and she was rising as slowly to her feet when the man entered.

From his manner and appearance she, too, knew that he wasn't 'one of them.' She looked at the card and said, 'Will you take a seat, Mr. Stevens?'

'Thank you, Ma'am.' He motioned with a gentle movement of his hand that she should be seated first.

When they were seated facing each other she said, 'It's a very raw day'; and he answered, 'Yes, it is indeed, Ma'am.' Then coughing twice, he went on, 'I won't intrude on your time more than is necessary. My firm is wishful to trace on your next-of-kin of the late Mr. Thomas Mallen and thought perhaps coming directly to his home would be the surest way of getting in touch with his relatives.'

'For what purpose?' Her back was straight, her voice was almost that of the old Miss Brigmore, and he, sensing her distrust, was quick to put her mind at ease, saying, 'Oh it would be something to their advantage, I should explain. Mr. Mallen had a son, Richard, that is so?'

'Yes.'

'Well, apparently Mr. Richard Mallen has sojourned in France for some years, but under an assumed name. This was the difficulty the French lawyers encountered when dealing with his estate. They eventually gleaned that he had left this country under troubled circumstances, and so their enquiries were slow and cautious, but recently they contacted us through a French associate we have in Paris, and asked us to ascertain the whereabouts of Monsieur le Brett's relatives.' Mr. Stevens again coughed twice before continuing, 'We became acquainted with the fact that Mr. Thomas Mallen had died intestate, unfortunately only a fortnight after his son's death.'

Miss Brigmore now said, 'He has two nieces, one is married and one still lives here.'

'No closer relatives? He was married twice, I understand.'

'Yes his two sons by his first wife died. He has a daughter, she's in Italy.'

'Ah, a daughter in Italy. May I ask if you have her address?'

'Yes, yes, I have her address.'

Yes, she had Bessie's address. She had written to her telling her briefly of the tragedy, and what had she received in return—a letter full of bitterness. They had scarcely got over the '51 affair. Did she know that it had even got into the Italian papers? Alfo was angry, his people were angry, she had barely lived down the disgrace of her father being turned out of his home for debts, and her brother almost killing a man of the law, and now this—well, they said there was a curse on the Mallens. . . .

There was indeed a curse on the Mallens, and all connected with them. If the last Mallen had married her, if Thomas had married her, this man would not be searching for his nearest relative at this moment. She asked quietly, 'Did he leave a large fortune?'

'No, when the recipient eventually receives it, it will amount to about two thousand five hundred pounds, somewhere in that region. There has been a great deal of expense incurred—You can understand. . . .'

No muscle of her face moved; not a considerable fortune, two thousand five hundred pounds! and they were now reduced to living on a hundred pounds a year. Their meals, other than Thomas's, had been frugal for a long time, for she had seen to it that he always had the pick of what was to be had, and when she became ill Barbara had continued along the same lines. . . . Poor Barbara, poor Barbara. She dared not think too much of Barbara's plight or her whole being would disintegrate in pity.

She thought in justifiable bitterness now that if anyone had earned Dick Mallen's legacy it was herself. Her cheating of the bailiffs had not only helped to get him out of prison but had likely afforded him a basis, through the selling of the snuff box and cameos, to start some nefarious business. But there, that was life, and life was bitter, like alum on the tongue, and she couldn't see time washing it away.

She rose saying, 'I will get you the address,' then she added, courteously, 'Can I offer you some refreshment?' As she watched his head move to the side and a thin smile appear on his face she added hastily, 'A cup of tea maybe?'

The smile slid away, his head shook. 'It's very kind of you,' he said, 'but I shan't trouble you; I had breakfast late and my dinner is awaiting me at the hotel, as also is the cab man.' He smiled again, and she went out of the room to see Mary scurrying towards the kitchen door.

In the study she took Bessie's letter from the desk drawer, copied the name and address onto a piece of paper, then going back into the drawing room, she handed it to Mr. Steven's.

'Thank you, Ma'am; I'm much obliged.' He looked down at the address written on the paper. Then, his eyebrows jerking upwards, he repeated, 'Countess.

Well, well! I don't suppose two thousand five hundred pounds will mean much to her.

He walked past her now as she held the front door open, and he doffed his hat and bowed to her, and he noted she did not close the door until he had entered the cab.

The door closed, she did not return to the drawing room but went into the study, and Mary coming into the hall and hearing the study door click shut stopped for a moment, looked towards it, then returned to the kitchen. That was one room she never barged into. When Miss went in there she wasn't to be disturbed. It had become a sort of unwritten law. She sat down by the kitchen table and, laying her hands on it, she joined them tightly together and, bending her head over them, she shook it from side to side. Two thousand five hundred pounds going to that Miss Bessie, and her an upstart if ever there was one, she'd never written to her father for years. Eeh! things weren't right.

She started visibly when the kitchen door opened and Barbara entered. She was wearing a long coat and had a shawl over her head.

Rising quickly, Mary went towards her, saying, 'Eeh! Miss Barbara, you'll get your death, I thought you were never coming back. Here, come and get warm.' She drew her towards the fire, pulling off her gloves as she did so; then taking the shawl from her head as if she were undressing a child she pressed her into a chair and, kneeling beside her, began to chafe her hands, talking all the while. 'You're froze. Aw, you're froze, lass; you'll do yourself an injury, an'—she stopped herself from adding 'the one you're carrying' and went on, 'You can't walk quick enough to keep yourself warm. You shouldn't go out, not on a day like this; wait till the sun comes out.'

'Who was that, Mary?'

'Oh. Oh, you saw him. Well, you won't believe it, you won't believe it even when I tell you. It was the solicitor's man. He came to find the nearest of kin to . . . to the master.' She never said your Uncle as she used to do, in fact no one spoke of the master to her in any way; but now, having mentioned his name, she

238

gabbled on, 'Master Dick, you know, well, well he's died and left some money and it goes to the next-of-kin. An' you know who the next-of-kin is? Miss Bessie. You wouldn't believe it, two thousand five hundred pounds! Imagine, two thousand five hundred pounds an' going to Miss Bessie. Eeh! if anybody should have that it should be her, meanin' no offence, Miss Barbara, you know that, don't you, but the way she's worked, what she's done. . .'

'And still doing.'

'Aye, and still doing.' Mary now smiled into Barbara's face. It was the first time she had heard her make a remark off her own bat, so to speak, since 'that business.' She rarely spoke unless to say yes or no; she moved around most of the time like someone hypnotised. She remembered seeing a man hypnotise a girl at the fair some years ago and the girl's mother went hysterical 'cos the man couldn't get the girl to come·back to herself and stop doin' daft things and there was nearly a riot. Miss Barbara put her in mind of that girl, only she didn't do daft things, except to walk; she walked in all weathers, storms had no fear for her. Since that night of the great storm when 'that business' happened there had only to be the sign of a storm and out she went.

She rubbed the thin white hands vigorously between her own now, saying again, 'You shouldn't do it, you're froze to the marrow. Look; an' your skirt's all mud. Go upstairs and change your frock. Go on, that's a good lass.'

When Barbara rose from the chair she pushed her gently towards the door, then across the hall and up the first three stairs.

Once in her room, Barbara didn't immediately change her dress, but walked slowly to the window and stood looking out. It was late October. The day was bleak, the hills looked cold and lonely as if they had never felt the warmth of the sun or borne the tread of a human foot; the wind that was blowing was a straight wind, bending the long grass and the dead flowers in the garden all one way; the garden was no longer neat and tidy, for the boy came no more, not since Constance

239

had been forced to deprive them of the second fifty pounds a year. She thought, as she often thought, that they had been cursed, that both of them had been cursed; the tragedy of the Mallens had fallen on them. But they weren't Mallens; there was no Mallen blood in them. He who touches pitch is defiled; perhaps that was the reason. It was like contracting a disease. She and Constance had been in close contact with the Mallens all their lives and they had caught the disease. Her stomach was full of it. She looked down at the mound pushing out her dress below the waistband. The disease was growing in her and she loathed it, hated, hated and loathed it. Given the choice she would have accepted leprosy.

She heaved a deep sigh. All life was a disease and she was tired of it. She would have made an end of it months ago if it hadn't been for Anna. She could not add to Anna's sorrow, she loved Anna, she was the only one left to love. Anna had given unselfishly all her life and what had she got? Nothing. Yet she knew that Anna would refute this. And now this latest injustice, two thousand five hundred pounds going to Bessie. Bessie was just a vague memory to her: a round laughing face and a white train which she and Constance held; it was connected with the memory of people saying, 'Isn't she pretty, isn't she pretty?' But they weren't referring to the bride but to Constance. Poor Connie! Connie, who was now virtually a prisoner on that farm.

Again she asked herself why this should happen to them. Three people who had done no harm to anyone. Her mind checked her at this point. Constance had done harm to Donald before she married him, and she also harmed him by marrying him; but nevertheless she did not deserve the treatment being allotted her. She had not seen Constance since her visit to the farm, but every now and again she had a letter from her, smuggled to the carrier no doubt. In each letter were the same words: 'Please write to me, Barbie, but don't refer to anything I have said.'

She had only once replied to the letters, and that was as recently as a fortnight ago when Constance had desperately beseeched a word from her. The letter was short and terse and held nothing personal, except to hope that she and the baby were well. Her own plight was bad but she considered that her sister's was worse.

She turned from the window and took off her dress and, standing with it in her hand, she said to herself, But what of Anna's plight should anything happen to me when the child is born?

It was the next morning at the breakfast table that Barbara said suddenly, 'Do you think we could afford to ask our solicitor to visit us out here?'

'Our solicitor? Why? Why do you want a solicitor, Barbara?'

Barbara lowered her head, rested the spoon against the side of her porridge bowl, then said slowly, 'Should anything happen to me, I . . . I want you to be provided for.'

'Oh, my dear, my dear.' Miss Brigmore rose from her seat and came around the table and put her arms around Barbara and, pressing her head against her breast, whispered, 'Oh child, my dear child, don't think about such things, please, please, for what would I do without you?'

'One must think about such things. If they had been thought of before you would be two thousand five hundred pounds richer at this moment.'

Miss Brigmore made no answer to this for she was surprised that Barbara had for the moment forgotten her own tragic condition and was concerned for her. It was the first time in seven months that she had made voluntary conversation. And she was right in what she said, if Thomas had thought of her. . . . Oh, she must not start that again. She had wrestled for most of the night with the bitterness in her, not against Thomas, she could never feel bitter against Thomas, but against the quirk of fate that would now further enrich the comfortably off Italian countess by two thousand five hundred pounds, for although the count had been classed as a poor man, his poverty was comparative. Patting Barbara's head now, she said softly, 'We will talk

241

no more about it; nothing is going to happen to you, my dear.'

Barbara withdrew herself from Miss Brigmore's arms and, looking up at her, she said, 'I don't want to go into the town but if I'm forced to I shall.'

'But . . . but Barbara, my dear, the money is in trust, Constance and you only receive the interest. It is something that couldn't be transferred. If . . . if what you say did happen, and God forbid, unless you left . . . issue, the money would go back into the estate.'

'I . . . I don't think so. I've been looking into Everyman's Own Lawyer, and there's such a thing as a Deed of Gift. Anyway, this is what I want to find out, and make it legal, that if and when I die, my allotment and share in the house will pass to you.' She paused here and, staring fixedly into Miss Brigmore's eyes, she ended, 'Whether I have issue or not.'

'But Barbara dear, you're . . . you're not going to die, you're so young and . . .' Her voice trailed away before she added, 'healthy,' for that would have been, if not a falsehood, a grave exaggeration.

'I shall write to Mr. Hawkins to-day.'

Miss Brigmore sighed a deep sigh, went around the table and sat down. She was not thinking of what Barbara's gesture might mean to her in the long run, but of the fact that they could not really afford the ruinous fees the solicitor would ask for coming all this way from Newcastle. If it had been from Allendale or Hexham it would have been expensive enough, but all the way from Newcastle. . . . She wondered what they could do without in order to meet this further expense. . . .

When half-an-hour later she saw Barbara going down the garden path towards the gate at the bottom which led on to the fells, she opened the windows in the study and called, 'Barbara! Barbara dear! don't go too far, please, please.'

She knew Barbara had heard her although she didn't turn round. She looked up at the sky. It was high and blue and the sun was shining. It was much warmer than yesterday, in fact it was a nice day, an enjoyable Indian summer day. Not that the weather had any effect on her now, except that she worried about the extended cold days, when they used more wood and coal than they could afford.

She closed the windows and sat down in the leather chair behind the desk. It did not pain her to sit in this chair, the chair in which Thomas had paid the price for his crime, the crime he had in all ignorance committed, for she knew he would have suffered crucifixion rather than knowingly perpetrate such a sin against Barbara, whom he had loved as a daughter.

She leant her head back against the top of the chair. She was feeling tired, weary, but strangely she was no longer enduring the physical weakness that had plagued her for so long following the pneumonia. Perhaps it was the shock of that night, and the call made on her inner resources, but since she had heard the gun shot she had ceased to be an invalid; necessity had made her strong enough to cope with the terrible circumstances.

'MISS! MISS! MISS! COME QUICKLY.'

As she pulled the door open she ran into Mary.

'Oh Miss! Miss . . .'

'What is it?'

'Miss Barbara, she's, she's in the kitchen with pains.'

'But she's just gone out.'

'No, she's back; like a ghost she is an' doubled up. . . . Oh! Miss! . . .'

When she burst into the kitchen Barbara was sitting by the table, gripping its edge; her eyes were tightly closed and she was gasping for breath.

'You have pains?'

She nodded, then muttered, 'Something . . . something seized me. I turned back, and then a moment ago it came again.'

Miss Brigmore now turned to Mary, saying sharply, 'Get an oven shelf, two, she's freezing, and more blankets. . . . Come along, dear, come along.' She put her arm around Barbara's shoulders and eased her to her feet. 'We must get you to bed. . . .'

After putting Barbara to bed with a blanket-covered oven shelf at her feet and one to her side, she and Mary had a quick consultation in the kitchen. 'It would be safer to get the doctor,' Mary said, 'It might just be a flash in the pan but on the other hand it mightn't.'

243

Miss Brigmore did not think it was a flash in the pan. She agreed with Mary that it would be wise to get the doctor; but the carrier had passed and how were they going to get a message to him?

'I could run down to Jim Pollitt's,' said Mary; 'he generally drops in for his dinner around one o'clock. He might be takin' the sheep over that way or going to the farm, an' Mr. Stanhope might let him run for he's not a kick in the backside from Allendale.'

Miss Brigmore did not check Mary for her coarse saying for she knew it was only when she was anxious that she made such slips of the tongue in her presence. She said, 'Get into your coat; wrap up well, for the sun's gone in and there's a mist falling. How long do you think it will take you to get there . . . I mean to Mr. Pollitt's?'

'I could do it in half-an-hour if I cut through the bottom of the Hall grounds, an' I will. An' if they catch me I'll explain; they can't hang me.'

As she talked she was winding a long woollen scarf around her head and neck. A few minutes later Miss Brigmore, opening the door for her, said, 'Tell him how urgent it is, Mary,' and Mary nodded at her and answered, 'Yes, Miss, I'll do that, never you fear. . . .'

It was two hours later when Mary returned. She had come back much slower than she had gone, for the mist had come down thick. After taking off her things she went upstairs and before she reached Miss Barbara's door she heard her groaning.

The doctor arrived when the dusk was falling into dark, and he confirmed what all three knew, the child was struggling to be born.

It struggled for the next ten hours, and when at last it thrust itself into the world it seemed to have little life in it, hardly enough to make it cry.

As Mary took the child from the doctor and hurried out, Miss Brigmore held Barbara's two hands close to her breast and whispered in a choked voice, 'It's all right, my dear, it's all right.' But how, she asked herself, could she say it was all right? Half the time words were stupid, language was stupid, for it did not convey what the mind was saying and at this moment her mind
244

was saying that no one should have to suffer as this poor girl had done in order to give birth. For what seemed an eternity she had sweated with her and her own stomach had heaved in sympathy; but even so she had not experienced the excruciating pain of the convulsions, although she would gladly have suffered them for her had it been possible.

The tears were spilling down her face as she murmured, 'It's all over, dear, it's all over.' But even as she spoke she experienced a new terror as she realized that for Barbara it was all over, for she was letting go of life.

Barbara had lifted her hand towards her and her lips were mouthing the name 'Anna, Anna' but without sound; then on a deep sigh her head fell to the side.

'OH NO! NO! BARBARA, BARBARA MY LOVE, BARBARA.'

Miss Brigmore's cry brought the doctor from the foot of the bed. He took hold of Barbara's shoulders as if to shake her while saying, 'No, no! Everything's all right. Come along now, come along now.'

There was a long silence in the room before he gently laid her back on the pillow. Then straightening his back, he looked across the bed at Miss Brigmore and shook his head as if in perplexity as he said, 'It was all right. Everything was quite normal. The child is small but . . . but everything was all right.'

Miss Brigmore brought her agonised gaze from his and looked down on her beloved Barbara, Barbara who had been like her own daughter. Of the two girls, it was Barbara who had needed her most, although she would never admit it; she herself had had to make all the advances. And now she was dead, as she had planned. If anyone had arranged their death she had. She had walked herself to death, she had starved herself to death, but more than anything, she had willed herself to death. 'Oh Barbara. Oh, my dearest.' She fell on her knees and buried her head to the side of the limp body.

A few moments later the doctor, raised her up, saying gently, 'Go and see if the child is all right.'

When she shook her bowed head he insisted, 'Go now, and send Mary to me.'

As if she were walking in a dream she went out of the room and down the stairs.

In the kitchen Mary was kneeling on the mat, a bowl of water at her side. She was wrapping the child in a blanket and she didn't look at Miss Brigmore but said, on a light note, 'She's small but bonny.' She placed the child on a pillow in a clothes basket in front of the fire, then turning her head to the side, she looked up at Miss Brigmore and slowly her mouth fell into a gape. She sat back on her heels and shook her head, and when she saw Miss Brigmore drop down into a chair and bury her face in her hands she exclaimed softly, 'In the name of God, no. Aw no, not Miss Barbara now. Aw no.'

When, rocking herself, Mary began to wail, Miss Brigmore got to her feet and, putting her hands on her shoulders, she drew her upwards. Then she held her in her arms, an unprecedented gesture, and Mary clung to her, crying, 'Oh Miss Barbie! oh poor Miss Barbie!'

After a time Miss Brigmore pressed her gently away and in choked tones said, 'Go up. Go up, Mary will you, the doctor needs you.'

Rubbing her face with her apron, while the tears still poured from her eyes, Mary asked helplessly, 'What'll we do? what'll we do, Miss? what'll we do without them?' and Miss Brigmore answered, 'I don't know, I don't know, Mary.'

A moment later she knelt down by the wash basket and looked on the child, the child that was the outcome of lust and terror. Thomas's child; Thomas's son, Thomas's daughter; she hadn't up till this moment thought about its sex. As if loathe to touch it, she took the end of the blanket in her finger and thumb and slowly unfolded it.

It was a girl child.

THREE

It was towards the end of November, the dreary
month, but as if to give the lie to the defaming tag the
morning was bright; there was no wind and the earth
sparkled with a thick rime of frost.

But the morning had no pleasing effect on Constance, she was numbed to the bone. She felt as if she
were standing on the edge of a precipice trying to work
up the courage to jump, and she knew she would jump
if something didn't happen soon to alter the situation.

Last week when they had returned from burying
Barbara she had almost gone mad with grief, and at one
moment had almost screamed at him, 'It's Matthew's!
Do you hear? it's Matthew's! Do what you like. Do you
hear? Do what you like!' Such an outburst would have
taken the implement of torture out of his hands, but it
was his mother who had prevented her. As if she knew
what was in her mind she had said, 'Be patient, lass, be
patient, it can't go on for ever'; but she had looked at
the older woman and said, 'It can, it can.' Jane had
shaken her head and answered, 'God's ways are
strange, they are slow but they're sure.' And at that
moment she knew that Jane was not only afraid of her
son, but she hated him as much as she herself did, and
the bond between them was strengthened.

The dairy door opened, and now Jane's voice came
to her softly, saying, 'Come on, lass, there's a drink
ready, and he's bawling his head off.'

Constance left what she was doing, rubbed her hands
on a coarse towel hanging on a nail in the wall, and

went towards Jane who was holding the door open for her. Then on the threshold they both stopped at the sight of Donald crossing the yard with a man and boy at his side.

They themselves crossed the yard and met up with the men at the kitchen door. Donald went in first, but the man and boy stood aside until they had entered; then they followed and stood just inside the room.

'Give them a drink of tea,' Donald jerked his head towards the pair as if they were beggars; but they were dressed decently if poorly and didn't look like beggars.

When Jane had poured out two mugs of tea, she motioned the man and boy to sit down on the form, then asked. 'Would you like a bite?' and the man said, 'Thank you, Missis, we would that; we've been walkin since shortly after five. The others are outside.'

'My! my!' she nodded at him. 'Where you from?'

'Near Haydon Bridge, Ma'am.'

'Haydon Bridge? My! That's a way. You must have found the hills cold this mornin'.'

'Aye, an' slippery underfoot; the rime's thick up there.'

'It would be, it would be.'

'Who told you I wanted a man?' Donald was standing with his back to the fire in his 'master' attitude, and the man answered, 'Mr. Tyler who I worked for, at least did afore he was bought out. He said he heard in the market you were goin' to set somebody on.'

'Aye, I was; but one man, not two of you and a family. You say you've got a family?'

'Only two, I mean a wife and a daughter; we lost the others. But Jim here, he's fourteen gone and can hold his own with any man. And the girl, she's thirteen, an' she's been the last four years in the farm kitchen an' the dairy. She's very handy, me wife an' all.'

'Huh! I daresay, but I'm not asking for your family. Anyway, I've got no cottage to offer you; the only place habitable, and then not much so, are two rooms above the stables.'

'We'd make do with anything.' There was a deep anxiety in the man's voice. 'As long as it's a shelter we'd make do. And you wouldn't lose by it, Sir. I'll promise you you wouldn't lose by it. We'd give you more than your money's worth.'

'What are you asking?'

'Well, well'—the man shook his head—'It'll be up to you, Sir. But I can tell you we wouldn't press as long as we had a habitation.'

'Aye, yes.' Donald walked from the fire towards the table and, lifting up a mug, he took a long drink of the hot tea before he said, 'Habitations are necessary in the winter. How long were you at Tyler's?'

'Over ten years, Sir.'

'Alway's been in farming?'

'No . . . no.' The man's voice was hesitant now and he said on a weak smile, 'I was a footman at one time in the Hall, High Banks Hall, over the hills.' He now jerked his head to the side and looked at the young woman sitting at the table. She had spilled her mug of tea and the liquid was running between the plates. She did not seem to notice this but she stared at him and he at her. He knew who she was. But that was hearsay, for he would never have recognized her from the child he remembered, and should she remember him that might be the end of his chances.

'What's your name?'

He brought his eyes back to the master of the house and said slowly, 'Waite, Sir. Harry Waite.'

Waite . . . Waite. The name sounded like a bell in Donald's mind awakening the memories of twelve years ago. Hadn't Waite been the man who started all the hubbub? the man Dick Mallen had wanted to shoot? He glanced from him to Constance and at the sight of her face a mirthless laugh rose in him. He had the power to engage a foorman, the footman who at one time had waited on her. Well, well! the irony of it. All round it was going to be a very exceptional day. He had a surprise for her but this bit was added interest.

'Drink up and I'll show you those rooms. If you're as handy as you say you are you should be able to make them habitable.'

Before he had reached the kitchen door the man and boy were on their feet, and the man, nodding first to

249

Jane, and then to Constance, and awkwardly muttering his thanks, followed him.

Waite. The footman who had lifted the lid of the armour box and got them out. The man who had tapped her on the bottom, had tapped them both on the bottom, saying, 'By! you're a couple of scamps.' The nice footman, as she had thought of him, but also the man who was the cause of her sitting in this kitchen at this moment. Without him having expressed his opinion of his young master it was doubtful if anything that had happened since would have taken place; but for that meek-looking man they might all still be in the Hall, Uncle Thomas, Barbara, herself. . . . Yet how could she blame the man. As Anna so often said, lives were cut to a pattern, all one did was sew them up. The man looked desperate for work and shelter for his family, and he would get it. Oh yes. She had seen the look in Donald's eyes; he thought that by engaging him he would be cutting another sinew of her pride.

The child began to cry and she picked it up and started to feed it. The clock ticked the minutes away. Jane bustled about the kitchen washing up the mugs, sweeping up the hearth, doing a lot of necessary and unnecessary things, and neither of them spoke.

When the door leading from the hall opened and Matthew entered they both looked towards him. He coughed all the way across the room, short, sharp coughs. When he reached Constance's side she did not raise her head and look at him but went on feeding the child as she said below her breath, 'He's engaging a new man, with . . . with a family. He was Waite, the second footman at the Hall.'

Matthew looked from the top of her head across the table to his mother, and she nodded silently at him.

His coughing became harsher. Sitting down slowly by the side of the table, he said in a low husky tone, 'Well, he was going to hire a man anyway, but where will he put a family?'

'In the rooms above the stables.' It was his mother who spoke.

'They're not fit.'

'The man's desperate.'

250

'There's no place for a fire or anything else.'

'They'll likely cook in the storeroom. . . .'

'In the boiler with the pig meat!'

Whatever response his mother would have made to this was cut off by the door opening and Donald entering, alone now. He did not walk towards the fire and stand with his back to it as was usual when he had anything special to say, but standing just within the doorway and looking at his mother, he said, 'You'd better set the dinner for one more, there'll be a visitor.'

'The man and . . . and boy?'

'No; what would I be doing with the man and boy at our table . . . Miss Brigmore.'

In one swift movement Constance returned the child to the crib and was on her feet.

'Why?' The word was so laden with apprehension that he laughed before saying, 'Because she's bringing the child across.'

'Bringing the child here?'

They all moved a step forward, and it brought them into a rough line facing him. His eyes swept over them as he said, 'Aye, bringing the child here. Where should it be but with its nearest relations, and we are that, aren't we?' He was looking directly at Constance. 'You're it's only relation; apart from meself, that is because what hasn't appeared to strike any of you afore apparently'—he now nodded first at his mother and then at Matthew—'is that the child is as much me half-sister as you, Matthew, are me half-brother, and so, therefore, I want her under my care.'

Constance's words seemed to spray from her twitching mouth as she spluttered, 'What . . . what do you mean? What are you doing? What's going to happen to Anna and Mary? There's the house.'

'I've been into all that.' His voice was calm. 'I saw the solicitor at the beginning of the week. Barbara's share of the property and her income naturally fall to the child, and as the child's coming here we would have no further use for the cottage. I have ordered it to be put up for sale.'

'NO!' She moved towards him until she was within touching distance of him. 'No, you won't! You won't

251

do this! You're a fiend, that's what you are, a fiend. You're mad. I won't allow it, I have some say, some rights.'

He looked down into her face. The hatred in his eyes rising from deep in their black unfathomable depths struck her like a physical force, yet it wasn't so frightening as his voice when he said quietly, You have no rights; you are my wife, what is yours is mine and'—he paused—'what is mine is me own.'

Seconds passed and no words came, as was usual he had frozen them within her. It was Matthew, after a fit of coughing, who said, 'But Anna, she worked for Mallen for years and brought them up.'

Donald took his eyes from Constance and looked at Matthew. He looked at him for a long moment before he said, 'She was paid for her services.'

'She was never paid, you know that, she ... she's worked for years ... without pay. ...' He was coughing again.

'There are more ways than one of receiving payment. SHE WAS A WHORE.'

His calmness had dropped from him like a cloak; every word was a bark; his face was contorted with passion. 'And she wasn't the only one, was she? You're all whores, every one of you.' His arm swung before him with such force that had Constance been a few inches nearer it would have felled her to the ground. Then he turned and stamped from the kitchen.

They all stood still for a full minute, then they looked at each other and their eyes said, He's come out into the open. What now?

It was eleven o'clock when Miss Brigmore got off the cart and walked into the farmyard, but she had no child in her arms.

Constance met her at the gate and they enfolded each other in a close embrace, and when Constance muttered, 'Oh! Anna, what can I say?' Miss Brigmore answered, 'I didn't bring her; I've ... I've come to appeal to him. I'll go on my knees to him, anything, as long as he doesn't take her from me. She's all I have; there's no other purpose in my life, nothing to live for.'

Constance said again in an agonised tone, 'Oh! Anna'; then added, 'I'm helpless.'

As they crossed the yard still clinging to each other, Miss Brigmore murmured, 'I couldn't believe it when I got his letter; he had given no indication of it when I last saw him. I thought, well, naturally I thought I would stay in the cottage with Mary and bring up the child. I . . . I never dreamed for one moment'—she paused and came to a halt and, turning her face to Constance, said, 'Yes, I did dream. I have been in terror for months now in case he should do something to force you to persuade Barbara to fall in with his plans and sell the house, because . . . because, Constance, it is a plan. It is a plan of vengeance. His letter was so cold, so ruthless, it was as if he had been waiting all these years to do this to me. In between the lines I could read that he blames me for everything that has happened.'

Constance could say nothing to this for she knew it was true. He had a hate of Anna that was beyond all reason. He had always disliked her, in the first place because she had not liked him, but the main reason was that she had been close to Uncle Thomas.

'Is . . . is he in the house?'

Constance shook her head. 'No, no, he's out walking his land. He walks it every morning. Legally he doesn't own a foot of it but no one would dare to resist his claim to it, for he *is* the farm. He works it, or has done up till now, almost by himself. But now he has engaged a man and his family. You will never guess who that man is.'

'Who?'

'Waite, the footman.'

'Waite! the footman?'

'Yes.'

'And he has engaged him?'

'Yes, Oh, I don't mind the man being engaged; strangely, I remember him as a very kindly man. It's the reason why he did it. He has no compassion for the man or his plight. He has a family and needs a home for them. Tyler's Farm, where he worked, has been sold and the new owner has his own men. Anyway, the

253

man heard that there might be an opening here. It . . . it was the first I knew of it, or, or Mam either. But then'—she shook her head—'he's determined to expand. He has bought another fifty acres. Most of the dairy produce is sold now. We have an allowance in the house, so much and no more. Oh! Anna. Anna'— she shook her head—'Life is unbearable. Why did I do this? Why?'

Miss Brigmore now drooped her head as she said, '*You* didn't do it; you wouldn't have done it, *I* forced you. On this at least I accept the guilt. You wouldn't have married him if I hadn't pressed you. But any shame you might have had to bear would have been better than your present state.'

'Oh, you musn't blame yourself, Anna; you did what you thought was best for me. There's one culprit in this business, and that is myself. When I look back and see myself distressed at the thought of not being married before I was twenty I think I must have been insane. But come inside, you're cold, and you look ill.'

They had just entered the kitchen and Miss Brigmore, after greeting Jane, was turning to Matthew where he sat crouched over the fire when the sound of hurrying, almost running steps across the cobbled yard froze them all.

Constance, turning to see Donald coming over the threshold, his face red and sweating, knew that he must have run at high speed from the far fields where he would have seen the carrier pass. The cart was well before its time this morning, the fine weather doubtless having set the pace.

No one spoke for a moment. Then the colour in Donald's face deepening to a purple hue, he demanded of Miss Brigmore, 'Where is it?'

'I . . . I didn't bring her, I wanted to talk to you.'

'You can talk till you're black in the face, and it'll be useless. What I said in that letter holds; as I've told you already I have the law behind me.'

'I . . . I know you have.' The placating sound of her own voice made Miss Brigmore sick at herself, but she continued in it as she said, 'You . . . are quite within your rights to want Constance to bring up the baby,
254

but . . . I have come to beg of you to be lenient and to leave her with me. You know I'll do all in my power to educate her and . . .'

'Aye, and teach her to lie and cheat and whore.'

Miss Brigmore put her hand to her throat and her body swayed slightly before she said, 'You do me a terrible injustice.'

'I do you no injustice; they took their pattern from you. Well, now you've come without her so there's nothing for it but for me to go back and fetch her.'

'You'll not, you'll not do this, I'll never let you.'

He moved slowly about until he was facing Constance and asked, quietly now, 'How are you going to stop me? You haven't a leg to stand on and you know it, so what I say to you now is, get yourself ready because you'll be carrying your niece back with you.'

'I won't! I shan't, and I'll fight you. Do you hear? I'll fight you.'

Still gazing at her, his lip curled in scorn as he said, 'Don't be stupid.'

He had turned from her and had put his foot over the step before his mother's voice stopped him. 'Don't do this, Donald,' she said.

He glared at her, his eyes narrowing; and then his voice low, he said, 'I'll advise you to keep out of it.'

'I've kept out of it long enough. When you're talking about legal rights you forget that Matthew is my husband's only son.'

Donald didn't speak for some seconds, and then he said, slowly, 'I forget nothing. To all intents and purposes I am Michael Radlet's eldest son; it's only hearsay that this'—he tugged at the white tuft of hair to the left of his brow—'makes me a Mallen, but it would be hard to prove in law. There are a number round about with white streaks; it wouldn't be possible they are all the results of frolics in the wood.' Their eyes held for some seconds before he finished. 'You're wasting your breath if you think you're going to achieve anything by that. Now'—he cast his glance over them all—'as far as I'm concerned the talkin's finished. In ten minutes' time I'll have the brake in the yard, an' you'—he nodded towards Constance—'be ready.'

255

The kitchen was weighed in a silence like that which follows an announcement of the plague. The three women stood where they were, and Matthew sat where he was, all immobile, until the child in the cradle gurgled; then Matthew turned his head and looked towards it. He kept his eyes on it for some minutes before pulling himself up from the chair, and the almost imperceivable motion of his head he made towards Constance told her that he wanted to speak to her.

As if awakening from a dream she looked first at Anna, then at Jane, then back to Anna again before, bowing her head deeply to her chest, she went out of the kitchen and into the hall.

Matthew was waiting for her just outside the door. He put out his hand and drew her to the far end of the hall and into a clothes closet that was near the front door, and there in the dimness he held her face as he said softly, 'Listen now; listen dear. You . . . you are not to go over there. You must make on you have taken bad, you must faint or something and I'll . . . I'll go with . . .' He pressed his hand tightly over his mouth as he began to cough. Constance whispered desperately, 'But . . . but you couldn't stand the journey, Matthew; it'll be dark before you get back, and the cold will set in and . . .'

'Don't, don't worry about that, just listen to me. Listen to me, dear. Pay attention, don't cry. Now listen, I want you to go into the front room and lie on the couch; just say you feel bad. . . .'

'But . . . but he won't believe me; and he'll never take you. . . . And why . . . why do you want to go with him?'

'It doesn't matter why, only do what I ask.'

She shook her head slowly. 'He won't take you, he'll bring her himself.'

'He can't, there's only a chain to the back of the brake, and a basket could slip through.'

'Oh, Matthew, don't be silly, you know him, he'll think of some way. He'll tie it on. But why, why? What are you going to do if you go?'

'Listen to me, dearest, please. Now you and I know that I've had much longer time than was due to me.
256

I might go the night, I might go in the mornin', but one thing's certain, I won't get through this winter. It was a miracle I got through the last. Now listen, listen. Look at me. We haven't much time.' He stared at her in silence for a moment, then whispered, 'Aw Constance, I love you. Aw, how I love you. It's this that has kept me alive, but now I'm suffering the torments of hell 'cos I know I'll be leaving you here alone to suffer him. 'Cos Mother's no match for him, no more than I am meself. He's turned into a devil. And to think that I once loved him, and he me! I know I wronged him but . . . but . . . Oh! my love, my love, I would wrong him again for you.' He touched her face with his fingers and his voice was scarcely audible as he said, 'I've . . . I've never kissed you but that once.'

Slowly his face moved towards hers and his lips touched her brow and her eyelids, then traced her cheek, but before they reached her mouth a fit of coughing seized him and he turned his head away and held a piece of white linen to his lips, then screwed it up tightly before he looked at her again.

The tears were raining down her face and when she went to speak he put his finger on her lips and muttered, 'No questions, nothing, no more. As he said, the time for talking's past. Come on, my dear; just do what I ask, go and lie down on the sofa.'

'No, Matthew, no.'

'Please, please, do this for me, make me happy, Constance, make me happy. Let me think there's been some meaning in me being alive. . . .'

'Oh, Matthew, Matthew, what are you going . . . ?

He had opened the door and drawn her into the hall again, and now pressing her towards the sitting room he said quickly, 'Don't speak to him when he comes in, not a word, be prostrate.' He bent quickly forward and kissed her on the mouth, then whispered, 'Good-bye my love.' He opened the door and pressed her inside, then closed it quickly as she went to protest. The next minute he was in the kitchen, and with a briskness in his voice that his mother hadn't heard for years, he said, 'Constance has fainted, she's lying down in the sitting room." Then putting his two hands out, one towards Miss Brigmore and the other towards his mother as they made to move towards the far door, he said, 'Leave her alone, please. . . . Leave her alone. I'm . . . I'm going over with Donald.'

'You? you're not!'

'I am. It's a nice day an' the drive will do me good.' As he stared into his mother's eyes, she put her hand to her mouth and whispered, 'What, what have you in mind, boy? What are you . . . ?'

Nothing, nothing, Mother; I'm just going over in Constance's place to bring the baby back.' He turned now and looked at Miss Brigmore. She was staring at him, her eyes wide and questioning, and he smiled weakly at her and nodded reassuringly before saying, 'Don't worry.'

'No Matthew, no!' Jane pulled him round to her. 'There's nothin' you can do, nothin'. What chance have you against him, or ever had for that matter? Things have got to take their course.'

'Be quiet.'

The door opened and Donald entered. He stood for a moment looking at them, and then he said, 'Where is she?'

It was Jane who answered, 'She's had a turn, she's lying down.'

'Huh!' His laugh was pitying. 'She's had a turn, she's lying down, is she?' He stalked across the room and they heard him going up the stairs, taking them two at a time; then his steps running down again and the sitting room door opening. In a few minutes he was back in the kitchen. Walking slowly to the middle of the room he looked from one to the other and said, 'Well, whatever you've planned, it won't work. I'll bring it back if I've got to nail the basket to the cart or lay her in a bundle under my feet.'

'There won't be any need for that. I'll come along of you.' Matthew's voice was quiet, tired sounding; it was like someone saying, Anything for peace.

Donald turned his head sharply and looked at him.

258

He looked at him for a full minute before he smiled grimly and said, 'Well, that mightn't be a bad idea after all. We could stay overnight and I'll load the brake up with the bits and pieces I want to bring across.' He had turned his gaze on Miss Brigmore, and she closed her eyes against the look in his; then swinging round he went outside.

Jane now ran into the hall and returned with a heavy coat, scarf and cap, and as she helped Matthew into them she kept whispering, 'What is it? Tell me, what is it? what are you up to?'

When he stood muffled up to the eyes he looked into her face and said gently, 'Nothing, Mother, nothing; what could I be up to? Now I ask you, what could I be up to? You go and see to Constance, she needs you. Good-bye.' All he did now was to touch her shoulder with his fingers. Then he turned to Miss Brigmore and, addressing her as he always had done, he said, 'Come on, Miss Brigmore, come along.'

'Can't . . . can't I see Constance just for a moment?'

He went close to her now before he spoke; then he said, 'It would be better if you didn't. You'll see her again. Don't worry, you'll see her again.'

She shook her head before letting it fall forward, and like someone in whom all hope had died she went out of the kitchen, without a word to Jane, and across the yard to the brake.

Donald was standing to the side of it. He did not speak to her but pointed into the back of it, and it was left to Matthew to help her up.

Slowly she covered her ankles with her skirts and sat, for once in her life, without any sign of dignity while the cart rumbled out of the yard and began the journey over the hills.

As they drove higher Matthew's coughing became harsher, but only once did Donald turn his head and glance at him and note there was more blood than usual staining the piece of linen. It would be odd, he thought, if he died on the journey. He wanted him to die, and yet he didn't want him to die. There were still grains of love left in him that at times would cry out

259

and ask, Why had he to do it to me? I could have suffered it from anybody else in the world except him. But such times were few and far between and his hate soon stamped on the grains.

They were nearing the narrow curve in the road where the guard or snow posts stuck up from the edge above the steep partly wooded hillside. It was the place where Barbara had experienced the terrifying fierceness of the gale as it lifted the carrier's cart over the ditch. The line of posts curved upwards for some forty yards and it was at the beginning of them that Matthew, putting his hand tightly over his mouth, muttered, 'I'm ... I'm going to be sick.'

Donald made no comment but kept on driving.

A few seconds later he repeated, 'I'm, I'm going to be sick. Stop, stop a minute. I'll ... I'll have to get down.' His body was bent almost double now.

The horse had taken a dozen steps before Donald brought it to a halt, and Matthew, a piece of linen held tightly across his mouth, got awkwardly down from the cart and hurried to the edge of the road, and there, gripping one of the posts, he leaned against the wire and heaved.

Miss Brigmore watched him for a moment from the side of the cart and as she slid along the seat with the intention of getting down, Donald's voice checked her, saying, 'Stay where you are.' Then he called to Matthew, 'Come on, come on.' But Matthew heaved again and bent further over the wire. After a short while he slowly turned around and, leaning against the post, he gasped, 'I'm ... I'm bad.'

Donald looked down at him. There was blood running from the corner of his mouth, his head was on his chest. He hooked the reins to the iron framework, then jumped down from the cart and went towards him, and as he did so he slipped slightly on the frosted rime of the road, which as yet the sun hadn't touched. When he reached Matthew's side he said sharply, 'Get into the back and lie down.'

'I ... I can't.' Matthew turned from him and again leant over the wire and heaved.

Donald, bending forward now, looked down. There was a sheer drop below them, before the trees branched out. He said harshly, 'Come back from there, you'll be over in a minute.' It was at this moment that Matthew turned and with a swiftness and strength it was impossible to imagine in his weak state he threw both his arms around Donald's shoulders and pulled him forward. Almost too late Donald realized his intention, and now he tore at the arms as if trying to free himself from a wild cat while they both seemed to hang suspended in mid-air against the wire. Donald's side was pressed tight against it; he had one foot still on the top of the bank, the other was wedged sideways against the slope. With a desperate effort he thrust out one hand to grab the post, and as he did so he heard the Brigmore woman scream. Then Matthew's body was jerked from him and he was free, but still leaning outwards at an extreme angle over the drop. As he went to heave himself upwards, his foot on top of the bank slipped on the frost-rimed grass verge, and the weight of his body drew him between the wire and the top of the bank, and with a heart-chilling scream of protest he went hurtling through the air. When he hit the ground he rolled helplessly downwards, stotting like a child's ball from one tree trunk to another. . . .

They lay on the bank where they had fallen, Miss Brigmore, spread-eagled, one hand still gripping a spoke of the cart wheel, the other clutching the bottom of Matthew's overcoat.

When, getting to her knees, she pulled him away from the edge of the drop and turned him over she thought he was already dead, for the parts of his face that weren't covered with blood were ashen.

'Oh Matthew! Matthew!' She lifted his head from the ground, and he opened his eyes and looked at her. Then, his lips moving slowly, he said, 'You should have let me go.'

She pressed his head to her and rocked him for a moment, then murmured, 'Try to stand. Try to stand.' Half dragging him, half carrying him, she got him to the back of the brake and pulled him up, and he lay on the floor in a huddled heap.

Before she got up into the driver's seat to take the reins she walked a few tentative steps towards the edge of the road and looked downwards. Far, far below a dark object was lying, but it could have been a tree stump, anything. If it was Donald he might still be alive.

She urged the horse upwards to where the road widened and, having turned it about, she drove back to the farm.

It was five hours later when the men lifted Donald from the flat cart and carried him into the farm kitchen, where they laid him on the wooden settle to the side of the fireplace.

Miss Brigmore, Constance and Jane stood together near the dresser; one might have thought they had their arms around each other, so close were their bodies.

Matthew was lying back in the wooden chair near the kitchen table. If his eyes had not been wide open and moving he too could have been taken for dead, such was the look and colour of his skin.

The four of them watched the men as they straightened their backs after laying Donald down but no one of them spoke, or moved.

It was Willy Nesbitt from Allendale, a man who had been on many winter rescue expeditions, who broke the silence. Looking at Constance, he said, 'He's fought hard; don't know how he's done it, Missis. He's smashed up pretty bad; he should have been dead twice over, but he's fought to keep alive. I thought he was gone two or three times, but even now there's still breath in him.'

The man's eyes seemed to draw Constance from the protection of Miss Brigmore and Jane, and like a sleep-walker she went around the end of the table, past Matthew, and to the settle, and there she stood looking down on Donald. He looked twisted, all of him looked twisted. His face was bruised and shapelessly swollen, all that is except his eyes, and these were open.

His eyes had always been dark, black when he gave

way to emotion, but now they were like pieces of jet on which a red light was playing, and the feeling that emanated from them struck her with a force that was almost physical, for she fell back from it. She even flung out her arms as if to protect herself; and then she cried out as it beat on her and bore her down. When she fainted away the room became alive with movement. . . .

She recovered lying on the mat in front of the fire. Miss Brigmore was kneeling by her side. Donald was no longer on the couch; under Jane's direction the men had carried him into the front parlour.

Miss Brigmore, stroking the damp hair back from Constance's brow, whispered, 'It's all right, my dear, it's all right, he's gone.'

Constance's breast was heaving as if she had raced up a hill. She did not need to be told he was gone, she knew, for with his last look he had tried to take her with him. The strength of his mind, the intensity of his hate, the futility of his life had all been in that last look and he had kept himself alive to level it on her. If ever a man had wished death on another he had, and as she had slipped into the black depths she thought he had succeeded.

When she went to rise, Miss Brigmore helped her to her feet, saying, "Sit quiet for a while, sit quiet.'

Matthew was still in the same position in the chair. It seemed that he hadn't moved and when she looked towards him and whimpered, 'Oh Matthew! Matthew!' he answered through blood-stained lips, and in a voice that had a thin flatness about it, 'It's all right, it's all right.'

Constance leaned her head against the high back of the chair and closed her eyes. It might be over, but it wasn't all right, and it might never be all right. Matthew had killed Donald, as surely as if he had stuck a knife between his ribs he had killed him, but the guilt was hers. She had known, as had his mother, when he set out in the cart to go over the hills that it wasn't in order to bring Barbara's child back, but to put an end to Donald. . . . Yet there had had to be an end, it had to come

263

in some way for she could not have stood this way of life much longer. Donald had not been a sane man; his jealously had turned his brain. . . . But there again, was she not to blame for that? Oh God! God! At this moment she wouldn't have minded if he had taken her with him, for then she would not have had to face the prospect of living with this feeling of guilt.

She opened her eyes to look at Miss Brigmore who was again stroking her brow. But here was something she could be thankful for; Anna's future, however long or short it might last, was secure, and Barbara's child would not be brought up in hatred. And that was another thing, neither would her own. She took in a deep breath. Some good could come out of this deed other than her own release. She'd have to think along these lines.

Matthew now moved in his chair and muttered. 'Get my mother,' and as Constance went to rise Miss Brigmore said, 'I'll go, sit quiet.'

Constance sat quiet and she and Matthew looked at each other, until Matthew closed his eyes to shut out the pain that the sight of her always brought to him. . . .

Miss Brigmore went from the kitchen and into the sitting room where the new woman Daisy Waite was helping Jane to lay out the body of her son.

Donald was lying on the table, the stairs having been too narrow for the men to carry him up. The two women had him undressed down to his long pants and vest, and Daisy Waite was unbuttoning the pants that were stained red around the hips, while she cried as she talked. 'God Almighty! To end like this. Did you ever see anything like it? Aw, the poor man, the poor man. And it was him who gave us shelter when nobody else would. And to come to this. Aw, dear God. Where's the sense in anything?'

Miss Brigmore turned her gaze away from the now partly naked body for she too felt on the point of fainting. She touched Jane on the shoulder and said softly, 'Matthew needs you.'

Jane nodded but did not turn and follow her or look

at her, but she kept her gaze on the face of her son. He was gone, he was dead, they were rid of him, they were all rid of him, they were free, and she was glad. . . . Then why was there this pain in her? She had never wanted him. When she was carrying him she never wanted him, and when he was born she had never wanted him for she had seen him as something that had been thrust on her—into her, and since the day he had breathed he had brought strife with him. He in his turn had never liked her, had even hated her. Yet what she was feeling was an overwhelming pity for him, as if she had sustained the loss of a loved one. She couldn't understand it. If it had been Matthew she could have. And she would be feeling like this again soon, for Matthew wouldn't be long in going now.

What would happen to Matthew when he died? Would he be brought before the Judgment? His father had instilled the good book into her, so she must believe in Judgment, but surely the dear God would take everything into account. But she didn't know, she didn't know. He was a fearsome God at times. Her poor Matthew! her poor Matthew! And Donald? At this moment she could say, if not, 'My poor Donald,' at least 'Poor Donald,' for he had never been hers, nor she his, but yes, she could say, 'Poor Donald.'

She turned her dry eyes on Daisy Waite and said, 'I'll be back in a minute.'

'Don't worry, Missis, don't worry, I can manage. He isn't the first, and he won't be the last I've put ready for a journey. But I never thought to see the day I'd be doin' it for him. Dear God! Dear God!'

Miss Brigmore took Jane's arm and led her from the room, but they did not go immediately into the kitchen. In the dim hallway they instinctively turned and looked at each other, and the look was deep. Neither of them said a word but their hands gripped tight for a moment before they moved on again into the kitchen.

When Jane stood beside Matthew's chair and he said. 'I want to go to bed, Mother,' she replied, 'Come away then, lad.' And tenderly she helped him to his feet, and with her arm around him led him from the room.

Constance had not moved, and now Miss Brigmore went to her and, bending over her, said softly, 'Try to think no more of it, what's done is done. It . . . it had to be this way, you couldn't have gone on, something would have happened, perhaps something more terrible.'

'But . . . but what will happen to Matthew?'

'Nothing will happen to Matthew, I've told you, I mean to explain it all as I saw it, and nothing will happen to Matthew.'

'Oh Anna.' Constance jerked to her feet, her hands gripping her neck. She seemed to be on the point of choking, until the tears, rushing from her eyes and nose, relieved the pressure. Miss Brigmore put her arms tightly about her and they both swayed as if they were drunk.

When the paroxysm passed Miss Brigmore, her own face showing her distress, murmured, 'There, there, my dear. You must forget it, all the past, all of it, all of it. Just . . . just thank God that you've been saved and you're still young and, and beautiful. There's a life before you yet, you'll see. There's a life before you yet.'

And to this Constance made a deep dissenting sound.

At the inquest a week later Miss Brigmore explained to the coroner exactly what had happened. Mr. Matthew Radlet, who had the disease of consumption, had been in distress, and because he was feeling sick had got down and stood at the side of the road. His brother Donald had gone to his assistance. She could not explain how it had happened because she was sitting in the back of the cart at the time, but she surmised he must have slipped on the frost-rimed verge; the frost had been very heavy the night before; all she knew was Mr. Matthew Radlet had made an effort to grab his brother, but without success.

It was an awful tragedy, everyone said so, for Donald Radlet was the most up and coming farmer in the district. They said this aloud, but among themselves in

266

the drawing rooms, the parlours, and the select ends of the inns they reminded each other that, after all, he was a Mallen and did anyone know of any Mallen who had died in his bed?

AFTERMATH

It was the end of the harvest supper. The barn had never witnessed such gaiety for it was the first time such a function had been held there. Michael Radlet had not countenanced harvest suppers nor had his father before him, nor, of course, had Donald Radlet, and they would all have stood amazed, not believing their eyes at the changes that had taken place during three short years. In Donald's case, he would surely have experienced chagrin that his farm, as he had always considered it, was now being managed by a woman, a young woman, his wife in fact.

Matthew Radlet had survived his half-brother by only six weeks, and his going had drawn Jane and Constance even closer together. Their guilt, their remorse and their relief were mingled and shared.

For months after Matthew's going they had lived a cheerless, guilt-ridden existence, until one day Jane, as if throwing off a mental illness, had stood in the kitchen and actually cried aloud, 'Look girl, let us put an end to this. If we're going to live in misery then it's a pity he ever went the way he did. That's how I'm seeing it now, and you must see it the same way. Oh yes, more so than me, you must see it like that, for you are young, and healthy. And you have a child to bring up, and he should be brought up amid cheerfulness, not the gloom that's been hanging over us these months past.'

It was from that time that, as Daisy Waite expressed

it, the Missis and the young mistress came out of their sorrow.

It would not have been considered unusual had Constance left the running of the entire farm to Harry Waite. Harry was quite knowledgeable on farming matters, and more, more than willing to do all in his power to assist her, as were his wife, son, and daughter; but no, from the day Jane lifted the curtain of guilt, as it were, from their shoulders, there had risen in her a determination to manage the farm herself.

And so she went to market, driven by Harry Waite, and stood by his side as he bargained in both the buying and the selling. She said little or nothing on these first visits but kept her head held high and her gaze straight, and her look defied the neighbouring farmers to laugh at her, at least in public. That in the inns it was a different matter she had no doubt, for on one occasion Harry Waite drove her home having only the sight of one eye, the other being closed and fast discolouring, besides which his knuckles were bleeding. She did not ask him if he had been drinking, for Harry Waite, she had discovered, was a moderate man; his main concern in life being the welfare of his family and, since being in her service, protecting her.

His loyalty had been well repaid, for two months ago he moved his family into the three-roomed cottage she'd had built for them in a small enclosure about a hundred yards from the farmhouse proper.

Harry Waite's son, Jim, who was now seventeen, was among other things, a shepherd on the farm, and his daughter, Nancy, now sixteen, divided her time between the dairy and the house.

The house had changed beyond all recognition, for the horsehair suite no longer adorned the sitting room, nor was there linoleum on the floor, but a new chesterfield suite now stood on a patterned carpet, and there was never a day in the winter but a fire was lit in this room. Jane no longer sat in front of the kitchen fire warming her feet and knees before going up into the spine-chilling bedroom, but she and Constance usually ended the day sitting side by side on the couch, slippers on their feet, and a hot drink to their hands. On ex-
270

tremely cold nights there was the welcome glow of a fire in their bedrooms, an extravagant innovation this, and there was always a fire, except on days that were really warm, in the room that was now called the nursery.

So in the late summer of 1866 when Constance did her books and found that the profit for the year was well up on the previous one, and this in spite of having to engage extra labour for the threshing and the hay making, which crops were the first results from the land that Donald had so proudly acquired, she decided, with a little glow of excitement, to give a harvest supper. She would bring Anna, Mary, and the child over; they would enjoy it. Then, besides the Waite family, there would be the Twiggs, the father, mother, and three children—they had been very helpful. Then there were Bob and Peter Armstrong, two brothers who had a farm in the next valley. They had been most kind from the beginning, going as far as to come over and offer her advice; and it hadn't stopped there, for their help had also been practical. She liked the Armstrongs, Bob in particular, he had a merry twinkle in his eye.

The supper had not been lavish as some harvest suppers tended to be. She had provided plenty of wholesome food, and a certain amount to drink; and no one had overstepped the mark in this direction, except perhaps Mary. Two glasses of ale always led to three with Mary, and three to four, and then she became very merry; but she had caused a great deal of laughter to-night and she had got everyone dancing. Constance herself had danced for the first time in years. It had been strange feeling a man's arms around her once again. At first she had felt stiff, resisting both touch and movement in such close proximity; then Bob's merriment, and young Jim's fiddle playing, seemed to melt the aloof encasement within which she had remained for the last three years, and she had ended the dance with her head back and laughing, laughing as she used to do years ago when life had spread out before her like a never-ending series of bright paintings.

But now the visitors had gone. Peter Armstrong, shaking her hand as if he would never let it go, had told her in fuddled tones that she was—a grand lass, which had caused great hilarity. Bob had not taken her hand, he had just stood before her and had said simply, 'We'll have to have a night like this again, but not wait till next harvest supper.'

In reply she had said formally, 'I'm so glad you enjoyed it,' and his eyes had laughed at her, but in a kindly way.

And now she and Anna were seated before the fire, to use Mary's term, taking five minutes off, and they were alone, for Jane always tactfully gave place to Miss Brigmore during her visits.

Turning her head from where it rested on the back of the couch, Constance looked at Miss Brigmore and asked quietly, 'Did you enjoy it, Anna?'

'Enormously, enormously, my dear. Now I can understand why there's so much fuss made about them. And to think that years ago when I used to hear of the excitement surrounding them on the Hall farms I used to turn my nose up!'

Constance looked towards the fire again as she said softly, 'We turned our noses up at so many things in those days, didn't we? Life is strange; you've always said that it's a pattern that is already cut. I wonder what shape mine's going to take from now on?'

'A good shape I should think, dear.'

'I'd like it to remain exactly as it is now; I'd like to keep everything and everybody static, Michael forever small, Jane happy and content, and all the Waites so loyal and good, and myself at rest.'

'You are too young to be at rest, you'll marry again.'

'No, Anna, no.' Constance's voice, although low, held a definite ring.

They were both looking straight ahead into the fire when Miss Brigmore said, 'I like that Mr. Armstrong, the younger one; I should say he's an honest man and he has a great sense of humour.'

Constance did not move as she replied, 'I like him too, Anna. He is as you say an honest man, and his company is enjoyable . . . but that's as far as it will go; I wouldn't risk a repeat of what I've been through.'

'Well, time will tell. You are so young yet and life,

272

in spite of the pattern being already cut'—she slanted her eyes towards Constance—'no doubt has some surprises in store for you . . . as it's had for me. Now who would have thought that I'd ever sit in the Hall schoolroom again! In your wildest stretch of imagination would you have said that was in my pattern?'

'No.' Constance shook her head as she laughed, then added, 'And you know, I still don't like the idea of you being there. I've always considered you belonged to Barbara and me exclusively, I mean with regards to education. But it would appear that he was determined to have you in the end, and his motto seemed to be: If at first you don't succeed. . .'

Miss Brigmore laughed gently and nodded towards the fire. 'Indeed, indeed, that is his motto, which he applies to everything, I should say. He's a strange man, Mr. Bensham; you dislike him, yet at the same time you admire him, except, that is, when he's speaking to his wife, for he not only considers her a numskull but tells her to her face she is one, using that very word. Poor Mrs. Bensham. Yet it's odd but I find no need to pity her, she's a woman who can hold her own in her own way. As I told you she's such a common type, it's almost impossible to imagine her in the Hall as one of the staff, let alone its mistress, yet it's very strange you know'—she turned her head now and looked at Constance—'the staff don't seem to take advantage of her. She bustles, shouts, fumbles her way through each day, but there at the end of it she sits in the drawing room quietly knitting. I think she must do this every evening after dinner, and he, when he is at home, sits there too, smoking and reading his paper. . . .'

'Smoking in the drawing room?'

'Yes, smoking in the drawing room, and not cigars but a long, smelly old pipe.'

'Have you been to dinner? You didn't tell me.'

'Well, there hasn't been much time. But yes, I went to dinner to discuss the new arrangement. And you know, Constance'—Miss Brigmore's voice had a touch of sadness in it now—'it was the first time I had sat down to dinner in the dining room of the Hall. It was a strange experience; I felt most odd.'

'Oh, Anna, it is unfair when you think of it, isn't it?'

'No, no.' Her tone became airy. 'Yet it did strike me as peculiar at the time. It was a very good meal, by the way, and well served. The butler had not the dignity of Dunn of course; apparently at one time he had worked in Mr. Bensham's factory and ill-health had prevented him from continuing, which doesn't speak well for the conditions there, yet such is the make-up of our Mr. Bensham that he took him into his house service when they were in Manchester. Mrs. Bensham addresses him as . . . Arry, as she does her husband. Oh, I shouldn't make fun of them, because they have been, and are still, very good to me.'

'It is to their own advantage.'

'Perhaps, but to mine also bacause I am using them for my advantage, or at least for little Barbara's. I was adamant at first against going every day; I said I had my ward to see to and couldn't possible think of leaving her except in the mornings for three hours as the arrangement stood, and then it was he who said, as I hoped he would, "Bring her with you, woman, bring her with you." '

'Does he call you woman?' Constance was laughing.

'Yes, very often. The only time he gave me my title was when he came to see me, and then that was only after he had said, "You're harder to get at, woman, than the Queen herself. I've written you three times. What is it you want, more money? A pound for six mornings a week, you'll not get an offer like that again." It was then I said, "My name is Miss Brigmore. Won't you sit down?" and for the first and only time he gave me my title, "Aye, well, Miss Brigmore," he said; "now let's be sensible. I hear you're a good teacher an' I want you to teach my young 'uns. Three of them I have; a boy seven, another six and a girl coming five. Three so-called governesses the missis's had for them in a year, an' what've they learned nowt. The boys will be going off to school in a year or so, private like, but I don't want them to go with nothing in their heads, you understand?" '

Miss Brigmore now stopped her mimicking and leant her head against Constance, and as they laughed together she recalled, but only to herself, how Mr. Bensham had ended that introduction by saying, 'I've heard all kinds of things about you but it makes no matter to me; I've always said, a man's reference is in his hands or his head. They say you're a good teacher, and ladylike at bottom, and that's what I want, somebody ladylike.'

Strangely she had not taken offence at the man. He was a common man who had made money—there were many such these days—but she saw it was to his credit that he was wanting to educate his children above his own standards. Moreover, as he said, a pound a week for morning work was a very good offer indeed and although she now knew security in so far as she owned half the cottage, Constance having transferred to her her own share by deed of gift, together with fifty pounds a year, and this with the child's income of a hundred pounds enabled them to live better than they had done since she had left the Hall, she now saw in this new addition to her income a means of carrying out the vague plans that had been formulating in her mind with regard to Barbara's future.

A young lady's education could not be accomplished without money. She regretted that there was no musical instrument in the cottage; Barbara must have music lessons. Then there were languages; she herself unfortunately had only French to her credit. Moreover, a young lady needed dancing lessons if she was to fit into any civilised society; added to this, riding lessons were necessary; and there were so many, many more things her child—as she secretly thought of Barbara's offspring—would need before she could take her rightful place in society, and this she was determined her child should do. God sparing her, she would see to it that Thomas's daughter was educated to fit into the life that was rightly hers.

She was recalled to the present when Constance, chuckling said, 'So you cornered him.'

'Just that, just that.'

'Does he know that she isn't yet three?'

'Yes; he's seen her.'

'And when do you start to take her?'

'She's already been there. I took her along on Thursday, and I must say that the first meeting didn't augur well for the future.' Miss Brigmore pursed her mouth and her eyes twinkled as she added, 'Barbara ended her visit by attacking the daughter of the house.'

'No! . . . What happened?'

'Well, she had never seen so many toys in her life before. She has three dolls you know. Betsy and Golly and Fluffy, but the nursery at the Hall is now stacked with toys and dolls of all shapes and sizes. Barbara became fascinated by a Dutch doll. It was neither big, nor small, nor outstanding, it was just a Dutch doll, but apparently it was Katie's favourite. She went to take it from Barbara, but Barbara refused to let it go. When Miss Katie forcibly took possession of her own, Barbara gave way to one of her tempers, and oh dear, before we knew what had happened she had slapped Katie and pushed her onto her back, and Katie yelled, as she is apt to do when she can't get her own way. Then . . .' Miss Brigmore now stopped and bit on her lip and her expression turned serious. She looked at Constance before adding, 'Something strange happened. There had been no surnames used between the children, just Christian names: "This is Barbara, Katie," and "Katie, this is Barbara." But when I lifted Katie to her feet she ran from the room crying, "Ma! Ma! the Mallen girl has hit me. The Mallen girl has hit me, Ma" '

They looked at each other in silence now; then Constance said quietly, 'You never told them her name is Farrington?'

'There was no need, the occasion hadn't arisen when I was required to give her full name, but it proved one thing to me, she's known already as a Mallen. Mrs. Bensham must have spoken of her in front of Katie as the "Mallen child," and Mrs. Bensham would have heard it from someone else. I think it's going to be difficult to get people to realise that her name is Farrington, and it's going to be awkward as she grows older. It'll have to be explained to her.'

Constance sighed now and, pulling herself to the

edge of the couch, she dropped on to her knees and having taken up a shovel, scooped from a scuttle some small coal and sprinkled it onto the dying embers; then she patted it down before saying, 'There's a lot of things that'll have to be explained to her. But in the meantime, let her be happy. . . . And she will be happy'—she turned and nodded her head—'because she'll have her own way or die in the attempt. Look how she dominates Michael already, and he's willing to let her. Oh'—she put out her hand and covered Miss Brigmore's—'she'll be all right. She has you, so she'll be all right. Come, let's go up; we'll look in on them before we go to bed.'

A few minutes later they stood in the nursery between the cot and the bed. The candle glowed softly in its red glass bowl, showing to one side the boy lying on his back, his fair hair curling over his brow and around his ears. The bedclothes were under his chin, and the body was lying straight; he looked in deep relaxed sleep. But on the other side the small girl lay curled up into a ball; her forearms were crossed above her head and her black straight hair half covered her face. The bedclothes were rumpled down to her waist; she looked as if she were pulling herself up out of some dream depth.

As Miss Brigmore gently brought the clothes up around the small shoulders she thought that, even in sleep, the children looked poles apart. They were full cousins yet showed no apparent blood link in either looks or character.

The two women turned and tip-toed quietly from the room, and on the landing they kissed each other goodnight.

Constance went into her bedroom, which now held no resemblance to the one she had shared with Donald, and Miss Brigmore went into the room that had been Matthew's.

Strangely, their thoughts were running along the same channel now, for they were both thinking they would be glad when tomorrow came. Constance so that she could fall back into the daily routine when she and Jane would be alone together, and the older woman would become her relaxed and motherly self again. Anna's intellectual presence always put something of a damper on Jane, indeed her whole outlook was foreign to the farm atmosphere. It was lovely to have her for a short time but it was, and Constance hated to admit this, a relief when she went.

She did not probe this feeling too far for it seemed to be linked up with the day of Donald's death, and Matthew's act. Would Matthew have taken the step he did if Anna hadn't come to the farm begging to keep the child? If? If? If?

But there was another reason why she was always glad when Anna departed. It concerned little Barbara, for the child, as young as she was, dominated Michael, and in a way that annoyed her. The little girl had an attraction that was unusual, to say the least, in one so young. Yet she herself had never been able to take to the child, and this seemed strange because she had loved her mother dearly. Anyway, she told herself, she'd be glad when tomorrow came.

Miss Brigmore too thought she'd be glad when tomorrow came for then she'd be home where she was mistress, really mistress now, and in the cottage she would have the child all to herself.

It was very nice visiting the farm but the atmosphere was—well, how could she put it, a little raw. And Constance was changing, changing all the time. She noticed it on each visit. She wouldn't be surprised if Constance did marry that Mr. Armstrong, and it wouldn't be a case now of marrying beneath her for, of late, she had become very farm-minded. She wasn't being disloyal to Constance, oh no, no, she loved her, and would always love her, she was just facing facts.

Almost the last thing Miss Brigmore told herself before dropping off to sleep was, I go to the Hall on Monday. It was exciting being back at the Hall. There were moments when in the school-room she thought she had never left it. Already she had a status in the house, and it would grow; oh yes, it would grow, for she was needed there. She had sensed this from the beginning. Mr. Bensham needed her. 'What's the best way to tackle an invitation like that?' he had asked her on one

278

occasion as he handed her a gilt-edged card; and then on another. 'Who do you think's best for running a house, a housekeeper or a steward?' Yes, Mr. Bensham needed her.

And Mrs. Bensham needed her. 'Do you think this is too flashy-like to go to tea in? What happened in the old days when you lived here and they gave parties? How did they go about it, were they flashy-like or se-lectish?' Yes, Mrs. Bensham needed her very badly.

And Katie needed her. Oh yes, Katie needed her to discipline and train her, and in the coming years to stand as a buffer between the young lady she would be-come, and the parents she would undoubtedly look down on, as was usual in such situations.

And the boys needed her, but their need would only be for a short time. Her influence on them would be felt mostly during their holidays; yet they were very important in the future she was mapping out.

As the necessity for her presence at the Hall grew with the years so would Barbara's future become more and more assured, for 'the Mallen girl' would always have one asset the young Benshams lacked, breeding; but they, in their turn, would have one thing the Mal-len girl lacked, money.

Who knew, who knew but Thomas would reign in the Hall once again—through his daughter.

Happy, she went to sleep, forgetting as she did so the adage she so often quoted, that the pattern of life was already cut.

ABOUT THE AUTHOR

CATHERINE COOKSON was born in northern England at Tyne Dock, the background which she re-creates so vividly in most of her novels. For years she has been a best-selling author in England, and now her readership is worldwide; two of her books have been filmed; some have been translated into as many as eight languages. American readers will remember her for *The Dwelling Place. The Glass Virgin, Kate Hannigan, Katie Mulholland, Feathers in the Fire, The Fifteen Streets* and *Fenwick Houses.* Her latest novel is *The Mallen Streak.*

Mrs. Cookson and her husband, a schoolmaster, now live in Hastings, England.

Catherine Cookson

For years a bestselling author in England, Catherine Cookson's readership today is worldwide. Now one of the most popular and best-loved writers of romantic fiction, her spellbinding novels are memorable stories of love, tragedy and courage.

☐ THE DWELLING PLACE	7246	$1.25
☐ FEATHERS IN THE FIRE	7289	$1.25
☐ OUR KATE	7599	$1.25
☐ THE MALLEN STREAK	7806	$1.50
☐ THE GLASS VIRGIN	7962	$1.25
☐ PURE AS THE LILY	8079	$1.25
☐ THE FIFTEEN STREETS	8174	$1.25
☐ THE MALLEN GIRL	8406	$1.50
☐ KATE HANNIGAN	8646	$1.25
☐ FENWICK HOUSES	8656	$1.25
☐ KATIE MULHOLLAND	8678	$1.25

ENGLAND'S "MISTRESS OF ROMANCE"
GEORGETTE HEYER

Georgette Heyer, England's best-loved novelist, combines history and romance into an enthralling blend of drama and emotion. All of her enduring stories will bring you many hours of enjoyment and satisfaction.

- ☐ THE CORINTHIAN (Q8321—$1.25)
- ☐ FREDERICA (Q8308—$1.25)
- ☐ COUSIN KATE (Q7861—$1.25)
- ☐ FALSE COLOURS (N7034—95¢)
- ☐ CHARITY GIRL (Q7867—$1.25)
- ☐ LADY OF QUALITY (Q7779—$1.25)
- ☐ PENHALLOW (N7284—95¢)
- ☐ ENVIOUS CASCA (N7118—95¢)
- ☐ THE UNFINISHED CLUE (N5792—95¢)
- ☐ DEATH IN THE STOCKS (N5995—95¢)

Buy them at your local bookstore or use this handy coupon for ordering: